DEAD
WHITE

Llyfrgelloedd Caerdydd
www.caerdydd.gov.uk/llyfrgelloedd
Cardiff Libraries
www.cardiff.gov.uk/libraries

GWEN PARROTT

Gomer

First published in 2019 by Gomer Press,
Llandysul, Ceredigion SA44 4JL

ISBN 978 1 78562 293 9

A CIP record for this title is available from the British Library.

This book is published with the financial support of the
Welsh Books Council.

Printed and bound in Wales at
Gomer Press, Llandysul, Ceredigion
www.gomer.co.uk

*This book is dedicated to
my parents and the people of
Bwlchygroes, Pembrokeshire, without
whom it could not have been written.*

Acknowledgements

My thanks to Gwasg Gomer for this opportunity to publish Dead White as an English paperback and for their help and encouragement along the way.

CHAPTER ONE
March 1947

Della could barely feel her fingers any more, and the cardboard case grew increasingly heavier. Transferring it from her left hand to her right helped a little, but her shoulders and arms felt weak and stiff with cold. She should have stayed in the station with her trunk and the stationmaster. Every step was hard labour by now and still the snow kept falling. It was pointless spitting it from her mouth and wiping her eyes. Ploughing on meant lifting one leg laboriously after the other, knowing she was getting slower and more exhausted with every step. The flakes came down from all directions, hiding everything, the high hedges, the ditch either side of the road, the narrow lane itself. She had no idea where she was any more.

She tripped suddenly on something invisible and fell full length. Coughing, she lay still for a moment and then got up painfully, without bothering to brush the snow from her clothes. It would have been so much easier just to have lain there and let the white blanket cover her. She ached to sit down. Her eyes searched for a slightly more sheltered spot in the hedge and she had taken a step towards it when she stopped herself and shook the thought away impatiently. She stamped her feet to try to get some warmth into them and bent down to pick up her case with a groan.

The hole in the back of her woollen glove had let in the wet. It had been impossible to find the right colour wool in Swansea, even after keeping a coupon especially. It served her right for being too proud to mend it with the wrong shade. And who would have noticed? Nobody. She'd never been pretty enough to turn anyone's head, although after the seven years of strict rationing she was no longer overweight. But being slim in a snowstorm in Pembrokeshire was of no use at all: she could have done with an extra layer of fat in this searing cold.

Had the station master said to the left, or to the right, as he pulled her trunk from the luggage car? Hard to remember because she hadn't really been listening. He'd seen her name on the trunk label.

'Miss Della Arthur. You've come to take the place of the old schoolmaster have you? The house key will be down with Jean, you can venture. It's not far but it's stormy to walk in. Why don't you stay here until it lets up a bit?'

The judgement in his eyes had been evident all the while as he tried to persuade her to stay in his office by the fire. It had been easy to refuse at the time because only a few flakes were settling and it was daylight, although there was plenty underfoot as there had been for months now. There had been no light visible anywhere for a good hour, nor anything to hear but the crunching of her footsteps and the storm shaking the branches of the trees. All roads were narrow here and all hedges high with trees growing through them. Every house and farm seemed to be hidden from her down twisting lanes. And now, suddenly, Della had a choice of lanes to follow. The right side was the obvious choice because it had no snowdrifts.

Suddenly, there was a gate. She leaned against it, knowing this was not the right road. A wave of exhaustion and something akin to fear swept over her. Feeling something pulling at her sleeve, it dismayed her to find barbed wire wound tightly round where the latch should be. Even when she stared hard over the gate she could see nothing through the dark and the snow which fell even more thickly now. Was there a farmyard the other side or just open fields? What did it matter? There was really no choice; there was no turning back now, because she would be frozen and buried before getting within a mile of the station.

Putting her case down for a second she tried to ease her frozen fingers. It caught on a plank that protruded from the snow. Della bent to clear a place for it but found that there was another piece of wood behind and above it. A stile. Aware that her heart was beating hard, she made herself stop and consider whether that, of necessity, meant a house. The wind dropped for a second and she thought she smelt something new and redolent of animals. This wasn't the usual stink of cow dung or pigs. A neighbour of Tydfil and Nest's, her adoptive parents, had kept a pig in his back garden all through the war, and she knew the smell of it too well to forget. She sniffed the freezing air, but the scent had gone. Della climbed onto the stile and tried again. No, definitely not pigs, but something sourer and lighter. And then she heard a tiny but unmistakeable sound and smiled.

'Chickens!' Someone was keeping chickens close by, and nobody keeps chickens in an empty field miles from anywhere. So, there must be a house.

It was easier to follow the sound and the smell more energetically now because she had hope buoying her. She had to lift her feet clear of the deep snow, but that gave her a chance to stare into the darkness. Even in the blackout in Swansea there had usually been some faint light, but here there was nothing at all. Despite this, away from the narrow confines of the lane she could make out different kinds of blackness. The smell came from her left now, but she went past it. Della had made out a large, more solid shape rising before her. It must be a building of two floors and when the clouds broke for a brief instant she saw the silhouette of a chimney. When her fingers touched a stone wall and then the glass of a window, she was nearly crying with relief.

Under the soles of her boots she could feel rounded stones and she pressed herself against the wall, arms outstretched, to see if she could find a door. Scraping her gloves on the rough surface she felt a kind of edge and then wood. She thumped on it and shouted out loud.

'Hello? Is anybody at home?'

Nobody came, but she didn't care. If she had to break a window to get in, she could pay to have it mended. No one would deny her right to do so in such a storm. She ran her fingers downwards and felt a metal doorknob.

The room was some kind of store smelling strongly of chicken feed.

'Hello?' she called again but only the storm replied. Quickly shutting the door and shoving her gloves into her pockets, she fumbled with frozen fingers in her bag for her matchbox and struck one with difficulty. Before the flame went out she saw that it was a high-ceilinged room which ran the whole depth of the house and that a tin washtub with its accompanying scrubbing board hung on the wall beside her. Leaning against the wall to her right were half-full sacks, a roll of barbed wire and a huge pile of firewood. Picking up her case she walked carefully through the darkness to the far end. Almost hidden behind a tall stack of cut branches there was a stable door. She pressed the latch and opened it. The faintest of lights came from somewhere and she realised she was on the threshold of a short corridor, with a window looking out to the back of the property. There were slate flagstones under her feet and another stable door in front. As she pushed that open, she felt a sudden evanescent warmth. She had reached the kitchen.

'Hello?' she called yet again, and then instinctively rushed to the open grate on her left, which showed a glow. In its base the last piece of charred wood was busily giving up the ghost. By falling on her knees and blowing on it, she willed it back to life. Half a dozen sticks stood in the inglenook chimney and she pushed them carefully through the bars, praying they would not put out the fire. She stayed where she was, stiff with cold, listening to the clock ticking on the tall dresser against the wall on her right. It chimed eight. Three hours had passed since she left the station. The sticks started to hiss encouragingly as they caught and she realised, from the pool of water around her, that she was soaking wet. Stripping off her coat she laid it over the back of a chair with a colourful cushion next to the fire and unzipped her boots. Thank goodness she'd worn a pair of socks over her usual stockings because the floor was horribly cold through them already.

As the fire gained strength and lit up the kitchen, it became evident that this was a clean and well-cared-for home. Immediately behind her to the left stretched a wooden settle, with knitted cushions over it like the chair. On the other side of the room, under the window, stood the kitchen table with two or three hard chairs. China winked on the dresser and in the middle of the floor lay a rag mat. But where were the owners? They'd gone out for the day, probably, and decided not to venture home in the snow. They had been wise, if so. The wind shook the house and she thought she saw the door by the table tremble.

'Is anyone there?' she called, annoyed that her voice was shaky. No, there was nobody there. That particular door must open directly to the outside. A row of sturdy boots and shoes stood next to it, with coats hanging from hooks above them. Their number suggested more than one owner.

She sat back on the settle and extended her feet towards the warmth, trying to think what would be acceptable for her to do, being little better then a burglar. Did she dare make a cup of tea?

A black kettle hung from a hook over the fire. The sandwiches, which Nest had cut for her in the kitchen of the Manse, had been eaten hours ago, but even though her stomach growled, it would be a dreadful thing to steal people's food, with everyone still struggling on the rations. But if she took the smallest pinch of tea and drank it black, that wouldn't be so bad, would it? Yet, once she'd risen, she couldn't see a food cupboard of any kind. There must be a back kitchen somewhere where they kept everything. Between the dresser and the fire hung a long curtain, and when she pulled it aside, she saw she had guessed correctly.

It was no more than four feet square, with no window, but it was full of shelves to the ceiling with an enamel basin standing on a little table opposite the entrance. Soap lay in a dish with a cloth and a packet of soda by its side, but the light from the fire did not penetrate sufficiently for her to see more. Then she spotted a candle on the dresser, and lit it from the fire.

With light, everything became clearer. Whatever lay on the bottom shelves was obscured by more curtains. When she pushed one aside, the stock of tins left her staring. She had not seen so many for years. There were at least ten tins of ham and more than that of fruit in syrup. The last time she had seen a tin of ham of that size was when Tydfil and Nest entertained that group of American soldiers around 1942, and were given one as an expression of their appreciation. She could remember the look on the soldiers' faces, a mixture of surprise and embarrassment, that so commonplace a foodstuff in their country could elicit such gratitude. She smiled in the darkness as she heard Tydfil say, 'Who would have thought that those foreign lads would have been such staunch Baptists!' That was the highest praise he could have given anybody.

Perhaps these people were Baptists too, but she would not be eating their treasures. However, despite her searches, there was no similar cache of tea. It was some comfort to find a deep churn of cold water, so she poured a jug of it into the kettle, setting it to boil and standing in front of the fire to dry the hem of her skirt. It was Nest who had persuaded her to wear a skirt instead of the warm trousers which had been her first choice.

'Perhaps they won't be used to women in trousers in Pembrokeshire. You don't want to give the wrong impression.'

Della had been on the point of mentioning the Land Army girls to her, because surely they would not have been mucking out and cutting hay in a skirt and stockings, but she kept her mouth shut. Nest might be right, and there was no way of knowing how welcome she would be in any case, with or without trousers, as a woman arriving to be headteacher of the local school. All vacant posts were being offered first of all to the men who were returning from the war and by now, in her vocation, what had been one or two former soldiers had swollen to hundreds.

How many times had she applied for jobs in the last six months without even making the shortlist? If she had been married it would have been worse still. She could not, in all conscience, feel that anyone who had spent the war fighting did not deserve a little preferential treatment, but the wonderful, more equal world that she had heard so much about, and indeed voted for, did not appear to extend to women. The official attitude seemed to be that they should be back in the kitchen.

She lifted the lid of the kettle and watched the bubbles rise. She hadn't expected to get this job either after so many disappointments, and Tydfil and Nest hadn't shared in her jubilation when the letter arrived. Nant-yr-Eithin was too far away from Cwm y Glo, and possibly utterly lacking in facilities, even though they had tried to look on the bright side. As they were not blood relatives, perhaps Tydfil and Nest had not felt entitled to express open opposition. She understood they were afraid of losing her. They had lost their only child Eifion, her fiancé, four years earlier when he was killed in the Far East and they could hardly bear to let her out of their sight since then. But although Della was sad to leave them, she realised that she longed for some freedom. Their love and care had started to feel claustrophobic, even though she felt guilty admitting it. She couldn't join them in their conviction that their future had died with Eifion. Perhaps bereaved parents of an only child always felt like that, but Della had known two years ago that her life was not over by a long chalk. She sighed to think that she had thoughtlessly endangered herself outside in the snow. What fate had driven her to the shelter of this place? Nest would insist that it was Eifion keeping an eye on her, and Tydfil would say that it was the mysterious hand of providence. And what would she herself put it down to? She didn't really know, but she suspected that pig-headedness had a lot to do with it.

From the corner of her eye she saw a small tin box on the shelf at the side of the inglenook and took it down. Tea at last! She returned to the back kitchen to ferret about. There was a drop of milk in a jug, but when she took off the fancy doily and sniffed, it gave off a sour smell and she put it quickly back in its place. There was nothing else she could take with a clear conscience, apart from dozens of eggs in their shells right at the back in a large vessel covered in some strange clear liquid. Waterglass, she thought. Where on earth had they got that? Nest had mentioned it once, and said that eggs kept in that way were fine as long as you didn't boil them. Pity.

The kettle was boiling by now and she made tea in a cracked cup. With her head up the chimney replacing the kettle on its hook, she noticed that a whole flitch of salt bacon had been hanging there all the time. In no time she had fetched a knife, a frying pan and two of the eggs from the back kitchen, had cut two thick slices of the bacon and had set them to fry. Then she counted out one shilling and six pence in change from her purse and put it on the dresser, in case she forgot later. When the bacon had sweated out some fat, she fried the eggs.

Sitting on the settle, chewing the salty, greasy delicious meat dipped in the yolk, she finally allowed herself to relax. She had shelter, food and warmth. If the owners walked in now, she had paid for what she'd eaten and used. A huge weariness stole over her, and because of it she went out again to wash the dishes. She then felt she had discharged her obligations, and could only hope that the owners would see it in that light.

She leaned back on the hard wood, pulling some of the cushions behind her. The fire looked fine for the next half hour.

Della woke suddenly. Everywhere was quiet apart from the occasional gust of wind whistling in the chimney and blowing snow down to melt on the fire with a hiss. She nearly closed her eyes again but saw that the clock showed some minutes past one. Her snooze had lasted much longer than she'd intended, as if she had any say in the matter. Her legs and feet ached like the aftermath of a twenty-mile hike. When she sat up and inspected the fire, she saw that it needed more fuel and so, with a groan, she stepped into her boots and trod the slate flags to the store. Two sizeable pieces of wood should be enough, although there was no sign of any coal. It was scarce that winter even though the colliers in the congregation at Bryn Seiont, especially the deacon who was a gaffer at the pit, had managed to keep Tydfil and Nest warm. That was the great advantage of being a minister of religion in the Valleys.

Out in the cold storeroom she felt her bladder protest. That was a problem she had not foreseen. She hurried back with the firewood and placed it carefully. What could she do about going to the lavatory? If they didn't have tap water, they wouldn't have a bathroom either, but there would definitely be a chamber pot in one of the bedrooms. Alternatively, she could dress up warmly and brave the storm. No thanks. The pot seemed a much better bet, and she could dispose of the contents the next morning, inconspicuously, outside. If there was a thick blanket or eiderdown on one of the beds, she'd borrow it and sleep on the settle. Bacon and eggs were one thing, but using someone's bed, uninvited, quite another. There was only one door left that she hadn't tried. Reason dictated that it must lead to the rest of the house.

A subarctic wind came to meet her the moment she pushed it open, and nearly put out the candle in her hand. She found herself at one end of another corridor, lino-floored with doors deeply recessed in the thick walls. Opening the first door on the right, she saw a parlour. The room only had one window which was open, and the heavy chenille curtains were blowing wildly in the wind. Heavens above, thought Della, and hurried over to shut it. The window had been open a long time because the backs of the curtains were wet and snow had accumulated on the sill and blown onto the floor. The lady of the house must be worrying about this, wherever she was.

Back in the corridor, she noticed that it had made little difference to the appalling draught. There must be another window open somewhere. She opened the door to the left and found a bedroom and another window, in the same state.

Who on earth were these people with their incredible enthusiasm for fresh air in the middle of the worst winter in living memory? Then she saw that steep stairs disappeared into the dark halfway down the passage. Perhaps there were more windows open up there. She climbed carefully, shading the light with her hand, her footsteps on the bare treads loud in her ears. A landing opened above her with three doors leading off it. The door in front of her yielded a junk room, with an enormous wardrobe taking up much of the floor space, but at least the window wasn't open. There was another bedroom to the left, and after she'd closed the window she looked under the bed. There, set down neatly next to a pair of ladies' slippers, was a china chamber pot. Seeing it was enough to make her want to use it on the spot, but the thought of having to carry it full down the stairs stopped her. The eiderdown on the bed would be a comfort on the wooden settle and she took them both, leaving the pot on the landing while she threw the eiderdown over the banisters to the corridor below. It would come to no harm for the moment down there. She'd take both items back in the morning.

Right, one more room and that would be it. She turned the knob and pushed open the door in the teeth of the gale. This was by far the biggest of the bedrooms, with a double window. She saw no more than that before the candle gave out completely.

'Damn it!' She felt her way over in the dark. 'Hell's bells!' She cursed again when she struck her knee against the footboard of the large bed that she hadn't seen on the right. The wind doubled its efforts and she had to fight the curtains and the swollen frame to get the latch to hold. It must have blown the clouds aside because it was no longer completely dark. Wiping her hands on her skirt she turned and reached out a hand to stop herself from suffering a third knock.

And then she saw them. For a second she thought they were pillows, piled up under the sheet, but pillows didn't have hair. There were two of them, one much larger than the other, with the bedclothes pulled up high, and the eiderdown, similar to the one she had borrowed, folded neatly over their feet. The moon hid once more behind the clouds and they faded into the blackness around them, but they were definitely there. She wasn't imagining it. She thought of saying something aloud to explain her presence, but in her bones she knew they wouldn't answer, and anyway her mouth was too dry to utter a word. Fearfully, she touched the feet of the body closest to her, but there was no reaction, and there was no sound of breathing, apart from her own, like bellows in her chest.

Almost without realising it, she had crossed over to the door, when it struck her that perhaps one of them might be still alive. She could not leave them without making sure. With all her instincts shrieking at her to escape she forced herself to go back to the bed and with finger and thumb pulled back the sheet a fraction. A man and a woman, she noted automatically, with the husband next to the window. The woman was lying on her side, her eyes shut and the high neck of her nightgown obscured by the grey curls on her nape. The poor soul looked very peaceful but it took all Della's self control to push her fingers under the hair and feel for a neck pulse. The moment she touched the woman's skin she knew that she was long dead, but she had to try. She felt under the sheet for a hand. It was stiff and she gave up. Rigor mortis had set in. Leaning over her, she did the same to the man, but he was colder still having been closer to the window. His skin felt like wax and she took her hand away. She lifted the sheet and covered them both, disgusted to realise that she was shaking. You saw things a hundred times worse than this during the bombing, she chided herself fiercely. Yes, she answered, but never on your own in a house in the middle of nowhere under feet of snow.

Out on the landing she closed the door quietly behind her. Hugging the chamber pot to her she sat down on the top stair. The darkness was nothing to the nausea that rose in her throat, but she swallowed hard and came down the stairs one at a time on her bottom, until her feet touched the soft eiderdown. There was nothing to do now but wait for morning.

Chapter Two

All waiting is endless, and during the small hours, curled up in the eiderdown on the settle, she glanced over at the window a hundred times, desperate for daybreak. She must have slumbered, however, because one moment all was dark and the next the kitchen was flooded with light. She got up and felt her knee ache. She rubbed it and shook her legs. Putting on her coat and zipping up her boots, both by now reasonably dry, she wondered whether another cup of hot tea would shake her out of her tiredness, but although she no longer had the worry of stealing the owners' provisions, perhaps it would be better to start finding a way out at once. If she got too tired, or if there was absolutely no way to clear a path, she could come back. She left the fire smouldering, in case.

Out in the store, the temperature was so low she was shivering even before she found the heavy spade by the door. It weighed a ton and could be more trouble than it was worth. She went back to fetch the small coal shovel by the fire. She eyed the heavy coats and rubber boots by the door covetously. Their owners wouldn't need them now. All the pairs of Wellingtons were too big, but the smallest would do, with the pair of knitted socks that she found inside them. She silently gave thanks for the housewifely skills of the woman who lay dead above her head and pulled them on, together with a coat which was a little tight. A beautiful scarf, in a complex Fair Isle pattern fell out of the sleeve and she tied it over her own cap. She felt she knew a lot about this woman by now – far more than she knew about her husband. As a knitter herself, she recognised someone who was a mistress of the craft. She could imagine them both sitting either side of the fire, she busily clicking away. What would her husband be doing she wondered? Reading the paper or snoozing, probably. She shook herself. The only kindness she could do for the pair of them now was to strive as best she could to let their neighbours know, and so she turned for the storeroom.

Even opening the door to the outside was by no means easy. When it finally groaned on its hinges and yielded, she saw why. The snow had drifted overnight to form a solid wall at least four feet high, with barely two feet of daylight above it. She dug away like a mole for minutes before making much impression, but then the last part fell away and she saw where she was clearly for the first time. A sea of white stretched before her, unblemished except for the spidery tracks of birds. To the right stood a variety of wooden sheds and to the left stone farm buildings. At least it was no longer snowing. She picked up the large spade and started shovelling a path directly to the gate that she could make out by its top two bars in the distance, stamping down the snow as she went. She'd cleared about ten feet when she suddenly remembered the chamber pot. There was nothing for it but to get it and empty it. She admired her handiwork on the way, although she had much more to do before reaching the stile, and after that she had to clear a way through the narrow lane, where the snow was likely to be deeper than on the open farmyard. And then she had to tackle the main road. All at once, she was less hopeful. One step at a time she thought. Don't worry until you have to.

She dug a hole in the snow and poured the contents of the pot into it, refilling the hole so that there was no visible sign. One less thing to worry about. She rinsed it and then left it in the storeroom. She would not go upstairs again for anything so she put the eiderdown back neatly in the bedroom downstairs. Nobody would be any the wiser.

Back in the kitchen she regarded her pile of belongings with dismay. She couldn't carry them and dig and there was nothing but lengths of binder twine that she could use to drag them behind her. She'd have to return for them once she reached the stile. Perhaps there was a shopping bag somewhere. She found one with the coats that would do. On her way back to the storeroom she noticed another bag stuffed down by the side of the wooden settle that she hadn't seen the night before. Opening it she found it full of knitting, with a piece that looked like the back of a woman's jumper half-completed on the needles and lots of small balls of wool. She studied the knitted piece for a moment. There was something not quite right about it, although she couldn't say what it was, exactly. She didn't have time to worry about it now, anyway, and the bag was less sturdy than the one she already had, so she put it back.

Out she went and started shovelling again. Breathing hard with the effort and with the snow crunching and hissing as it fell off the spade, she didn't hear the noise immediately. She'd become accustomed to the wind and the crows croaking high above, but when she heard a door close she stopped and looked around. A young man was slowly appearing from behind one of the furthest sheds wiping his hands on a bit of straw. He saw her too, and surprisingly, gave her a jaunty wave before turning back to his tasks. It took her a moment to realise that he'd mistaken her for the owner of the coat and scarf. He looked no more than eighteen although he was very tall and well built. Where had he come from, and more importantly, how on earth had he managed to get through the snow?

Without a second thought, she started to cut a hurried path towards the shed where she'd seen him. Before she was halfway there he appeared again. She could feel his eyes upon her and she gave up shovelling and tried to wade instead.

'Do you know the best way to get to the road from here?' she called, but the lad didn't answer immediately. He looked bewildered.

'You're a relative, are you?' he asked after a pause.

She stopped to get her breath back and shook her head.

'No. I took the wrong turning from the station last night and ended up here.'

The boy looked over to the stile.

'Last night?' he asked. 'In the middle of that storm? On your own?'

'I was lucky to get here, wasn't I?' she said, smiling. 'I could be over my head in a snowdrift by now and you'd be having to dig me out.'

He laughed, showing a row of large, uneven teeth.

'Where were you supposed to be then?' he asked.

'At the school.'

His face changed again to something resembling pride.

'You're the new miss. Instead of the master. Miss Rees told us you were coming on Thursday before the school closed because of the snow.' He wrinkled his brow as he tried to remember. 'Miss Della Arthur, that's who you are.'

Was this great lad still in school then? He must be well over six feet tall. Della extended her hand.

'I'm very pleased to meet you,' she said formally. 'And what's your name?'

'Norman Davies, Miss. I'll be in your class.'

He shook hands with her, but then fell silent and looked around awkwardly. Della faked joyful enthusiasm.

'So now I've met the first of my pupils,' she said. 'And I'm so glad it's you. One of the infants wouldn't be much use to me here, would they?'

This evidently pleased him. 'D'you want me to take you to the sglouse?' he asked confidently.

It took her a moment to understand his pronunciation of the word. He meant schoolhouse.

'Yes, please,' she answered. 'But I have a case and a bag. Do you think we can manage them between us?'

'Course we can,' he said importantly, and then his brow

furrowed again. 'D'you mind if I feed the fowls first. I won't be a jiffy.'

It was a comfort to hear him treading heavily behind her in the direction of the store, but she decided she would not tell him about the two bodies if she didn't have to. He could be no more than fourteen. If he took fright and galloped off, where would that leave her?

Norman hurried over to the sack of corn and handed her a bucket.

'Ask Glenys for some water from the churn, please,' he said. 'The trough's frozen.'

Della was back with the bucket in seconds, hoping that he wouldn't notice that she hadn't spoken to anyone in the interim, but he took it with a smile.

'If you can carry your things as far as the chicken coop, I'll take them then.'

Della shut the storeroom door carefully behind her. Norman waited for her on the path looking uncomfortable.

'I'm supposed to lock up,' he said, 'but I've lost the key.' He turned his trouser pocket out and pushed his finger through the hole in the corduroy. 'They haven't noticed yet. You won't say anything, will you?'

'Not a word,' Della promised, blessing the loss on the quiet.

He fed the chickens in no time and then they both clambered awkwardly through the snow, she following in his footsteps.

'You look after Glenys's chickens, do you?' she asked, hoping she'd remembered the name correctly.

'No, I don't,' he answered over his shoulder. 'The chickens are mine. Glenys and Leonard get eggs from me as rent. I started with a couple of chicks. I've got nearly twenty now. Nanty gave me a cockerel Christmas before last, but he's not much cop. I'd like another one but I'll have to save up. We'll have the old one for dinner then.'

'How do you know he's not a good cockerel?' asked Della thoughtlessly as she was concentrating on keeping her balance.

Norman turned and looked at her, with the words 'Is this one all there?' written clearly across his face.

'Eggs' he said. 'There ought to be more of them than there are, and there ought to be chicks in them.'

Della nodded wisely and thought hard before forming her next question. She had a pretty good idea, having seen all the eggs under the isinglass, that the cockerel was not as hopeless as Norman believed, but she wasn't going to mention it.

'So what do you do then, Norman? Leave the hen on the nest to see how many chicks hatch?'

'No, that's a waste. I hold every egg in front of a candle – you can see what's in them if you do that. A chick is like a spot or a shadow.'

'I can see that you really know your stuff.'

Norman laughed. 'Yes I do. Master said I was an "eggs-pert".'

That was kind of him, thought Della. They reached the hedge and Della cast one last look back at the farm over her shoulder. By the time she started to climb, the boy was already standing on top of the hedge and holding out a strong, hard hand to her. They stood together and looked out over another field stretching away in front of them.

'Right,' said Norman. 'You're going to have to watch where you put your feet now. The snow's deeper in this field and we'll have to stay on top of the hedge until we come to the road. Rees Clawdd Coch and some of the others had brought the mare and the gambo as far as Garreg Ddu as I was coming out this morning. You'll get a ride then.'

She stepped after him obediently, grabbing at the occasional bare trunk as she saw him do. Norman stopped every now and again and let her catch up, smiling encouragingly at her. Della was no longer worried about reaching 'sglouse', but what she would do after that lay in a cold lump in her stomach. She'd have to contact the authorities somehow. She was on the point of trying to elicit more information from Norman regarding this when he spoke again.

'You'll like the sglouse,' he said. 'Master used to say it had "mod-cons". I think that means a bath and tap water.'

'Is there a toilet there too?' she asked hopefully.

'Yes there is, a proper one with a chain, inside. Like the ones in school, at the top of the yard except those get frozen up easily. But Jean puts a spoonful of paraffin down each one. She did it Thursday, when the message came from the office to close the school.'

How had that message arrived? 'Is there a telephone in the school, then?'

'No. Jean happened to hear the one in the sglouse ringing when she was cleaning ready for you to arrive. My Nanty would be very glad of a toilet and a telephone, but nobody's offered, so far. The farm's too far from the road, I think. When Nuncle's really ill I have to run to the square to call the doctor. There's a red box there, too.'

That solved two mysteries at once. Nanty was his aunt and there was a telephone in the house. Della could have kissed him.

'Is your uncle often ill?' she asked, instead.

'Yes,' he nodded. 'In this weather he doesn't get out of bed at all. In the summer he sits in the kitchen sometimes in his overcoat.'

'I'm sure they're very glad of your help Norman. There's a lot of work on a farm.'

He shrugged and Della sensed this was a sensitive topic.

'I've got two cousins … They're the ones who sort things. But once I've finished in school …'

He stopped mid-sentence and listened. Suddenly, from afar,

voices could be heard. Without another word they hurried towards the source of the noise.

By the time she got there, Norman was quite a distance ahead and was announcing her arrival like the Queen of Sheba.

'I've got the new miss,' she heard him say. 'Miss Della Arthur. She'd been staying with Glenys and Leonard overnight.'

Della stared down at the scene. It was like a tableau from a medieval painting. There was a gang of men, old and young, one of them holding the bridle of a mare which was harnessed to a cart and others with meal sacks over their shoulders, without a glove between them, shovelling snow for all they were worth. One or two wore flat caps and others had woollen ones, but two or three, darker in complexion than the rest, were bare-headed.

'Good morning,' she said and saw their eyes assessing her from head to toe.

One of the men came forward, a short, plump, red-faced person, and looked up at her with startling blue eyes.

'We never thought to see you here in such weather, Miss Arthur. I'm Eirug Rees, from Clawdd Coch farm. You'll be wanting the key to the schoolhouse, I expect.' He called over his shoulder. 'Carwyn, mun, go down to Jean, there's a good boy, and ask for the key, will you?'

One of the younger ones glanced up and instantly leapt like a hind up the opposite hedge. He nodded briefly in her direction and then he was gone, at a pace, across the field. The short man turned back to her.

'He won't be two minutes,' he said and then laughed. 'Well, perhaps he'll be a bit longer than that, but he'll be quicker than I'd be in his place.'

As he was speaking, one of the darker men approached, clearing a way for her down the side of the hedge. He reached out a hand to her.

'*Prego, Signorina,*' he murmured turning his eagle profile to the side so that she could only see one grey, intense eye.

'*Grazie,*' said Della automatically and stepped down in as dignified a manner as she could.

This drew an admiring whistle from several of them. Eirug Rees tutted at the lack of respect but they didn't care.

'You can see she's a teacher,' said a voice from the back. 'Talks Italian and all, hell's bells.'

'Now then, my girl,' he said. 'You come and sit in the cart. You must be frozen stiff.'

'Thanks for the offer,' replied Della, shaking her head. 'But the poor mare's having a hard enough time without having to pull my weight as well. The case shall go into the cart, if that's not inconvenient.'

She saw gratefully that she'd said the right thing. This was not the time or the place to be a grand lady. The others nodded and the Italian who'd helped her down from the hedge had a half smile on his face. Della walked slowly with them, noticing that Norman had found a spade and was shovelling with the others. A metal flask appeared from someone's pocket and was passed from hand to hand. She was offered some but she refused as courteously as she could.

'I'd better not. I'm not used to it.'

There was a good deal of leg-pulling when Rees accepted the flask.

'I thought you were one of the leading lights of the Band of Hope,' said the owner. 'I saw you sign the Temperance Pledge. And you a deacon in chapel and all. For shame!'

Rees wiped his mouth, and smiled bashfully. 'Medicinal purposes,' he said, adding in an aside to Della, 'I was only six when I signed, fair play.'

With the snow crunching like broken glass under her feet, the sky a deep blue above, and with the laughter and chatter echoing from one hedge to the other, Della felt quite content and safe for a moment. And then she remembered that she had a difficult task ahead. What if she told these men? She turned and stared around her. When they weren't shovelling, they were throwing snowballs, like schoolboys, even though several of them looked old enough to be grandfathers. Norman's presence was also an obstacle, and anyway, it would look very odd if she mentioned it now. But how could she have announced it from the top of the hedge before they'd even greeted her? The truth was that there could be no perfect moment to tell people bad news. She'd lost her chance. She was dragged from her thoughts by a shout from a nearby field. The one who had been called Carwyn was returning with another man. Rees waved at him.

'I said he wouldn't be long,' he remarked. 'And he's brought help with him.'

'That one, a help?' said a tall man with a cigarette apparently glued to his lower lip. 'Since when?'

He raised his voice slightly.

'Hide the flask boys, Stevie's coming.'

'Don't listen to them,' muttered Rees. 'They're an uncouth lot.'

They had reached a turn in the narrow road and the drifts were now almost all on the right, curling over like beaten egg whites.

'I think we can get to the school from here,' he suggested. 'The cart won't go through, but we can go on foot – if that suits you? I'll come with you to carry the case and see you're alright.'

As she was fetching her possessions from the cart, Della saw that the two men had reached the bank that separated the field from the road. Carwyn jumped easily up and then down the other side, but the other one was less confident. She fancied she saw his hands shake as he grasped at clumps of grass to steady himself.

'On the pop last night again, Stevie?' said the cigarette man and received a mumbled reply that Della could not make out amid the general laughter. His eyes, rimmed with red, looked bloodshot and bewildered.

Before following Rees, Della went over to Norman.

'Thank you very much,' she said. 'I don't know how I would have managed without you …' She didn't finish her sentence because the boy had turned bright red. She was saved by one of the others.

'There you are, Norman,' he said. 'No homework for you now for a whole month!'

She knew, as she walked away, that the men were already plying the lad with questions. They must regard it as strange that she'd come from the farm on her own. She could imagine the interrogation. Why had the owner of the farm – what on earth had Norman called him? – not come with her? She had to hurry. Rees was rapidly covering ground up ahead, kicking the snow out of the way to make things easier for her.

Her new home was indeed a handsome house. It stood whitewashed and solid in the snow, with the school, built of grey stone, only a step away across the yard. She was led up the four slate steps to the side door and into a kind of back kitchen with a large porcelain sink. A long lean-to shed ran out for yards to the back garden from a door next to the sink and another door to the right took her into the rest of the dwelling. Mr Rees chatted all the while, pointing out where everything was but Della wasn't listening. Rather, she went through the place like a whirlwind, seeing the Rayburn in the kitchen and feeling its heat from a distance, through the living room with its two easy chairs flanking the fireplace and the heavy sideboard and out into the front lobby that brought her to the front door. Her hand was on the receiver of the telephone that stood on a shelf in the corner before Rees had left the kitchen.

But her efforts were in vain. The instrument was quite dead. She put it back on its cradle with a thump and suddenly felt like crying. Rees appeared through the living room door to find her sitting on the stairs disconsolately. She lifted her head.

'The phone doesn't work,' she said miserably.

'Were you expecting it to in all this snow?' he asked quietly. 'Perhaps things are different in town,' he added, more to himself than to her.

'Will the phone box on the crossroads be working, do you think?'

He spread out his hands.

'I don't know, but I doubt it. The line comes up from the bottom, see, from the direction of the station. If your telephone isn't working, the one on the crossroads won't be either.'

Della looked at his sincere face. She had to tell someone.

'I've got to call the authorities immediately,' she began. 'It's my duty.'

'My dear girl,' said the farmer with a smile. 'The education office in Haverfordwest won't be open on a Saturday.'

Della tried to explain.

'No, not the education office. I've got to call the police. Do you have a policeman here?'

She could not have surprised him more if she'd suggested ringing Buckingham Palace.

'The police? Well, we've got Aneurin, but he lives a good two miles from here.'

When she didn't react, he watched her squeezing her hands between her knees and cleared his throat. Something seemed to have struck him.

'Nothing happened to you last night, did it? With Glenys and Leonard? Is that why you left the farm all on your own?'

Della suppressed a gust of inappropriate laughter.

'No,' she said. 'Nothing happened. The owners of the farm aren't in a position to harm anyone. They're both dead.'

There was complete silence and Della heard the slow ticking of the clock in the parlour opposite the stairs. Then she saw that Rees had taken his cap off and that he was waiting for her to continue. She took a deep breath.

'I found them last night. I thought there was nobody there. Perhaps it was the cold. They didn't look young.'

He nodded slowly, thinking hard.

'No,' he said at last. 'They were both getting on. Leonard was older than Glenys I'd say. Where were they? In the farmyard?'

'No, in the big bed in the front room upstairs. Apart from the kitchen the place was freezing and the windows all open. I couldn't make out where the draught was coming from. I'd been there a couple of hours before I found them. I thought the owners were away for the night.'

Rees scratched his bald head and chewed the inside of his cheek.

'In bed, then,' he muttered. He seemed to sense that something more was required. 'Glenys was a terrible woman for cleaning,' he added hurriedly. 'I wouldn't be surprised if the windows were open night and day. She'd be up on a ladder polishing them in the rain.'

Then he shook himself, as if he'd come to a decision.

'The best thing we can do is go up to see the minister,' he said. 'He lives in Chapel House on the crossroads. His telephone won't be working either, but at least you'll have told someone. He'll think of what we should do next.'

He turned suddenly and looked back towards the kitchen. Footsteps were approaching.

'Here comes Jean,' he said. 'We'll be a while yet clearing the road. You'll be more comfortable with her for an hour or two.'

And quite evidently relieved to be able to transfer the responsibility, he went out to her, shaking his head sadly.

Della watched him go frustratedly. If this Minister was anything like Eurig Rees, she could see herself struggling back down to the railway station and catching a train to somewhere where the phones still worked.

CHAPTER THREE

'A nice boiled egg and a slice of bread and butter,' said Jean, determinedly. 'You'll feel much better when you've had something to eat.'

From her chair near the black-lead stove, Della could only murmur thanks. She could recall this unpleasant sensation of near collapse from her years of fire-watching during the bombing raids. You could keep going for ages, like a machine, without sleep and swallowing nothing but tea and the occasional biscuit, but it would finally get to you, and you'd suddenly be as useless as a rag doll.

'Can you spare a whole egg?' she asked.

Jean laughed and bent over the saucepan, the better to settle it on the fire. She was a tall, thin woman, with dark hair that was beginning to go grey.

'Good gracious, Miss Arthur, of course we can. Now, if you were to ask for a hundredweight of coal, I don't think the whole neighbourhood could scrape it together. The wood will be an open field here before the end of the winter if we get much more of this snow.'

Della smiled sleepily.

'It's the other way round in Cwm y Glo,' she answered. 'Powdered egg is like gold dust but every back garden is full of the best anthracite. The colliers get it as part of their pay, you see.'

'Do they really? That's nice.' Jean thought about this. 'But I don't think I'd want to go below ground to get it, though. Your family were colliers, were they?'

'No, my father was a carpenter, but he died very young, when I was a baby, and my mother too when I was eighteen. I have no other family, as far as I know.'

'And here am I with more family than anything else.'

Three, if not four children had come into and gone out of the kitchen since Della's arrival, one in the arms of an older sister and all of them with cheeks burned red by the cold.

'How many have you got?' she asked.

'Six and the baby,' said Jean. 'And four of them will be in school with you. The oldest girl, Eirian, works in a shop in Cardigan, but the others are all at home with us.'

Where exactly, wondered Della. This was one of the smallest cottages she'd ever seen. As if she'd read her mind Jean continued, 'The two youngest sleep in our room, the three middle girls in the second bedroom on the landing and Gareth in the parlour. Holidays are the worst.'

'I'm sure you must miss Eirian.'

'You're right, I do. But she lodges with a widow and gets spoilt to bits. Gareth is tamping mad that she's been able to get a job away and he's stuck here on the farm. But what can we do?'

Della tried to do the arithmetic in her head, but failed. 'So has Gareth finished school as well?'

'No, but he will have done by the summer. He'll be with you in the big class – as much as you'll see of him.'

Jean smiled apologetically and showed unnaturally white false teeth.

'I do my best, but they're cunning at that age. I told him the other day – it'll be between you and the whipper-in, my lad! Mind you, I've never seen the whipper-in round these parts. Scarcer than the coal lorry. And Gareth's no more afraid of him than the bogeyman, the little devil.'

She laid a tray with a crocheted doily, and the best china, in front of her. Della roused herself to compliment it all and Jean smiled again.

'What did you think of the School House?' she asked. 'Lovely, isn't it?'

Della took the top off the egg and nodded. She was hungry.

'Yes it is. And somebody's been working hard keeping it clean.'

Jean acknowledged the praise with a nod and poured herself some tea.

'There's nobody tramping in and out of there, is there? And Master had nice things. Did you see the china cabinet in the parlour, and the mahogany piano?'

No, she hadn't had time. The only thing she'd managed to do was take off Glenys's coat and scarf.

'And of course you've got the Rayburn – they had a heck of a job to get it in, mind, but it's worth the trouble.'

'The master arranged to have it, did he?'

'No, it was the Education Office in Haverfordwest. We got the toilets at the top of the yard at the same time. Like living in a hotel, Master used to say. Did you ever stay in a hotel?'

'Only once, in London, before the war. I walked miles and slept all the way home on the train.'

Jean got up and refilled her cup. 'Good practice for last night,' she said. She'd said nothing about the previous evening before then. 'You were really lucky to reach Glenys and Leonard's farm. A lot of people would have given up and died in the hedge.' She wasn't smiling now.

Della looked down at her empty plate. 'It was my own fault for not thinking enough about the weather before setting out.'

Jean shook her head. 'Nobody could have told you how bad it would be. You've got to live here to know. But you'll be fine in School House. There are plenty of candles and paraffin and wood in the back shed. You won't have to worry about anything.'

Not a word about the deaths, noted Della. Hadn't Rees told her anything? Or was this woman a far deeper person than she appeared to be? She couldn't think of a reason why the farmer hadn't told Jean instantly. Was it perhaps because Della had talked about calling the police?

In the end she got a ride to the crossroads in the cart. Somehow they'd managed to break through and all Mr Rees's helpers had disappeared back to their homes by the time he came to get her. He walked in a leisurely manner, holding the mare's bridle and murmuring comfort in her ear when her feet slipped. There were only two or three smallholdings between the school and the crossroads and she felt the isolation of the place weigh heavily on her. It was difficult not to long for the continual human motion of the streets around the Manse in Cwm y Glo. She remembered guiltily that their safety during the storm hadn't crossed her mind.

'Is it as bad as this in other places?' she asked.

'I'd be surprised,' answered Rees. 'But someone did say that everywhere's affected.' He glanced back at her. 'You'll be wanting to let your family know that you've arrived safely.'

'Have you got a carrier pigeon then, so that I can send a message?' joked Della.

'A letter might get through. They'll clear the railway tracks before the road. There was some mention of putting the milk on the train, but I think there's too much of it.'

Oh yes, the all-important milk. It was a large part of their livelihood.

'What will you do if the lorry doesn't come?'

'We'll feed the calves with it and the other animals. We'll make butter and rice pudding and blancmange. And there'll be enough left over for us all to have a bath in it afterwards. Here we are at last.'

The narrow road had opened out unexpectedly and Della saw the crossroads for the first time. Because it was so wide, the snow hadn't got such a grip. Straight in front of her stood the shop and post office with two petrol pumps. To the right of the shop a long incline stretched up between the hedgerows and on the corner stood Eynon Chapel attached to its vestry and Chapel House. Some children played in the empty space, throwing snowballs like mad things.

'We'd better not be long,' said Rees as they negotiated the narrow path between the half-buried gravestones. 'It looks like more snow's coming.' He sniffed the air like an old dog.

The front door was opened by a busy little woman in a colourful apron, her face deeply wrinkled. She smiled broadly showing more gaps than teeth, but her welcome was warm. Della shook hands with her and learned that she was Hetty, the minister's housekeeper.

'Go into the study to Mr Richards,' she said. 'And I'll bring you a cup of tea.'

Then she disappeared into the nether regions of the dark building with Rees at her tail, leaving Della standing outside a door stained brown like a chapel seat. She knocked and heard a deep voice answer within, so she entered. The minister sat at a large desk by the window with his back towards her. He didn't turn to see who it was.

'Excuse me,' ventured Della.

Hearing an unfamiliar voice the man leapt to his feet, and she was shocked to see him reach for a walking stick before crossing the room to greet her. He didn't look old or frail. Her first impression was that he was in his thirties, as she was, but as she stared at him she could see his hair was already turning white.

After shaking her hand, it was evident that he didn't know what to say, unlike every other minister of religion that she'd ever met, but then he motioned her to one of the two armchairs by the fire and moved painfully to the other. Something was definitely amiss with his right leg. The pain from it could be responsible for the web of fine lines around his eyes. He'd been good-looking once.

'I apologise for calling unannounced like this, Mr Richards,' she began, while he poked the fire. He looked up and gave a half smile.

'I've been expecting you for weeks,' he said. 'But perhaps not today.'

So he knew who she was. He wiped his long fingers on a white handkerchief before tucking it back in his pocket.

'You take your social duties very seriously, quite obviously, calling on your minister before even organising the house. It bodes well.'

There was something sarcastic in his tone which he didn't bother to hide.

'This is not a social call,' Della answered sharply. 'If the telephone had been working I wouldn't be here at all. But as it isn't, I was advised to come to you, failing a policeman.'

That caught his attention.

'And what do you want a policeman for?' he murmured, in the same mocking voice. 'When you've just arrived.'

Della took a deep breath. She understood now why Rees had left her to explain on her own, but there was nothing to do but plough on.

'I'm afraid I have bad news,' she said. 'Last night, I got lost in the snow on my way from the station to the school.'

He interrupted her.

'What on earth were you thinking of, coming here last night? Couldn't you have stayed with the stationmaster?'

'Of course I could, but it was only starting to snow.' She stopped herself from sounding as annoyed as she felt. 'I walked for ages, but there was nowhere much to take shelter, and then, when I was beginning to despair, I found a farm.'

He nodded and leaned forward to warm his hands.

'The door wasn't locked and so I went in. Nobody seemed to be home and the fire was almost out. I thought the owners were away – but they weren't. They were there all the time, dead, both of them, upstairs.'

She stared long and hard at him, but apart from a tiny movement in the corner of his eye, he didn't react. Della drew off her gloves and warmed her own hands.

'From what Mr Rees told me this morning, they were called Glenys and Leonard. And before you ask, I took their pulses. They were both stone cold.'

She sat back in her chair, and waited. When he did speak, it was to ask an unexpected question.

'Where did you learn to take a pulse?'

She was thrown off balance for a second, but she answered evenly enough.

'I watched fires for years in Swansea during the war, and I did a first aid course. I got enough experience there with dead bodies to last a lifetime.'

He made a gesture with his left hand that she couldn't interpret, but she was saved from having to say anything by a knock on the door, which announced that Hetty had brought the tea in on a tray. He made to get up, but Hetty waved him back to his seat.

'Stay where you are,' she said, adding, as if he wasn't present, 'He was daft enough to clear the path to the house this morning and now he's paying for it.'

From her cheerful demeanour, Della guessed that she hadn't heard about the bodies from Rees, and she left them with a command to shout for more tea, if needed. The minister poured for both of them, waiting until Hetty closed the door behind her before speaking.

'And what did you do then?' he asked, as if his housekeeper had never been there at all.

'Pulled the sheet up over their faces and left the room. After that there was nothing to do but wait for daybreak and try to find a way out.'

He drank his scalding tea in one gulp and set the cup down on the saucer. Della sipped at hers in the silence.

'To whom have you spoken about this, apart from me?' he asked again.

'Nobody but Mr Rees.' And why was that important? Wasn't letting people know the whole point?

There was another long pause.

'And where were they exactly?'

'In bed in the largest room upstairs. As if they'd died in their sleep.'

'Both of them?'

'Yes!' It was so difficult to hide her frustration in the face of such purposeless questioning.

He got to his feet and with the aid of the walking stick went over to his desk. She saw him rifle through a number of documents. He turned back to her, holding one.

'I had a letter yesterday,' he said, 'from the renowned Reverend Tydfil Owen introducing you to me.'

Della was torn between annoyance at hearing him call Tydfil renowned in an ironic voice, and annoyance at Tydfil for sending such a letter. She didn't doubt that it was full of praise for her, and asking his brother in the faith to smooth the path of a newcomer, but it was also a way of keeping tabs on her.

'I'm sure he writes volumes,' she said drily.

The tall man smiled humourlessly.

'It's a kind of reference, if you like.'

'I can believe it – running to four pages.'

'And more.' He looked at her seriously. 'There's one sentence that strikes me as being particularly relevant. "*You can depend on Miss Arthur to know when to speak and when to keep silent.*" I wonder if I can?'

The silence between them stretched out. Della stood.

'Let me be quite clear about this,' she said coldly. 'You're asking me not to say anything about the two bodies to anybody, not to report their deaths to the police or to any other authority. Have I understood you?'

He nodded slowly.

'And you're intending to leave them there without doing anything?'

'Yes, for now.'

'What if someone else finds them in the meantime? Someone like Norman, for example. Do you think that's fair?'

He waved the letter about impatiently.

'He won't go into the house, and he definitely won't go upstairs. He wouldn't dare.'

'But if he doesn't see them for days, isn't he likely to go looking for them?'

He made a contemptuous sound in his throat. Della glared furiously at him, slapping her gloves from one hand to the other.

'I can't believe I'm hearing this,' she said. 'I thought things had got as bad as they could be last night, when I found a married couple stone dead in bed, hours after I'd arrived. But I'm now being warned by a minister of religion not to mention it to anybody! It's unbelievable!'

The smile appeared again.

'If you'd been here a month and not a day, you'd understand that I have to think very carefully what to do next.'

Della was about to protest, but he raised his hand to stop her.

'I'll tell you one thing that may, perhaps, give you some idea of the extent of the problem. Glenys and Leonard were not a married couple, but brother and sister.'

Chapter Four

She was so deep in thought as she left the Manse, she barely heard Hetty talk about the shop. She came to when Rees said, 'Yes, this is the best chance you'll get.'

By now, one of the children was holding the mare's head, and the rest of them were watching. She saw Rees give the boy a ha'penny and he leapt away gleefully. The children were already at the shop counter as she crossed the threshold.

'No you can't!' she heard a peevish female voice say. 'You haven't got a sweet coupon between you – off you go!'

Della looked over to where a small woman stood behind the counter, with her hair in long metal combs all over her head. The little band turned away, disappointed, but a deeper voice came from the back.

'You can have a couple of broken biscuits, if you like?'

The woman scowled, and then, seeing Della, her expression changed completely.

'Iori!' she called. 'The new teacher's here. How are you, my dear? We never thought to see you in this weather. And you were lent Glenys's coat and scarf, a little bird told me.'

She lowered her voice but the children were busy choosing biscuits from a tin held out by a large, untidy man.

'It's a wonder you didn't have to pay for the honour. They didn't charge you for staying there overnight, I hope?'

Della smiled, ignoring the question.

'May I register my ration book with you here?' she asked, searching for it in her bag. The woman went through it curiously, as if hoping to find her life history written on its pages.

'Of course you can,' she said, and then leant over the counter. 'And I've got post for you.'

She bustled over to another part of the crowded shop and started to ferret about.

'Two letters,' she announced triumphantly. 'One from the Education Office. It didn't take them long to start bothering you, did it? And whoever wrote the second one has got lovely handwriting. Someone who's been to college, I'd say.'

'Ceinwen …' murmured her husband wearily under his breath, but the woman was unabashed.

'You've had more letters before arriving than most people get in six months.'

Della thanked her and took them, recognising Tydfil's commanding hand instantly, but revealing nothing. She bought a variety of things and Iori was sent out to get milk for her.

'And you'll want a can to carry it,' said Ceinwen, noting it down on the bill. Della paid for her purchases and watched Ceinwen rip the necessary coupons out of her book. What would it be like not to have to weigh and measure every mouthful of food and be allowed to buy whatever you liked? Doing so was nothing but a memory by now. She looked around her. This was a general store that sold everything, from washtubs, to barbed wire, and from flannel combinations to sugar and flour.

'You've got a very good stock,' she remarked.

Ceinwen just sighed.

'It's nothing to what it was before the war. I used to be able to get dress material and china and all, but now all I can get is a bit of knitting wool and the occasional cup.'

Della suddenly recalled the hole in her glove, and in a couple of minutes Ceinwen had found a card of darning wool that was roughly similar.

'It's not quite the same,' she said critically. 'But you could always put a little flower on the two gloves to hide it. If you aren't much of an embroiderer, you could always ask Glenys.'

Mercifully, Della didn't have to reply to this, because Iori had gathered her purchases together and was preparing to carry them out to the cart for her. She took her leave, grateful to go before Ceinwen could think of any more questions.

Rees hardly spoke for most of the way back, and Della was glad of that too, but he insisted on carrying everything into the house for her.

'I'll fetch your trunk up for you from the station when I can – perhaps tomorrow, if we don't get another storm tonight,' he said watching her arrange the bags on the kitchen table.

'Thank you very much for everything,' she answered. 'You've been such a help. May I offer you a cup of tea?'

'No, thanks. Lilwen will be wondering where I've got to. That's my daughter. She teaches the infants' class. You'll meet her on Monday, if not tomorrow.'

Yet he didn't leave, but stood on the back door step, as if considering whether he should say something more. Della decided to break the impasse.

'We're not supposed to say anything,' she said significantly.

'No, we're not,' the farmer answered with a hint of relief. 'I knew that's how it would be when you told me where you'd found them. But he'll have to think of something quickly.'

'Yes, he will. Do you have any ideas?'

'Heavens above, no. Much too deep for a simple man like me. But at least we don't have to worry that anyone will go and look for them.' He didn't expand further but added, 'I'll be here to fetch you to go to chapel in the morning, around ten.'

Then he bounced like a rubber ball down the steps. The first thing Della did after he'd gone was go to the far end of the long lean-to shed to the fuel store and fetch enough wood to feed the fire before it grew really dark. She peered through the window next to the door and saw that she had a small back courtyard that led to a garden up on the bank. Back in the warm kitchen,

45

while looking for suitable places to store food, she found the crockery and the saucepans and put water in the kettle.

On the mantelpiece in the living room stood an enormous paraffin lamp, and she carried it back into the kitchen, before going back to explore the place more thoroughly. In the parlour, the clock still ticked patiently, keeping company with the china cabinet and the mahogany piano. She opened the lid and struck a note. To her amazement it was still in tune. She stood there a moment and played a hymn from memory.

Out by the front door near the bottom of the stairs, she tried the telephone again, but it remained silent. She'd have to stuff something into the letter box as it flapped like a flag with every gust of wind. To the left of the door stood a wooden coat stand. One lonely black umbrella lurked in it. She noticed a small white door at the side of it and clicked the latch. A row of slate steps led down to a spacious glory hole. Apart from a wooden chair which was missing a leg leaning sadly against the furthest wall and a strange smell, it was empty. Perhaps the master had used it as a bomb shelter during the war. It looked solid enough. No, she thought, they never saw any bombs here.

Upstairs on the first landing was another door that revealed the famous bathroom. It shone, black and white apart from a piece of pink soap on a saucer at the side of the bath. She could see it was wet. If I were Jean, she pondered, with a house full of children, cleaning somewhere with a convenient bath, I too would bring them all here to wash them. But she wouldn't tell her that she knew.

She followed the turn in the stairs to the top landing. There were three bedrooms, a small one to the right with an airing cupboard, looking out over the garden, a medium-sized one facing the fields at the back of the house and a large one, facing the school yard, where the master had slept. She knew this immediately from the smell of tobacco which met her at the door. From the holes in the mat and the scorch marks on the bedside table, it was evident that the master had smoked in bed. Here again, Jean had done her best. She could imagine her tutting under her breath to see the damage, and she opened the large, empty wardrobe. Even though there was more room here than in the other bedrooms, it retained too much of its previous owner's personality to think of using it, and anyway, she only had single bed sheets. Or rather, that's what she would have when her trunk arrived. She'd have to manage somehow until then.

She came down the stairs to the kitchen, glad to hear the kettle whistling. She dragged one of the armchairs from the living room and set it next to the fire. She drank her tea, wondering where the master could have gone to in such a hurry, leaving so many of his possessions. Nothing had been said to her in the interview, and she'd been too determined to get the job to ask. She remembered the two letters and went to get them. She opened the one from the Education Office first of all and ran her eyes over it quickly. It contained plenty of instructions and information regarding pupil numbers and the maintenance of the building, but nothing about her predecessor. At the bottom of the second page she saw a paragraph bearing a name. She read it more carefully.

'The recent incumbent, Mr Dafydd Jones, is undergoing a lengthy course of treatment in hospital, and is not expected to be well enough to resume his duties for quite some time. In the circumstances, it was felt that allowing you, as a single lady, to live in the authority's property was the most practicable solution, despite its having been furnished at Mr Jones's expense. We trust that you will take all reasonable precautions to ensure that Mr Jones's effects are not misused or damaged. The rent will be payable in the normal way.'

Della sniffed at this. She now knew why she'd got the job. They hadn't been able to find a man with a family who was prepared to move into a house full of someone else's furniture, and they didn't want to lose the rent. But what kind of illness could have caused him to leave with little more than his clothes? Perhaps he'd had some kind of accident, but it sounded more like a long term illness. TB perhaps? She pulled a face. If so, she definitely wouldn't be using his bedroom. She'd ask Jean once she'd got to know her better.

The other letter lay on her knees, but she needed to unpack before tackling it. It gave her an unpleasant jolt to find that the contents of her small case were wet at the sides. That's what you got for putting it down several times in the snow, but they'd dry soon enough on the wooden rack above the fire. She cursed herself for not putting in some sheets, but the utility ones that she had were of heavy cotton and there would have been no room for anything else. Rolling up in a blanket would be the wisest course tonight.

With the place now resembling a laundry she sat once again and opened Tydfil's letter. She could expect to receive one weekly from now on, and she'd have to reply. Yet, seeing his greeting, '*My Dear Girl*' she warmed somewhat towards the correspondent. He explained that he had written to Huw Richards, who would be certain to tender an enthusiastic welcome to someone with her talents. Della shook her head and then bit her lip. She dared not breathe a word about the two bodies, not because of the irrational embargo placed on it by the minister, but because Tydfil would either bombard his brother in the faith with correspondence or travel there, with Nest, expressly to carry her back to Cwm y Glo.

The rest of the letter was a kind of lecture regarding the problems that she would encounter, but reminding her that she had '*taught in the land of coal and steel*' and had also '*energetically tackled the task of civilising those evacuees from London*' and, because of this, the behaviour of the country children would not be an insurmountable obstacle. However, she needed to remember – and Della could almost hear him lowering his voice at this point – that the people of Pembrokeshire lived far '*closer to the land*' and so she should not expect the same '*moral standards*' there as she'd been used to. As the children's moral standards were the least of her worries at present, Della leapt over the final libellous clichés because she had spotted Nest's spidery writing at the bottom of the page.

They were mostly exhortations to be careful about, amongst other things, not sleeping on any mattress '*with a mildewy smell*' and to remember that she was more than welcome to visit the Manse for a weekend any time she liked. She looked up from the page, her eyes damp, and swallowed. If they had only known how desperate she'd been to get away. Then she glanced at it again. In tiny handwriting, verging on the illegible, crawling up the margin, there was something else. She held it closer to the fire to read it.

'*Be careful with the minister. He has a HISTORY. Not a word to Tydfil.*'

She turned the letter over, but there was nothing else to be seen. She stared at the envelope and noticed that the flap had been set slightly askew. Nest had reopened it in order to add the warning. And as the most important word had been printed in block capitals, it must be a story worth telling.

She lit the paraffin lamp, made supper and ate it in front of the fire. She took out a piece of paper and pen, intending to make a start on an answer, but the effort was too much. She was exhausted, and without caring whether or not her nightgown had a 'mildewy smell', she made sure the fire was damped down, that the lamp had been turned off, and then, candle in hand, she made her way to bed.

Standing for a second in the lobby by the front door, she saw the patterns that the candle flame threw up onto the walls shake in the wind. The stairs stretched up ahead into the blackness. Rejecting the shameful idea of sleeping in the kitchen, she climbed them and had a quick wash in the bathroom. Despite the hot water, she would not have a bath that night. It pleased her that the airing cupboard gave out enough heat to make a difference to the smallest bedroom. She left its door open to benefit from it. She made up the bed as comfortably as she could without sheets, but it didn't matter. She could have slept on a stone that night.

CHAPTER FIVE

'*Signorina!*'

Della jumped and nearly dropped the inkpot on the cloakroom floor. She been cleaning out the pots from the inkwells in the desks ready for Monday and her hands were already blue-black.

Even though she'd slept heavily she'd awoken suddenly from a nightmare where she'd found Glenys and Leonard in a bombed-out house, and even though they were bloodied corpses they'd sat up and recited a litany of accusations against her involving the theft of bacon. Despite her telling them to shut up and lie down, they'd carried on with their complaints.

She'd lain wound up in the blanket that was wrapped too tightly around her and then, when sleep had refused to come, had risen. That was why she was standing at the sinks up to her elbows in cold water, being so virtuously industrious at such an early hour. She smiled over at the Italian, the one who had helped her down from the bank the previous morning.

'Good morning,' she said, trying to think what, apart from '*grazie*', she could say in Italian.

He nodded courteously.

'*Signor* Rees say not to wait for cart for chapel. He fetch you big bag. He says he's late.'

'Thank you,' Della answered and looked curiously at him.

He was a square, powerfully built man, about medium height, with his hair cut brutally short, which would have given him a villainous air, except that he had large grey eyes fringed with thick, black eyelashes. He saw her staring and smiled suddenly, running his hand over his crown.

'No hair, no problem,' he said, cracking imaginary lice between his thumbs.

'Do you live on Mr Rees's farm?' asked Della.

'Yes. Me and Giuseppe and Salvatore.' He extended his hand even though he could see the state of hers. 'Enzo Mazzati.'

After shaking hands it was difficult to know what to say.

'You'll be going home to Italy before long, I expect,' Della ventured.

'Don't know,' he answered, shrugging. 'Waiting for letter.'

Before she could say anything else, Enzo cast his eyes up at the building.

'This small school,' he remarked. 'Like my mother's village. You are new *professoressa*. Like *Signorina* Rees. She teach *bambini*. Hard work after …' and he jerked his thumb in the direction of the house.

'After Mr Jones fell ill. Yes, I'm sure it was,' Della answered.

He looked at her sharply.

'Hard work before also,' he said quietly raising his hand as if lifting a glass. Then he smiled again, transforming his heavy face. 'But everything OK now. *Ciao!*'

He waved at her and stepped confidently across the slippery yard to the road, leaving Della thinking hard as she hurried back to the house. She opened the door to the glory hole and sniffed the air inside it. Unfamiliar as she was with strong drink, she hadn't recognised the smell at first, but now she knew exactly what it was. Evidence of where the master would come to slake his thirst without leaving discernible signs. She pitied her co-teacher. And what effect had it had on the children's education? It looked like the hard work wasn't over by any means.

The clock in the parlour struck half past nine. It was high time she scrubbed her hands and dressed respectably.

Hetty was already at the harmonium as Della slid into a seat near the back of the chapel. Rees hadn't made an appearance as far as she could see and she hoped that fetching her belongings hadn't caused him a lot of bother. Aware of the curiosity that had followed her entrance, she was glad her gloves covered her grey hands. The chapel wasn't empty by any means and there were a good number of children to be seen also. The deacons emerged suddenly from a door to the left of the pulpit, with the minister close behind them. A hymn book was passed over her shoulder by a kind hand and the service began.

Looking down at them from above Huw Richards looked even more sardonic than he had the previous day. On the other hand he didn't seem to be limping quite so badly as he climbed the stairs. He read and prayed competently and then the children all filed out to the Sunday School. While they were doing so she heard the door open behind her and saw that Rees had arrived. He came into her pew, red in the face, and she made room for him. He leaned over and murmured.

'They didn't want to give it to me – the idiots!'

Della pulled an apologetic face, as 'The Old Rugged Cross' swelled around her. She settled herself for the sermon. This would be something she could describe to Tydfil and Nest in a letter without any danger at all, so she listened intently. There was no question but that he was clever and had prepared thoroughly, but in comparison to Tydfil, he was as dry as dust. She doubted whether his audience could follow half his arguments, and indeed she herself could not maintain an interest in the tribes of Gath for a whole half hour. With relief she saw him close the big Bible and the children came back in from the vestry to the deacons' seat to say their verses. The minister greeted them as warmly as if they were a pack of wild dogs. Della leaned forward with renewed interest, but the only thing she learned was that they all had conscientious mothers and were experts at keeping tiny bits of paper hidden in their fists.

They got up to sing and she noticed that a couple of people were frowning and looking in her direction significantly. However, she had no time to think any more about it because Rees whispered in her ear.

'The trunk's down with Jean. The children will bring it up to you. There's enough of them, after all.'

Outside, Della shook hands with a number of people whose names she didn't catch. Hetty hurried up, tutting impatiently.

'He should have welcomed you to the area,' she said. 'For a clever man he's not all there sometimes, honestly.'

Rees coughed.

'Would you like to have dinner with me and Lilwen?' he asked, but before she could answer Hetty broke in.

'She's coming to us today,' she said. 'Orders – you shall have her next week.'

Rees smiled gently and said goodbye before Della could thank him properly for his neighbourliness. She would have far preferred to go to Clawdd Coch and meet her colleague, but he had accepted the minister's claim on her without argument. Was Huw Richards's word like the law of the Medes and the Persians in this place? He'd better not try to influence matters in the school in the same way. She turned and followed Hetty into Chapel House without an ounce of enthusiasm.

If the conversation hadn't been so difficult to keep going, Della would have enjoyed the lunch greatly. After a roast fowl, plenty of vegetables and a glorious sponge pudding swimming in golden syrup (which blessed substance had never been on the rations, although, of course, getting hold of a tin was quite another matter), she and the minister were left alone in the study once more, while Hetty, refusing all help, went to wash the dishes and make tea.

'So you don't drink alcohol, then,' he said, when they'd sat down.

The first flippant reply that leapt to Della's lips was, 'Yes I do, mine's a double brandy,' but she managed to suppress it.

'No, not really, not spirits on an empty stomach, anyway,' so that he should know that she'd guessed about the flask that had been passed from hand to hand on her journey to School

House. And then, when he didn't react, she added, 'In contrast to my predecessor, poor soul.'

He raised his eyebrows. She'd succeeded in surprising him, which pleased her.

'And I thought we'd found every bottle,' he murmured. 'But then, there were so many, we could easily have missed one.'

She wasn't going to tell him that Enzo had spilled the beans. 'A stink like a brewery in the glory hole under the stairs,' she said casually. 'But there again, the old master had some sterling virtues, despite all that. He was kind to Norman, for one thing, which is more than can be said for Glenys and Leonard.'

Despite trying to hide his curiosity, he failed.

'What leads you to that conclusion?'

'They were stealing his eggs. Dozens of them. Norman thinks that the cockerel's a dead loss, but I think that from now on, he'll be delighted at his effectiveness.'

Before he had the opportunity to take the conversational lead again, she asked, 'Have you decided yet what to do with the bodies?'

He took a deep breath and smoothed out the wrinkles at the knees of his trousers.

'No, I haven't,' he admitted. 'The snow creates problems, although it keeps people away. I doubt whether Eirug Rees and I could carry Leonard down the stairs. Glenys wouldn't be so heavy.'

Della doubted whether his gammy leg would allow him even to do that. If he was less irrational about letting folk know, there would be no difficulty. An idea struck her.

'Would you consider using the Italians? They're foreigners, physically strong, without any real connection to the area and about to be sent home. And I'd be more than willing to lend a hand. I've carried a number of bodies in my time.'

He gave this some thought.

'Of course. During the bombing. Your shining hour.'

When she didn't rise to the bait, he glanced over his shoulder to his desk.

'Tell me, are you a relative of Tydfil's? He thinks the world of you. Are you a niece or something?'

Della decided not to answer resentfully. She shook her head.

'No, there's no family relationship. I went there to lodge at the beginning of the war when I had this huge crowd of evacuees to organise. That's where I met their son, Eifion, and in time, became engaged to him. They're the nearest I have to a family, however. My parents died young.'

He nodded.

'And now here you are far away in the depths of the country. How's Eifion going to cope with that, I wonder?'

'Hard to say. He was killed in forty-three.'

The silence that followed was broken by Hetty knocking on the door with a tray. Della got up swiftly to let her in, hiding a malicious smile. That put a spoke in his wheel, the patronising devil!

'That was a meal fit for a king, Hetty,' she said. 'I can't remember when I last had such a good lunch.'

'I told him last night that you needed feeding,' answered the housekeeper, smiling. 'She's been living on fish and chips in town, I bet, I said.'

Della agreed that she had eaten her share.

'But I couldn't face snoek at all,' she said, and then, seeing them look blankly at her, explained, 'You know, that oily fish from South Africa. Horrible!'

'Good gracious, I'm not surprised. Enough to turn your stomach.'

Hetty placed the tray on the little table between them.

'You'll need to keep an eye on the clock if you want to get home before dark. I'll walk part of the way with you. He's not fit.'

When she'd gone, Della poured the tea. Huw Richards had not spoken all the while.

'It's interesting that Hetty always refers to you in the third person,' she said provokingly. 'As if you weren't actually there.'

He looked at her suspiciously and shrugged.

'It's quite common here. But I agree it's interesting linguistically, a kind of distancing mechanism, or perhaps extreme politeness. Sometimes the men round these parts call each other only by the names of their farms.'

'Did anyone ever call you Chapel House?' enquired Della innocently and then changed the subject before he could answer. 'I too had a letter from Tydfil. Warning me not to expect the same moral standards here because they live closer to the land. Is that your experience?'

She could see him considering whether this was some kind of trick question.

'It's true that there are different priorities here,' he replied cautiously. 'The farm comes first in all things. Insofar as that affects you at the school, you won't see some of these children at potato picking or harvesting time. And you'll have to deal with a number of much older children who are desperate to leave and start working on the family farm. That's how it always has been, and always will be forever more.'

Della felt that she had to offer some opposition.

'Surely not!' she said. 'Raising the school leaving age to fifteen this year will make some difference, and they're talking about building a secondary school in the vicinity. Perhaps it'll take a couple of years to change attitudes, but it'll be a great opportunity for some.'

He shook his head sourly.

'It's going to take longer than a couple of years. Their horizons are unbelievably narrow. The only time most of them go anywhere at all is on the Sunday School trip. And not one of them has been inside a library, or has learnt to swim. I don't think you realise that living in the country can be an incredibly bleak thing.'

'No bleaker than living in the industrial valleys,' Della answered. 'What's the point of a swimming pool or a cinema if you don't have the money to go there? And there are plenty who can't go to the County School in the next street because their parents can't afford the uniform and the books. The only other choice is the pit or the foundry. At least the children here won't spend their entire working lives in the bowels of the earth or in some red hot cave.'

'No they won't. Instead, they'll be out in all weathers, and bent double with rheumatism before they're fifty. Don't think that they look at the beauty of the landscape with the same eyes as you or me. It's either arable land or grazing land. If they can't eat it, or turn pigs onto it, they're not interested.'

Della would have liked to ask why he was still here, if he held such a low opinion of the place, but she stopped herself. She knew, that as a Baptist minister his moving somewhere else was dependent on his receiving an offer of a pastorship from another chapel. And who would do so, having heard him preach? He was a disappointed and frustrated man, she decided, full of bitterness.

'Right then, are you ready?'

Hetty's voice came from the doorway and Della got up thankfully. Huw Richards followed them out to the hall and watched her put her coat on and change her shoes for Glenys's rubber boots.

'Lucky you thought of bringing those with you from Cwm y Glo,' he remarked quietly.

'Isn't it, just?' she answered, without looking at him, knowing that it was a kind of oblique warning to her not to say anything to her companion on the way home. But he hadn't finished with her yet.

'Perhaps I'll pop over to the school during the week, if it thaws a bit.'

Della gritted her teeth but smiled.

'Send a message before venturing out,' she said pleasantly. 'We might have gone on a nature walk.'

Hetty's company was so much easier. They were hardly out of sight of the crossroads before they both started to slip and slide, laughing. They grasped each other's arms and stepped more carefully.

'I'm indebted to you for the dinner, and for this,' said Della.

'Not at all. You've come all this way in the snow, so someone needs to give you a bit of a welcome. Can you see him limping all the way to School House? Mind you, his leg does hurt. That's why he's so awkward to deal with.'

Della saw her chance to learn more.

'Did he have an accident, then?'

'No. Something happened to him in India while he was in the army. He was months in the hospital out there, too ill to come home. They say he's lucky to have a leg at all. And now we're leaving India for good. What was the point of it all?'

Interesting. Della pretended to be surprised.

'What was he doing in the army? I though ministers of religion were exempt. Or did he go in for the ministry after coming home?'

'No. He was already the minister here. But you're right, he didn't have to go.' She considered briefly. 'That's how he is. He gets an idea in his head, and there's an end to it. Like a lot of men. You won't see women doing something so daft.'

They reached a turn in the road and saw that the sky was growing grey around them.

'I'll be fine from here,' said Della. 'I've got to fetch the trunk up from Jean's house. Mr Rees was kind enough to fetch it from the station for me. I'll have bedclothes tonight.'

Hetty looked askance at her but didn't argue. Della thanked

her again and took her leave. Hetty took a few steps and then turned back.

'Watch Eirug Rees,' she said, with a wry smile. 'He's a widower. When he isn't chasing the lads away from Lilwen, he's looking for a wife.'

Heavens above, thought Della, as she stepped along the path left by the cart and the men. Complications on all sides. She ploughed on thoughtfully, yet she wasn't worried. Although the hedges were as heavy under the weight of snow as they had been two nights ago and the light was fading fast, she now knew where she was going. She went past the turn leading to Glenys and Leonard's farm, deliberately averting her gaze, but despite this she fancied she saw a flash of light in the distance. By the time she'd turned her head, it had gone. Fifty yards from the house, she was spotted by Jean's children, who shouted cheerfully as they ran ahead of her to announce her arrival to their mother.

Chapter Six

'How many will turn up, do you think?' Della asked, sipping tea as she stood by the large classroom window that faced the front.

When Lilwen didn't answer at once, she turned and looked at her, amazed for the second time at the golden strands of her hair and the creamy texture of her skin, as if she had been formed entirely from butter and milk. She saw that she was counting under her breath.

'About ten, I'd say,' she answered. 'The other farms are too far from the road, and some of the children are too small to come through the snow, anyway.'

Della would have liked to meet the whole school but she could see the advantage of this gradual introduction.

'Short Morning Service then, a hymn and the Lord's Prayer?'

Lilwen nodded, keeping her eyes on the contents of her cup. Even though she couldn't be accused of not being friendly – after all, she had made tea for her immediately on the fire in the infants' class – she possessed a certain reserve. Perhaps it was nervousness in front of a new headteacher.

'Do you normally play the piano?' asked Della. 'Or would you rather I did it?'

'I can't play a note,' confessed the girl, with a shy smile. 'The old master was really good at it.'

Of course. Della remembered the perfect condition of the piano in the parlour.

'I can't say I'm good,' she answered with a laugh. 'I'm afraid I play standing up with one foot on the soft pedal to hide the mistakes.'

Lilwen looked up at the big round clock above their heads.

'They'll be here before long,' she said. 'I might as well put the writing slates out.'

Lilwen's estimate of the numbers wasn't far out. As Della walloped out the accompaniment to 'Onward Christian Soldiers', with one eye over her shoulder, she could hear a variety of voices coming from the rows behind her. Only four of the infants had found a way through the snow, and two of those were Jean's children. From the six or seven older ones, she could see that she had children ranging in age from seven to fourteen, and a couple of those looked old enough to have children themselves. She could clearly hear Norman's voice. He stood head and shoulders taller than anyone else but his voice ground along a monotone subterranean furrow. Next to him stood a sharp-looking boy and a girl with fair plaits. Keeping them busy and maintaining their interest would be one of her more difficult tasks, and from the look in the eye of the sharp boy, she believed she was already being weighed and measured in this respect.

Yet, having marked the register, received the dinner money, asked the plaited girl, who was called Delyth, to refill the ink pots and set them all an essay on the topic 'Despite the Snow', an encouraging silence descended. Early days, she warned herself and went to look in the vast cupboard in the corner for one of the colourful geographical pictures she'd seen there the previous day, portraying the life of the Eskimo. She foresaw frantic igloo building in the yard at lunchtime.

On his way out at playtime at half past ten, Norman paused at her desk. She'd seen him eyeing the fire a number of times when he should have been writing his essay.

'The fire needs feeding,' he said, all of a rush. 'I used to do it every playtime. Do you want me to carry on, or is somebody else going to be coal monitor now?'

His longing was so evident, Della couldn't refuse.

'I'd be grateful if you'd carry on doing it, Norman,' she

answered. 'I need someone experienced and strong. You shall certainly be coal monitor.'

He smiled his great crooked smile at her and hurried out, waving the bucket triumphantly. Della followed him from a distance and saw Gareth, the sharp boy, loitering by the back door. She suspected that someone had put the idea in Norman's head that he might lose his important job. She made a show of rearranging the hymn books on top of the piano, while trying to think of something that would show Gareth's maturity.

'Gareth,' she called. 'Would you be so good as to make sure that the little ones are not doing silly things in the snow? If they're soaking wet, they have to come in and be dried. And nobody's to put a stone in a snowball. I don't want anyone losing an eye.'

He peeled himself slowly off the wall he'd been leaning against, but his sulky look didn't change. She supposed he'd had a bellyful of looking after small children at home, and tried to offer something more attractive.

'You're the only big boy I've got while Norman's carrying coal. If it's needed, I've got a first aid box in the house. I'll go and get it dinner time. You'll be responsible for it.'

The faintest glimmer of interest passed over his features.

'Bandaging them and things?' he asked.

'Yes. I'll teach you how to do it properly. It's quite complex and there's a lot to remember. Of course, it's entirely up to you …'

He shifted his weight from one foot to the other and thought. Enthusiastic shovelling sounds could be heard from the coal shed outside the back door. He came to a decision.

'Say one of them broke their arm,' he said. 'Could I put a sling on it?'

'Yes you could.'

'What if we need a stretcher? Is there one?'

'Not at the moment, but I'm sure we could make one,

between us. I have a book that shows you how to do things like that. We could go through it together, if you like.'

He nodded slowly, reluctant to appear too keen, but when Della turned back to the books she saw him go out to where the younger children were engaged in a fierce battle. She heard him raise his voice above the screaming. 'Hey, Gerwyn Jenkins! Leave it, will you?' and allowed herself to smile. As her old college principal used to say, '*Turn poachers into gamekeepers wherever you can.*' Wise words, but not always easy to put into practice.

'If something doesn't come through the snow quickly, there'll be no dinner here after Wednesday.'

Mrs Jefferies breathed deeply through her nose and glared challengingly at Della over the serving table. Snow or not, she remained dignified in her starched apron and cap and the food looked hot and tasty. Behind her, Jean flitted to and fro from the kitchen to the dining hall, which was situated at the top of the yard, winking mischievously at Della behind the back of the head cook.

'They could always have Spam, Mrs Jefferies,' Jean offered humbly. 'There's still two big tins of it in the back of the cupboard.'

'Spam!' Mrs Jefferies spat out the word. 'The poor little mites. And I thought we'd won the war.'

Della was saved from having to solve the Spam problem by a shout from the hall door.

'The milk lorry's coming!'

As one, the little band leapt to their feet, hurriedly swallowed the last of their pudding, and half carrying the youngest between them rushed, sliding, sometimes on their backsides, down the slope to the gate. Della followed, calling for care and calm, but she was largely ignored. Hanging over the gate or staring through the bars they gave a conqueror's welcome to the slow moving truck as it trundled up the road.

Della was reminded of the newsreel she'd seen, showing the Allies reaching Paris some years before. Even Lilwen was all smiles.

'I was worried that we'd have a repeat of January,' she said. 'The milk freezing solid in the churns and bursting the lids before the lorry got through.'

Unwillingly, when it had disappeared into the distance, the children trickled back for the afternoon session, that was spent drawing or doing crafts. Della hoped that they wouldn't get the impression that every afternoon was to follow the same pattern. Yet, she was exhaustedly pleased to see them pick up their wet gloves from the fender at the end of the day. Jean was already clanking about with her bucket and mop as the last one went through the door.

'Well then, Miss,' she said, poking her head through the half-open doorway to the classroom. 'How did it go?'

'I can't complain,' answered Della. 'With only a handful of children, and two of those being yours. Everyone behaved very nicely.'

Jean snorted through her nose.

'You wait,' she said. She glanced over her shoulder and then came in and shut the door.

'Don't you let Gareth take advantage,' she said confidentially. 'If he starts, give him a clout.'

'But he was a terrific help with the smaller children in the yard today,' said Della, pretending astonishment. 'And I think he's going to be really good at first aid.'

'Our Gareth?' asked his mother, as if there had been half a dozen Gareths in the class. She had to think about this for a few seconds.

'He's pretty good with his hands, I suppose,' she admitted.

Della picked up the bundle of essay books. From what she'd managed to read so far, he was pretty good with a pen too. She put them on the window sill so that Jean could run her duster over the desk. At the front gate she could see Lilwen standing talking with a familiar red-haired young man. Jean followed her eyes and made a significant face.

'Tecwyn again,' she said.

'I thought his name was Carwyn. I must have misheard.'

'No, you didn't,' said Jean. 'There's two of them. Twins. Sons of Sara and Benj Pantglas. Cousins to Norman, poor dab. Identical. He'd better hurry up, because Rees will be tamping mad if he sees them.'

As she was busy analysing all this information, Della almost missed her cue to ask more.

'Why will Rees be tamping?' she asked.

'He's not good enough,' answered Jean. 'Seeing as she's been to college and all.'

'Has he got anyone else in mind, then?'

Jean didn't answer directly this time, but flicked her cloth over the mantelpiece.

'It would have been much better if she'd got a job further away,' she said.

She was prevented from saying more. They heard the clump of hobnailed boots coming through the hall and Norman appeared, breathless, at the door.

'I'll do the coal buckets for tomorrow for you now,' he said to Jean.

And without any further word off he went again. Jean smiled and shook out her duster into the fire.

'He saw me struggling one afternoon when I was expecting Mefin, the youngest, and now he does it for me every night. He's a good old boy, is Norman. I don't care what anyone says.'

There was no opportunity for Della to ask who said otherwise. A shy knock was heard at the front door of the school, and when she peered through the window, she saw Eirug Rees standing there. He must have come through the gate without her noticing. There was no sign of Tecwyn or

Lilwen. Della sincerely hoped he wasn't going to try to enlist her support to keep them apart. But when she opened the door, he seemed eager not to be seen.

'We'll be moving them tonight,' he whispered. 'Mr Richards is asking do you still want to come?'

'Of course I do,' answered Della without hesitation.

'That's what he said you'd say. Are you sure? It's no place for a lady, is it? I can't imagine Lilwen wanting to come.'

'Nor can I,' said Della. 'But then she's not a tough old bird like me, is she? I'll be waiting for you.'

She watched him cross the yard and around the corner of the building, shaking his head as he went. She returned to Jean who had started to wash the floor.

'Mr Rees, coming to fetch Lilwen,' she said loudly, knowing that Lilwen herself was most likely putting on her coat within earshot. 'Fair play to him. This snow's slippery.'

Jean waited until Lilwen's footsteps faded into the distance before answering.

'He's much too careful of her,' she remarked. 'He moved heaven and earth to get her into this school. But that was the worst thing he could have done, because when the master fell ill, she was too young and inexperienced to keep things going. I know she couldn't help that, but the place went to rack and ruin.'

'Poor girl,' said Della sincerely. 'I was in a similar situation myself, years ago, and I wouldn't wish it on anybody.'

'I grant you it wasn't easy.' Jean was willing to concede that much. 'But I doubt if I'd have found you crying as often as I found Lilwen. The little devils were running amok – but for goodness sake, they're only children after all!'

Della laughed.

'To you perhaps. But then you're used to a houseful.'

Jean leant on her mop and squeezed it dry in the colander at the top of the bucket with a practised twist.

'Well, I was fed up to the back teeth of standing on the yard reading the riot act, I can tell you. But then Mr Richards got to hear of it, and started coming down to keep order. You should have seen it! He taught them to march, "Left right, left right" and they were doing PT until they were running with sweat.' She smiled reminiscently. 'And the funny thing is, they used to look forward to seeing him. They like a bit of order, children do. They know where they stand.'

Nursing her cup of tea after her evening meal, her words came back to Della. Seeing that he had a finger in every pie, when Huw Richards came to see them she'd have to make sure that the school was being run on Hitler Youth lines. If she could get hold of the chairman of the selection panel, she'd give him a piece of her mind. It was deeply unfair to throw any teacher into this kind of situation without so much as a hint. Was this why they'd appointed a teacher from another county, because nobody local was prepared to take on the job? Nothing at all had been said about the long term dipsomania of the master, nor even that the school had been run for a long period by one young woman, straight out of college. The only thing she could remember from her interview, which should really have raised her suspicions, was the chairman staring hard at her over his half moon spectacles, as if he were judging a milking cow, to see how many productive seasons she had left.

When the knock on the back door came at last, it was so quiet Della almost ignored it. By the time she got up to answer, Eirug Rees had returned to the road, where the patient mare and the cart stood silently in the darkness. Sitting with him on the driver's bench was the minister and she could make out the dim figures of the Italians on foot.

'I'll only be a second,' she called, grabbing her coat and hat and shoving her feet into Glenys's boots which she'd left by the back door. She was helped into the back of the cart, where numerous mysterious objects lay under sacking, including a number of spades.

'There's blankets there, somewhere,' said Rees over his shoulder. 'Put them over your knees now, because there's likely to be a long wait. We'll have to clear a path.'

The minister said nothing, but Della knew he was glancing back at her from time to time under the brim of his homburg hat. Nobody much spoke as they went on their way, with the snow crunching under wheels, hooves and feet. It looked as if it would be another icy night. Above her head, the moon seemed to play hide and seek behind the occasional cloud, but at least the high hedges sheltered them from the vicious wind.

'Where shall we say we're going if we meet someone on the road?' asked Della, feeling that the silence had become oppressive.

'Temperance meeting,' answered the minister without turning his head.

Rees laughed briefly.

'Not if they see the beer in the back,' he said, adding apologetically to the man at his side. 'I had to promise the boys something. It's not going to be easy.'

He was telling the truth. Once they reached the narrow lane to the farm, even with four of them shovelling as fast as they could, Della felt as if she'd been sitting for hours moving along an inch at a time. It was Salvatore, one of the Italians, who was first to reach the stile and the gate. He came back to the cart, shaking his head and wincing.

'Wire,' he said, sucking his gloveless fingers.

The minister turned to Della, clicking his tongue to reassure the mare.

'There should be clippers in that sack there,' he said and watched as she fumbled for them. When she found them and gave them to Salvatore, she noticed that he now had gloves, good leather ones, and that Huw Richards's fingers were bare.

In the end, they lifted the wooden gate off its hinges and laid it in the hedge to save time. Ahead of them lay the wide yard, under a thick white blanket, but they could see the farmhouse by the light of the moon. The minister got down painfully from the cart and tied the reins to the gate post. He moved round to the back and pulled some of the sacking aside. A storm lamp stood next to a large earthenware bottle – the home-brewed beer, guessed Della. He succeeded in lighting the lamp, throwing an eerie glow over the proceedings for the first time and up over the sharp planes of his face. Della shivered and drew a deep breath to control herself. He looked at her.

'I'm not surprised,' he said expressionlessly, 'but it's your own fault for insisting on coming.'

She grimaced at him.

'I'm fine,' she snapped. 'It's just that you look like the Gestapo in that hat. Enough to make anyone shiver.' She pushed her hands into her armpits.

Rees appeared out of the darkness, his face flushed from the effort despite the temperature.

'I think we need to give the lads a bit of a boost,' said Huw Richards, as if Della hadn't spoken, and Rees looked at him gratefully. Della waited to see whether he would take some beer and when he did, to their surprise, she reached out her hand for the bottle, but Rees had brought a metal cup especially for her. She drank the bitter liquid bravely, even though she didn't care for it, just to feel the heat.

'We three can walk to the house from here, while they clear a path for the cart,' said Rees, wiping his mouth on his sleeve. 'There's no point wasting time. By the time they get through, we'll be ready to carry out.'

Holding the lamp, he led the way. Della followed in their footprints, having to lift her feet up to knee level until they reached the path she'd cut.

'Who did this?' she heard Huw Richards ask.

'It was here this afternoon when I arrived,' answered Rees, 'but I cleared a bit more.'

'Anybody see you?'

'Oh yes. I made sure of that.'

On the point of claiming the path as her own handiwork, Della kept her mouth shut. She realised that the whole expedition had been carefully planned. Hence the wire clippers in the sack. Rees had been here doing a recce beforehand, under orders, with the minister overseeing the campaign. By the storeroom door, the farmer put the lamp down, and pulled away a stout stick that kept the door closed before clicking the latch and entering. There was very little difference in temperature between the storeroom and the outside, but Della shut the door behind her. The other two were already at the far end with the lamp, but she noticed that the wood around the lock was splintered. So Norman had found his key, then. She hurried through to the kitchen where the two men stood, looking about them curiously. Della went straight to the dresser where she'd left the candle and lit it with the matches in her pocket.

'You know this place better than anybody, Miss Arthur,' said Huw Richards and, when Della raised her eyebrows, Rees nodded in agreement.

'I never came into the house before this afternoon,' he said. 'Didn't you either?'

'No. I called shortly after they arrived, but I was kept standing in the farmyard. I suppose it's an apt place for a spiritual shepherd to be, but it was pouring with rain.'

'Was this before the war?' asked Della.

'About six months after it began.'

'So the rations were already in force,' said Della. She pulled aside the curtain which hid the back kitchen and showed them the treasury of tinned goods. 'Perhaps this is why.'

Rees stared at them with big eyes, but from Richards's

casual glance at them, Della doubted whether he was in the least bit surprised. The farmer moved over to the dresser.

'Look,' he said. 'There's money here,' and picked up the pennies that Della had left there. 'I imagine there's a lot more of these here somewhere.'

'We shan't be looking for them tonight,' said Huw Richards decisively. 'There's no need to put temptation in anyone's way.'

She knew quite well that he was referring to the Italians, but Della felt she had to explain.

'I put the money there,' she said. 'To pay for the food I ate, and the wood for the fire.'

She gestured towards the inglenook and Rees went over and peered up to where the flitch of bacon hung.

'And where did this come from, I wonder?' he murmured. 'There hasn't been a pig here for years. Not to mention that it's all got to be signed and approved by the Ministry of Food.'

Huw Richards coughed and Rees turned away quickly.

'It was very honourable of you to think of paying,' he said hurriedly, 'considering the situation.'

Della sensed that all this had some significance but she shrugged self-deprecatingly.

'I couldn't just eat people's food uninvited. And anyway, I was expecting the owners to walk through the door at any moment.'

The minister scooped up the money from the dresser and handed it to her.

'Take it back,' he said. 'You were never here.'

He'd opened the door to the corridor before Della got her breath back. She stared at the cash in her hand.

'But I was seen!' she said disbelievingly. 'By Norman and all the gang on the road, and wearing Glenys's coat and scarf, too. Where did I get those from if not from here? Did I find them in the hedge? Or did I perhaps strip Glenys's body and put them on?'

Rees was shifting about in a sweat of embarrassment but there was no sign of that on his general's face.

'You shall decide,' he snapped. 'But if I were you, I wouldn't admit to being inside the house at all unless someone in authority asks a direct question, and even then I should deny moving out of this room.'

He turned and disappeared in the direction of the stairs. Rees pulled an apologetic grimace.

'He's thinking of your reputation,' he whispered. 'As far as anybody around here knows, I found them this afternoon. Nobody had seen them for days, see, and I started to suspect something had happened.' He recited this like a verse committed to memory.

Seeing that she was about to protest he put his hand on her arm.

'Everything will be alright, you don't have to worry. He knows how to organise things. Now then, I'd better go and tidy them up before the boys get here.'

Della had no need to stand at the bottom of the stairs without the candle and listen to know what their first task was, but she did it anyway, moving back into the shadows as they carried Glenys's limp body, wrapped in a sheet, across the landing to her own bedroom. That's where she would be when the Italians arrived to carry her downstairs, dead, but respectable. And if the Italians spoke of it in the pub, as they were sure to do, the neighbourhood would hear the sanitised version that had been designed for them by Huw Richards. She shivered again and tiptoed back to the kitchen, pushing her hands deep into the pockets of her coat to stop them shaking. Ignoring the heavy sounds from above her head, she went over to Glenys's knitting bag. She remembered the moment she'd seen the knitting for the first time and noticed that something was wrong with it. What was it, she wondered? A dropped stitch, a wrong line of pattern? She pulled the piece on the needle out of the bag and held it up. It took her a little time to realise what it was, but even when she did, it remained a total mystery. For some reason, the knitting was on the needle the wrong way round, with the side where the next row of knitting should start, denoted by the long tail of wool, up by the blunt, stoppered end, and not next to the point, where it should be. Why would Glenys have left it like this? To continue to knit, she'd have had to take the whole piece off the needle and pick up the stitches, one at a time, so that they were facing the right way. It was a nuisance, because you always risked missing a stitch and making a hole. And why had she turned it the wrong way to start with?

She heard Giuseppe's harsh voice calling from the storeroom door and shoved the whole lot back before going out to light their way with the candle.

There was no room for anyone in the back of the cart on the way home. Della walked – after refusing Huw Richards's offer to take his seat – trying not to look at the two forms lying covered in front of her, jolting heavily as the cart lurched over frozen ruts in the snow. She kept her eyes on the two men on the driver's bench, the one in his high crowned hat and the other in his flat cap. It didn't look like either of them had much to say. She knew why, and was glad she hadn't gone upstairs. Apart from Enzo and the minister, all the others had come down white-faced and had emptied the earthenware bottle between them. When they finally reached School House, Della stood on the highest step and watched them trundle slowly down towards Rees's farm. That was where the bodies were to rest for the time being. The Italians had cheered up by now and Salvatore whistled quietly between his teeth and exchanged the occasional remark with Giuseppe. As she put her thumb on the latch she glanced once more at them. Enzo had turned his head and was staring at her. Then he too turned and joined in the conversation.

Chapter Seven

'Now that we have an accompanist,' said Mrs Jefferies from the head of the table, looking very much at home in a large carved chair from some turn of the century eisteddfod. 'I suggest that we sing 'Jerusalem'.'

The constant hum of chatter turned into grumbling, but the chairwoman would not be denied. She scowled at them.

'It says in the constitution that we're supposed to sing it in every meeting of the WI but we never do.'

She pushed a ragged book in Della's direction who saw, with a sinking heart, that it contained the musical notation for the hymn. Up to that point, she hadn't been paying much attention, especially through the chairwoman's long-winded lecture on 'Recipes on the Rations'. As she hadn't got to bed until well after midnight the previous evening, she wouldn't have gone to the meeting of the Women's Institute at all, but Jean had mentioned it and said it would be an opportunity for her to meet some of the mothers. She'd spent the time thinking and listening to the talk around her, which suited her mood. Unwillingly, she got up and went to the piano. She heard the women behind her sighing as they stood, scraping their chairs over the wooden floor.

The singing wasn't enthusiastic, it had to be admitted. Only Mrs Jefferies knew all the words, and out of the corner of her eye Della could see that Jean had positioned herself behind that large lady and was pretending to turn a handle in her back. Suppressing a smile Della ploughed on. Walking back to her seat, she suddenly noticed that Lilwen was no longer there. One or two of the other women were glancing at the door and exchanging significant glances. She saw the word 'Tecwyn' being mouthed by one and the other nodded. One of the women in the row behind hers leant forward.

'Gerwyn said you played standing up. I didn't believe him.' Della smiled.

'I started doing it in my first school,' she explained, 'so that I could nip any misbehaviour in the bud. And now I can't play any other way.'

'I can't eat sitting down for the same reason,' remarked Jean.

The meeting appeared to be winding down slowly, but nobody was in a hurry to leave. Truth be told, Della was astonished that so many had made such an effort to turn up, but perhaps this was their only opportunity to leave daily responsibilities behind and have a good chat. Like their children in school earlier that day, the news of Glenys's and Leonard's demise was a topic of never-ending interest and she heard the same tales – quite untrue for the most part – regarding the event. What surprised her most of all was that not one of them asked her about the night she'd spent on the farm. She could see Ceinwen from the shop among the crowd, but despite eavesdropping unashamedly on her conversations, Della did not hear her own name mentioned once. This could have been because she was sitting there in the flesh, but there might have been other reasons.

No enlightenment came until she was walking back down the yard with Jean. They stood by the privet that surrounded the front garden of School House.

'There'll be a funeral before long then,' said Jean casually. 'If they can dig a grave. The snow will be enough of an excuse to keep most people away.'

Della pretended to be surprised at that.

'Were they not popular?'

In the moonlight she saw Jean roll her eyes.

'Good God, no. Especially not Leonard. They lived at arm's length with all the neighbours. Wouldn't let the children cross their land even when it cut a good two miles off the journey to school and back. I could never see why. It wasn't as if they grew anything or kept livestock. They didn't farm at all, or do much with anybody. Although, he was a regular at the Hut.'

She must have felt she'd said too much because she added, 'But there we are, you only saw their better side. Like I said to Stevie, no one could refuse somebody shelter in that storm.'

Della made a small ambiguous sound in her throat. So, the general belief appeared to be that they'd died some days after she'd left there. Without doubt, her behaviour would strike them as extremely odd if they'd known that she found the bodies. She really should have announced her discovery to the road gang as soon as she saw them. This was all her own fault. She said goodnight thoughtfully to Jean and went into the house. The parlour clock was striking half past ten as she took off her coat. She stared at her reflection in the hallstand mirror. As faces went it was alright, she supposed. The grey eyes were serious, the straight nose independent, and the frame of carefully rolled dark hair gave no hint of feminine softness or weakness. That's my problem, she thought. I've seen too much, and learnt to fence off my feelings until I have the time to deal with them. Crying and grieving publicly and showing fear are no longer part of my nature, if they ever were.

She climbed the stairs and changed into her nightgown and warm dressing gown. Rolling her stockings into a neat ball she recalled Huw Richards's strange attitude in the farmhouse, telling her that she should decide on her own story, and Eirug Rees's awkward attempt to take the sting out of his words by talking of her reputation. Was that the real reason – that her reaction to the deaths had been so unnatural that it would breed suspicion if the community got to hear of it? Was all the careful planning so that she shouldn't be accused of hiding the deaths, or worse still, of having caused them in the first place? She shook her head angrily and pushed her feet into her slippers. Would hysterical weeping have been more appropriate? Surely not. There was some other reason for all the secrecy, something other than concealing the fact that the brother and sister had been sharing a bed when they died. After all, if nobody liked them, what did it matter how they were found? If they'd been pillars of the community and everyone's friend, she could easily understand why their pastor would wish to keep that quiet, so that they'd be remembered fondly and not with disgust.

She went back down the stairs and put a saucepan of milk on to heat. She'd just poured the warm milk into a cup when she heard a footfall on the back steps and a knock on the door. Oh no, she thought, who's there again now? She had no choice but to answer the door as she was.

'*Signorina*,' said Enzo's voice from the darkness, 'I hope I don't wake you. We need to talk. About the bodies.'

If she hadn't been turning the subject over in her mind already, Della would not have let him into the house. He smelt of beer for one thing, although not strongly, and there was no way of knowing who'd seen him standing there. She shut the door quickly after him and offered him warm milk, but he refused it.

'I have been to Hut,' he said. 'Plenty to drink.'

He lifted one of the hard chairs and set it down by the fire. He perched there, warming his hands while she settled herself in her usual chair.

'This last night,' he began. 'Many questions … many things …' He searched for the right words.

'Are hard to understand?' suggested Della, wondering how exactly she could answer these questions without revealing too much but he nodded enthusiastically and leant his elbows on his knees.

'Why was wire on gate? They use car. No other gate from farm to road. Have to take away wire each time to get out.'

This was not the first question that Della had been expecting, but she thought about it.

'Jean told me tonight that they didn't want anybody crossing the land. Perhaps they put the wire on the gate to keep people out.'

'New wire,' he said. Della shrugged. She didn't know the difference between old wire and new. She didn't want to mention that it had been there the night she'd reached the farm. He saw that he was looking at her hard and hoped he couldn't read her thoughts. When he spoke again it was to make a statement.

'*Signora* don't die in big bed. She die in other bed. *Signor* Rees and Napoleone move her.'

It was a good name for Huw Richards, she thought, but she was, nevertheless, puzzled by his conviction.

'Marks on sheets. Two bodies marks in big bed. No marks on her bed. Body liquid, after you die …?' He made gestures indicative of leakage to illustrate his point. Della looked at the skin that was slowly forming on her milk and set it aside.

'They were brother and sister, after all,' she said, hoping he would get her drift. Enzo puffed impatiently.

'Of course. Don't want scandal. But problem. How can two die in bed the same time? One perhaps, old and ill. But not two.'

Della gnawed the inside of her cheek and cursed herself silently for assuming that the cold had killed them. But could that not still be true?

'It was terribly cold,' she said carefully. 'And Mr Rees said that they used to keep all the windows open.'

The look of sheer disbelief that answered her remark spoke volumes. Enzo shook his head.

'Old house,' he said. 'Walls like this.' He held his arms out wide. 'Plenty wood for fire … plenty food. Why did they die of cold?'

Della felt distinctly uncomfortable now.

'Do you think they might have killed themselves?' He looked at her drily.

'How? No gun, no knife, no tablets.'

'Couldn't they have taken sleeping tablets before going to bed and thrown the bottle away?' She went on, elaborating her theory with increasing enthusiasm. 'Perhaps that's why they were together, so they wouldn't face the final hours alone. And perhaps there were tablets by the bed. Mr Rees or Mr Richards could have removed them before you got there, again to avoid a scandal.' She saw him think and then he shook his head again, but less definitely this time.

'Why not want scandal? Nobody cry. Nobody care. Glenys and Leonard – phut!' He turned down his thumb like the Emperor Nero. 'Now lie in shed on farm. Wait for Hetty.' This was news.

'Why Hetty of all people?'

'She wash dead bodies.' He crossed his arms over his chest and closed his eyes briefly. 'Then they bury them. Gone.'

Della didn't know what to say. How blind she'd been! Why had she not looked around the room when she had the chance? Because you were shocked rigid and couldn't wait to be out of there, she responded silently. She regretted opening the door to the sharp Italian. She hoped the interrogation was finished, but there was more to come.

'One thing more,' said Enzo, and this time he didn't look at her. 'Why they ask you to come and move them?' Della pretended indifference.

'Because I'm a stranger I suppose,' she said as carelessly as she could. 'Like you and Giuseppe and Salvatore. Perhaps other people refused. Who knows? But you're right about one thing, I'm sure. They really don't want a scandal. This is a small place. They could have been afraid that Hetty, for example, would let the cat out of the bag.'

'What is this cat?'

'It means talk too much. Tell secrets.'

He nodded slowly but she didn't know whether she'd convinced him.

'Could be,' he muttered. 'Or perhaps because you were last person to see them.'

Della never knew whether it was this sentence that made the dawn break over her, or whether it had been dawning on her slowly throughout the interview, but suddenly she knew one thing.

'You're a policeman, Enzo,' she said. 'That was your job back in Italy.' She searched for the right word. 'You were one of the *carabinieri*.'

For a second it looked as if he was about to deny it, but then he smiled.

'Very good, *Signorina*,' he said admiringly. 'I am here four years and nobody say, Enzo, you are policeman. You are first.'

'Not even Mr Richards, the minister?'

He drew a breath in through his teeth and winked.

'With him, I am careful.' He made forelock tugging gestures. 'With him I am always stupid.'

'And what about Giuseppe and Salvatore? Do they know?'

'No. They understand nothing.' He got up. 'I must go now, or questions. Hut is closed.'

He saw that she hadn't understood and added, 'Hut close half past ten. Walk home to farm half an hour. When you are drunk, three-quarters of hour. Tonight I am drunk.' He took a few mock-unsteady steps and laughed to see her smile. 'It is good place. See and hear much. Leonard drink whisky. Master drink gin. Stevie drink everything. People let the cat out of bag.' He repeated the idiom, evidently intending to remember it.

Della followed him to the door. Even though she didn't know whether she could trust him any more than anyone else, he was, at least, taking an intelligent and unbiased interest in the matter.

'Tell me,' she ventured. 'Is there any way I could see the bodies? I've seen a lot of dead people. Perhaps I could get some idea of how they died.'

She saw his back stiffen but when he turned back in the darkness of the scullery she realised that he was pleasantly surprised with her.

'Not easy,' he answered. 'Shed locked. Have to think. But also we must go back to Leonard's farm. You and me. We need to search and look.'

'What for exactly?'

He shrugged.

'Don't know. But you must put coat and scarf back. You don't have with you the other night.'

Della was taken aback. She'd completely forgotten about them. She bit her lip and sensed his smile.

'People see you wear them,' he whispered. 'They talk.'

He opened the back door and glanced swiftly up and down the road.

'*Ciao, Signorina!*' he said and melted into the night.

Della shut the door behind him and went to wash up her cup. She stood there for an age, turning it this way and that under the tap in the candlelight, trying to think what else she could have forgotten. Napoleone had been right to insist on her taking her money back. She was already in the bathroom when she remembered the chamber pot sitting in the storeroom. Hell fire, she thought. How on earth could she put that back without Enzo noticing? If he saw her doing so, he'd realise immediately that she'd been upstairs. Could she say that Glenys had brought it down for her to use? Would he believe her? Would anyone believe that she'd done nothing but discover the bodies, if they knew the truth?

CHAPTER EIGHT

'Well, I must say it's nice to see a fire in the grate in this room. The old master, poor soul, never lit one.'

Aneurin the Policeman settled himself more comfortably in the armchair in the living room and a small shower of crumbs fell on the floor.

'More tea, Mr Jenkins?' Della asked, seeing the second of the half dozen small cakes that one of the children had given her that morning disappear before her eyes.

'I won't say no,' he answered, all smiles, reaching out his large red hand with his cup in it. 'I would have called before now,' he said when Della came back from the kitchen with it refilled, 'but this old snow's lethal on a bike, see.'

'I think even the children are getting tired of it,' answered Della. 'I know I'll be glad to see the back of it. When they come in from the yard at dinner time, the place is like a laundry all afternoon.'

It was a stroke of luck that she'd set the fire that morning, because otherwise she'd have had to entertain him in the kitchen, and he was evidently a man who appreciated the comforts of life. When school finished that day, she'd been looking forward to a quiet evening reading in front of the fire, but the heavy figure of the representative of law and order had been standing patiently at the door of the house, waiting for her, and he didn't look as if he did anything in a hurry.

'The missus said she'd met you at the WI – the Wild Indians!' He smiled at his own joke.

'You wouldn't believe how wild we are there,' replied Della, joining in the game, 'with Mrs Jefferies leading the high jinks.' Aneurin winked to show that he understood.

'I was surprised that Mari wanted to go the other night, but now I know why.' He leaned forward confidentially. 'What do you do there?'

Della sucked her teeth, thoughtfully.

'If I told you that, I'd be thrown out.'

Aneurin laughed like a squeaky gate. He brushed the rest of the crumbs off his knees. Then he looked serious.

'I had another reason for calling. There are a couple of things I want to ask you.'

Della felt her heart speed up. She'd been suspicious since she'd seen him on her doorstep that this wasn't just a social call. She prepared herself mentally.

'I've had a word with the Reverend Richards, and he said that you were the woman to ask. On the spot, as it were.'

The swine, thought Della, throwing me to the dogs at the first opportunity, but she managed to smile. She saw that the constable was squirming slightly as if he felt awkward. Perhaps he'd never had to question anyone about such a matter before. He certainly seemed to be choosing his words carefully.

'The thing is … and I want you to feel you can tell me the truth here … has our Gerwyn got any hope of passing the Eleven Plus? His mother's got her heart set on him going to the County School, but really, if there's no hope, is it fair to push the child? What do you think?'

Five minutes later, out in the kitchen, filling the teapot for the third time, Della allowed herself a tiny sigh of relief. Even though she doubted whether Gerwyn Jenkins would be the brightest star in the firmament of the Grammar School, he wasn't hopeless by any means, and if his parents were willing to employ the minister to coach him, then he did have a very fair chance of passing the exam. Gerwyn was lazy, taking after his father to all appearances, but that didn't mean there was nothing in his head. The same was true for Aneurin, she realised. She should keep her guard up.

'This will have to be a quick cup,' said the policeman, back in the living room. 'I'm all of a rush tonight to go over and see John Ffynnondderw's widow.'

Could have fooled me, thought Della, but it was not a name she'd heard before and she said so.

'No, you wouldn't have known him. He went out to see to his sheep the night of that terrible storm and never came back. They found him dead in the field.' Aneurin shook his head sadly. 'He didn't need to go at all, because the sheep were fine. It was this perishing cold again, you see Miss Arthur. You take Glenys and Leonard now. Same thing. And they were in the house!'

Della nodded.

'Tragic,' she murmured.

'It is,' agreed Aneurin, swallowing tea like a calf from a bucket. 'And awkward, you wouldn't believe! I don't know when I can get the doctor out to Clawdd Coch to give a certificate, and then have to send that away again. And how are we going to bury them? The ground's as hard as iron.'

'It's a lot of work for you, Mr Jenkins.'

'Don't talk! And that's only the beginning. If they had family somewhere it would help. But they came from away somewhere, like yourself.'

'Perhaps you'll have to put a notice in the paper, if all else fails,' suggested Della. 'Don't you have any idea where they came from originally?'

He thought hard.

'Funny you should mention it, because I was talking about this last night with Mari. I seem to recall Leonard talking about a village in the south, but I can't put a name to it. Somewhere between Carmarthen and Llanelly. And then somebody said that they had another sister, but that she'd died – I'd give my right arm for her to be alive, I can tell you. What's going to happen to the farm? And all the furniture? Endless paperwork for me, that's what.'

'It's very difficult,' said Della, who had been thinking as he spoke. 'You could always ask in the bank in Cardigan or Newcastle Emlyn in case a will had been left with them. Or even go round the solicitors there.'

For a dreadful second she thought she'd shown too much interest, because he looked at her far more sharply than before.

'That's the value of a college education,' he said. 'Knowing where to go.' Della smiled at him.

'Unfortunately, that was something I had to learn on my own,' she said. 'While I was fire-watching in Swansea during the war, it was one of the things I had to do. There were occasions when a bomb would fall and kill everyone in a lodging house down by the docks. And you can imagine how difficult that could be, when there was nothing left but rubble without any indication of who anybody was.'

'Heavens above!' Aneurin finished his tea with a final gulp. 'At least the house is still standing here.' He looked at her again. 'You wouldn't be willing to come with me, would you?' Della demurred.

'Wouldn't your warrant card be enough for the bank and solicitors?'

'Not to see them. To the farm. There could be papers there that would help us contact people. I don't remember anything like this happening before. Everybody's related to everybody else – you can't hear yourself speak above the crowing of people claiming to be related. Usually, they're like a plague of locusts. But not in this case. You'll know what to look for.'

She could have refused. She told herself so, over and over, as she tossed and turned that night. But the problem was how, without appearing unnecessarily uncooperative, and anyway it was better that she was present than that Aneurin should find things in her absence which would cause him to ask unwelcome questions. As she said goodbye to him, she'd nearly blurted out the whole story, but was prevented by the knowledge that, at this late stage, it would place Rees and Huw Richards in a difficult position. She believed that Eirug Rees was acting, at least partly, in order to save her from the attentions of the authorities. She hoped that Huw Richards was spurred by the same motivations, but she wasn't sure. She felt, in her bones, that there were other reasons behind his decisions. He wasn't called Napoleone for nothing. He was just like some army general in his study, planning and organising a great battle, expecting his soldiers to obey without hesitation. However, she had no intention of sacrificing herself without a very good reason. The last thing that struck her before she dropped into a comfortless doze was that she and Enzo would have to go to the farmhouse very soon, before Aneurin. And she would have to warn him to wear gloves. In complete contrast, the more fingerprints she could leave the better, especially in Aneurin's company. Perhaps, after all, by agreeing to go with him, she'd chosen the wisest course.

It was the middle of the afternoon on the following day when a child, returning from the toilets, mentioned that 'one of the Italians had brought food for the kitchen'. Della hurried up the slippery slope to the dining hall. She sincerely hoped that it wasn't either Giuseppe or Salvatore. If they were as dim as Enzo had claimed, perhaps Rees would not have sent them. Mrs Jefferies stood at the kitchen door and from inside a sack could be heard being thumped about.

'Good news, Mrs Jefferies?' called Della as she approached.

The chief cook sniffed and folded her arms.

'To a degree,' she answered. 'They can have turnip mash if nothing else.'

She moved out of the way to let a dark figure go past and then disappeared back to her work. Aware that the door was still open, Della thanked Enzo formally. He smiled knowingly.

'*Signor* Rees say plenty more if you need.'

'He's very kind indeed,' said Della in a loud voice. 'Do remember to thank him. The school is in his debt.' Then they strolled down towards the gate where the mare was tethered. When they were out of anyone's earshot Della murmured, 'The village policeman called yesterday. He's asked me to go with him to the farm to look for official papers, like a will. So you and I have to go there quickly.'

Enzo untied the reins from the gatepost.

'Tonight?' he asked and Della nodded silently. Then Enzo looked around before climbing onto the driver's bench.

'Snow is going,' he remarked. 'No more freeze and suffer. *Ciao!*'

Would that were true, thought Della, wrapping her arms around herself, as she scurried back into the warm building.

CHAPTER NINE

'I've got a torch.'

Della offered it as she saw her co-conspirator trying to cut off a piece of barbed wire from the gate in the shadow of the hedge.

'No,' he said. 'Only in house.'

Although Della couldn't imagine who could possibly see them in the narrow lane, she obeyed. Cursing quietly in Italian, he succeeded at last, and she followed him through the gap and across the farmyard. Seeing that he was almost running, she quickened her pace to catch up. His whole attitude, although not exactly a surprise, was unsettling. He pulled away the stout stick that wedged the door shut and ushered her into the storeroom in front of him.

'Now torch,' he said, rubbing his hands until the beam lit up the bare room. Della shone the light over the walls.

'I remember seeing wire here the other night,' she said, but Enzo was already reaching up with his sample in his hand. She directed the light so that he could see better. He made a sound in his throat.

'Wire different,' he muttered, tucking the small piece into his pocket. He offered no further explanation, but turned towards the door to the kitchen.

Once there, his first act was to look at the window behind the large table and then he went straight through into the passage. While she was hanging Glenys's coat and scarf back in their proper place, Della watched him going through the rooms on the ground floor. Then he came back and took the stump of a candle out of his pocket, lighting it.

'Curtain closed everywhere,' he muttered. 'Even in best room and empty bedroom. Why?' He saw her pause and added, 'Why close curtain in room where nobody live?'

As it was she herself who had done so when she'd shut the windows, she could only shake her head, and try to think of a good reason.

'Perhaps Mr Rees thought he should,' she ventured. 'You know, because it's a house of grief. It's our tradition when somebody dies.' He appeared to be satisfied with that.

'Yes, maybe so. *Signor* Rees came here in afternoon. That's why I think strange.' Then he shook his head as if to reject a premise and Della's heart sank. 'But why not more wet on floor? Windows open three days. Much snow.' However, to her relief he didn't wait for a reply but continued.

'We look now everywhere,' he said, miming pulling out drawers. Della nodded, and then remembered the need for gloves. She found a pair in the pocket of one of the coats on the rack and gave them to him.

'Dead man gloves,' he said grimly, but put them on despite this.

Della waited for him to go into the parlour and hurried back to the storeroom. The chamber pot sat just where she'd left it and she felt grateful that they'd chosen a time when it was too dark to see much of anything without a candle. She knew there was no way she could take it back upstairs, and so she carried it through to the scullery behind the kitchen. There would be somewhere there she could hide it behind the curtains. She was on her knees, having shoved it right to the back of the lowest shelf when she heard the heavy drape move behind her.

Enzo gave a low whistle and Della, after a jolt of panic, realised that he hadn't seen the stock of tins before now.

'Treasures,' she remarked. 'All manner of food you haven't been able to get hold of for years. I saw them the other night with the minister and Mr Rees.'

He crouched and stared.

'Black market?' he asked with a dry smile.

'Definitely. They didn't buy these in Iori and Ceinwen's shop.'

She looked at them again and then shone the torch over the stack.

'What you seen?' asked Enzo but Della was counting under her breath.

'Some have gone,' she said. 'When I was here the other night, there were more of them I could swear. There were three rows – there are only two rows now, even though they've been arranged to hide the gaps.'

Enzo tutted and got to his feet.

'Another week, all tins gone,' he said.

The thought of this didn't bother Della as much as what else could already have disappeared, but when she said so, the Italian wrinkled his nose.

'This is children,' he said dismissively. 'Boys. Eat, then throw.' He went back into the main kitchen and opened the dresser drawers. 'You look for papers,' he said stepping towards the passage door. 'I must look at beds.'

Della would have liked to go with him, but she knew he was right. With his limited English, he would have no means of knowing instantly what could be significant on official stationery. She bent to her task, and when nothing had appeared from the innards of the dresser, she moved on to the parlour. She remembered seeing a chest of drawers there. Above her head, she could hear him pulling furniture about and a scraping sound as he lifted the mats. She closed the last drawer in the chest and leaned back on her heels. There was nothing. So far, she'd found table and tray cloths, knitting wool, sets of knives and forks, china, everything that you would have expected a careful housewife to keep tidily and at hand. But amongst it all there hadn't been a single scrap of paper, no bank statements nor even a letter or bill. She looked around her. Were they illiterate? It was quite possible that they couldn't read, but everybody got post. What about the car that Enzo had mentioned? Cars always involved paperwork. And what about their ration books and identity cards? Everyone had those.

She went to the empty bedroom and resumed her searches, but there was no item of furniture there that could hide anything. When she came out and went to the bottom of the stairs, Enzo could be seen on his knees with the candle peering intently at the long mat that ran from one end of the landing to the other. She climbed up to him.

'There's nothing at all,' she said. 'Which makes me think there must be a secret place where they kept all their important documents.'

He nodded, but his mind was far away. Then he jerked a thumb in the direction of Glenys's room.

'One thing,' he said. 'On bed.'

She stepped past him and went in. The room was exactly as she remembered. Then she saw a small piece of paper, some four inches square on the coverlet. She picked it up, holding up the candle to make out the writing on it: 'Glenys and Robin, Christmas 1938'. Turning it over, she saw that it was a photograph of a woman standing outside a house with her hand on the shoulder of a boy of about nine or ten. The woman smiled proudly, but the boy stared sullenly at the camera. Why was he sulking, Della asked herself, if it was Christmas? Was it because he'd had to leave his new toys, have his hair combed, and stand in the cold to have his picture taken? He was wearing an Arran sweater, full of extremely complex cables. Glenys's work, more than likely, which explained the look on her face. She shone her torch on the background. Behind them, the front door to the house stood open and in the passage she thought she could make out, although indistinctly, a wheel and a mudguard. Was a new bike the toy he'd had to leave? And who was he? He'd be about eighteen now. This photo was something Aneurin the

Policeman should find. Perhaps this boy would be the inheritor of the whole farm, if he could be found.

She went back to the bedroom door.

'Where was this?'

'Left drawer,' replied Enzo, who was still holding the candle to illuminate the mat. 'Under woman's things.'

Della went to the dressing table and opened the drawer, seeing neatly folded underclothes. She put the photo carefully back among them, and returned to the landing.

'Anything interesting?'

Enzo shrugged.

'Could be.' He pointed to a spot that was somewhat lighter in colour than the rest. 'Somebody wash this,' he said rubbing his fingers over the place and sniffing them. 'Soap.'

'Is that suspicious?' asked Della. 'Mr Rees did say that Glenys was always cleaning.'

Enzo straightened his back and rubbed the nape of his neck.

'If Glenys do this,' he said, 'why don't she wash here too?'

He held the candle so that she could see what he meant. Along the wooden skirting there were half a dozen little dark spots. Della stared at them.

'Blood,' said the Italian.

'How do you know?'

As a reply he licked his finger. They stood silently for a moment.

'No blood in other places,' said Enzo thoughtfully. 'So why here? What happened?'

Della could think of a hundred and one perfectly innocent things, but she sensed that this was not the place to start listing them.

'So there's nothing in the big room, then?' she asked.

He shook his head.

'Man clothes. Shoes, suit.'

'Anything in the pockets?'

'No.'

'So where are their identity cards and ration books?'

There was only one room left and they searched it together. Enzo gave a groan to see all the rubbish but then he glanced over at the window.

'Curtain open here,' he murmured.

'Too much trouble to move things out of the way,' said Della and saw him nod.

'You go left, me right,' he said. 'We hurry now. He took out a large pocket watch. 'Hut close in one quarter of an hour.'

It was Della who found the brown leather case. It was one of a pile of cases and boxes in the corner. To be honest, she only lifted it in order to see what was behind it and was surprised at its weight.

'There's something in this one,' she said, putting it down and pressing the latch. 'But it's locked.'

She moved aside a saw Enzo take off his right glove, pull a long length of metal from his pocket and fiddle about in the lock for a second. She held her breath.

'Has it occurred to you that Aneurin might wonder why it's open if it's full of important papers?' she asked.

There was a dull click and Enzo laughed quietly as he lifted the lid.

'Not my problem but yours,' he said smiling at her over his shoulder.

Leonard had been the guardian of the case, Della decided, seeing the jumble within. On the top lay the ration books and the identity cards. She flicked through them quickly and looked at the weeks of coupons ripped out. They weren't registered with the local shop, which was interesting in itself, and they had dozens of loose coupons, unused. Taken with the store of food in the scullery, perhaps that wasn't so surprising. She looked at their personal details.

'Hughes,' she said. 'They were Glenys and Leonard Hughes.'

'Yes,' nodded Enzo. 'Mister Hughes. Very important man. He have his own bottle of whisky in Hut.'

'Did he offer anybody a glass out of it?'

Enzo started to shake his head, then stopped.

'I only see once. Gave to schoolmaster. He drunk. He spill it.'

Della raised her eyebrows and began ploughing through the rest of the contents. She knew she dared not take anything, so she'd have to remember what she saw. Enzo stood just behind her and watched. Five minutes passed and then Della put everything back as she'd found it.

'You see enough?' asked her companion.

She nodded emphatically.

'Indeed I have, but I can't work out what it all means. They got money regularly from somewhere – nearly thirty pounds a month paid altogether into the bank in cash. That's a lot in ready money.'

'Rent,' said Enzo. 'For the land. Every field.'

'But who was paying it?'

He shook his head.

'Nobody say. Some fields nobody do nothing to them. Maybe not farmers.'

This was a puzzle.

'Why would somebody who didn't need the land for farming pay rent for it?'

Enzo didn't answer but closed the case and put it back carefully among the others.

'We look at car, then go,' he said.

Della followed him from the room, deep in thought. As they crossed the landing, Enzo swore. His candle had spat hot wax and burnt him. She saw more drops fly as he shook his right hand.

'It's your own fault for taking off your glove,' said Della. 'And now we'll have to wipe those up from the floor.'

But he wasn't listening. He was, yet again, crouched down over the mat. He gave a quickly suppressed cry and then grinned broadly up at her.

'Look!' he hissed, pointing to the marks left by the wax which had already congealed in the cold.

'I can see,' said Della wearily. 'Perhaps we could scratch them off with a fingernail.'

'No, not wax. The blood. Big, less, less, small.' He realised that she didn't understand and searched for the right words. 'Pattern,' he said and shook his fingers once again to show how the blood had fallen.

'Did one of them cut themselves?' tried Della.

With a despairing snort Enzo put the candle down.

'I show you. OK?' and suddenly grabbed her around the waist, lifting her up and over his shoulder. 'You hang down,' he ordered.

Too surprised to protest, Della obeyed and lay limp, letting her arms swing. Enzo took a few steps back and then rushed in the direction of the largest bedroom. At the door, he set her back on her feet. 'You see now?' he enquired urgently.

Della opened her mouth ready to remonstrate, but then she saw what all the physical jerks had been about.

'Was Glenys carried from her room to her brother's?' she whispered. 'But you said yourself that she'd died in Leonard's bed. This could have happened when Napoleone and Mr Rees carried her back.'

'No, no, no!' Enzo was almost dancing in frustration. 'Too late then. Dead for days. No blood. She is killed in there!' He pointed at the door to Glenys's bedroom. 'Blood run. She is carried over, put in big bed. Then stains.'

Della took a deep breath. Amidst all this one word had leapt out at her.

'Killed?' she asked quietly. 'They were killed?'

Enzo threw his arms in the air.

'Of course they are killed,' he said as if speaking to a small child. Then he collected himself. 'But how? That is the next problem.'

Out on the farmyard, having extinguished all lights and put the gloves back where they belonged in Leonard's coat pocket, Enzo cast a glance over at the farm buildings that were mere shadows off to the left.

'No time for car now,' he said and grasping her elbow he led her towards the lane. Della said nothing until the more intense darkness of the hedgerows had closed over them. She'd been feeling quite sick since the demonstration on the landing. The worst thing was that she had to come back here and be possessed of enough guile to make Aneurin think he'd discovered everything. But did she want him to come to the same conclusion as Enzo, for if the two had been killed, who but she would be the first to be suspected? Pure fear shot through her. She battled to overcome it.

As she wasn't watching where she put her feet, she tripped on a clod under the snow, and felt Enzo grip her arm more tightly. She heard his voice in her ear.

'Not worry,' he said. '*Signor* Rees say doctor will come. He will see how killed. No more problem.'

Della doubted that very much. That would merely be the start of her difficulties. She shook her head.

'That's not true,' she whispered and turned her head to look at him. 'I was the last to see them – or the first, depending on how you see things.'

She saw him ponder.

'First, last?' he asked.

'The first to see them dead. I found them. Not Eirug Rees. The night of the storm.' She heard him groan but he kept on walking.

'Why you don't say?' he enquired gently. 'Why you don't shout, run?'

She smiled sadly although she knew he couldn't see her.

'There was nowhere to run to that night – and the next morning the first person I saw was Norman. I couldn't tell him, could I?'

He exhaled loudly.

'*Si, si.* Norman. When you tell *Signor* Rees?'

'As soon as we reached School House. I was looking for a telephone to ring the police but it wasn't working. It was his idea to tell Huw Richards.' She felt him nod.

'Napoleone organise all after that.'

They went on in silence. The main road was now discernible in the distance. On the point of asking him whether he believed there was something dubious about Huw Richards's actions as regards the deaths, she was shocked to hear voices. Enzo stood still, then as one body they scuttled to the blackest shadow of the far hedge and listened.

'And you had a lift from the station to the Hut, did you? That was a bit of bloody luck.'

The words slithered from the speaker's mouth, oiled by drink.

'Wasn't it?'

The answer came sharply in a female voice. She sounded as if she regretted it.

'And then there I was going past conveniently to see you right.'

They heard two sets of footfalls approach and squeezed themselves out of sight behind a tree that thrust its trunk out into the lane. Della had a pretty good idea who owned the male voice. It would take more than the worst snow in living memory to keep Stevie, Jean's husband, from the Hut. But who was the woman? They were nearly at the entrance to the lane now. She prayed that nothing would make them turn their heads in the wrong direction. She dared not look, but she needn't have worried. Stevie was so shaky on his feet that the strange woman had to grab his arm to keep him from falling and they went past. Della heard Stevie's voice again.

'You'll like the teacher who lives in School House now. A real lady she is – teaching band … bandadaging to our Gareth.'

'Teaching him to play the banjo? Hell's bells!'

She heard no more because Enzo poked her in her side. He whispered into her hair.

'Wait five minutes then go. I go home through fields.'

And then, completely silently, he disappeared back in the direction of the farm leaving Della scraping the furthest corners of her mind to think of a reason why she should be out this time of night.

Chapter Ten

'You haven't got anything stronger to put in this, I suppose?'

Della stood with one hand on the kettle and watched the strange woman stare resentfully into the cup of tea she'd just handed her. As they had been introduced in the darkness outside the front door by Stevie, she hadn't had the chance to study her properly. Mercifully, nobody enquired where'd she been. So this was the sister of Dafydd Jones, the previous master. A fondness for alcohol was evidently a family failing. And where on earth did she get those nylons?

'I'm very sorry, Miss Jones,' she heard herself say. 'I don't keep any in the house.'

The woman tutted in disappointment and crossed her legs, letting her high-heeled shoe hang from her foot. She sipped the tea, leaving a red lipstick mark on the cup.

'Doesn't matter,' she lied, and then smiled. 'Call me Lena, everyone else does.'

She raised a hand with nails painted as red as her lips and tidied her complex, unconvincing blonde curls. Della sat down on a hard chair opposite her.

'I'm surprised the authorities didn't let you know that your brother was ill,' she said. 'This must have come as dreadful shock to you.'

'Oh, it is. Terrible.'

Lena pulled a serious face but the tone of her voice was insincere.

'But you see I've moved more than once. Perhaps the letter went to an old address. And Dai isn't one to keep in touch. Never has been, not since he was a boy. I'm different. Sending notes to people every ten minutes.' She realised suddenly what she'd said and added swiftly, 'There was no point sending a letter beforehand to say I was on my way. I'd have arrived before it in all this snow.'

'A surprise visit then,' Della answered smoothly.

'Yes.' Lena looked around her and smiled again. 'You keep Mam's furniture lovely, fair play to you.'

Della lay awake a long time that night listening to her putting away her things in her brother's bedroom across the landing. What else could she have done but offer her a bed? Or rather, not object when Lena got up and announced that it was time she turned in. There was nowhere else she could go. For someone who only had one case, she'd brought endless stuff if all the opening and closing of drawers and cupboards was anything to go by. Della wondered why she didn't have her own share of the family furniture. Perhaps 'Dai' had been the mother's favourite, who knew? If she decided to make off with it all, she had the right to do so, but Della was paying rent for the house and intended to stay put – if she wasn't accused of murder in the meantime. She felt awake and churned up. She sat up, lit the candle and fumbled for her bag of knitting from the floor. Sleep would not come easily now so she might as well do something useful. She'd hardly knitted a row of the jumper she'd started before leaving Cwm y Glo, and the evenings she'd spent with Tydfil and Nest in front of the fire listening to the wireless for hours seemed like a dream. The nights in this place were even busier than the day. One of the needles insisted on sticking, and without thinking she ran it through her hair to oil it a little, as she normally did. It caught in the knot of one of the rags she used to curl her hair and jabbed hard into her scalp. She rubbed the spot, and stared angrily at the sharp end of the needle. She could see the tiniest smear of blood on it. She lay the work on her lap. The urge to knit had completely gone. She also had a nasty feeling that she knew how Glenys and Leonard had been killed. She had to see the bodies. How she could accomplish that, she had no idea.

'Still got your visitor?'

Jean and her bucket and mop were busy as usual a couple of days later, after the children's muddy feet had left their daily mark on the floors.

'Yes,' Della lifted her head from the pile of marking and stared through the open door to the assembly hall. 'I believe she's trying to make up her mind what she should do. It's a pity nobody thought to contact her about her brother.'

Jean moved out of the way to let Lilwen go past. The infants teacher hurried towards the back door making a little sound that might have been a goodbye. Jean watched her go pensively and then turned back to Della.

'Big family,' she remarked, and seeing puzzlement on Della's face, added 'She's a lot younger than the master. But nice clothes, all the same.'

As Della considered that Lena's clothes were garish and tasteless, she could not agree directly.

'There's probably more choice in town,' she said.

'No there isn't, believe me! There's no choice anywhere! Although I'm glad to get things a bit cheaper with our Eirian working in a clothes shop. But it's worse than it was during the war, if anything.' She smiled and mopped vigorously. 'She'll be company for you,' she added, changing tack. 'It's a big house.'

Not big enough, thought Della, remembering Jean's words as she sat in the chapel the following Sunday morning. Between the nylon stockings drying in the bathroom and the knickers made of parachute silk hanging on the rack above the kitchen fire, Lena's presence announced itself everywhere. There was no escape either from the bottle of cherry brandy that had appeared one night after Lena had returned from the Hut, which was fast becoming her spiritual home. And when she wasn't propping up the bar there, she was cleaning School House like a tornado. The cupboards had all been turned out and rearranged and whenever Della happened to pop back to the house from school during the day, she was presented with a view of Lena's backside, on her knees before some item of furniture with her head in its depths.

'You're too busy,' had been the reply when Della had told her she really didn't need to do all this. It didn't look like Lena was planning to leave any time soon. Della tried to concentrate. If such a thing were possible, Huw Richards's sermon was even more highbrow than the one he gave last week, full of Greek and Latin words and frequent references to 'the original Aramaic'. Who did he think he had in his congregation? A chapel full of divinity students? Her mind wandered, despite herself, to the dinner that would follow down in Clawdd Coch with Eirug and Lilwen. She must try to steal a look at the bodies, but for the life of her she could still not see how to do it.

'Thank you very much for inviting me, Lilwen,' she said, as they washed the dishes in the spacious kitchen. 'I'm sorry you had to miss the service to prepare.'

Lilwen smiled in her shy way.

'I don't go most Sunday mornings,' she said. 'I worry too much about things burning. I generally go at night. And it's no bother – I have to feed the Italians anyway.'

That was the longest speech that Della had heard her make so far.

'So they haven't asked you to take on the Sunday School?' she enquired.

'Yes, they have, actually,' Lilwen admitted. 'But Dada put his foot down. There are plenty of others to do it, after all.'

And more of a chance of getting an unburnt dinner, thought Della. Her attention was drawn by an unfamiliar noise and she leaned over the sink to see better out of the tiny window. At the far end of the farmyard an ancient car was trundling forward carefully under the direction of her host, Eirug. It came to a halt and Aneurin the Policeman climbed out of the passenger seat, while a thin, white-haired man whom she hadn't seen before emerged from the driver's side. She realised that Lilwen was standing beside her.

'Who's that?' she asked.

'Dr Davies,' the girl replied, folding the drying up cloth. 'It's a wonder that Aneurin has got him to come out on a Sunday.' She said nothing about why he was there, but went, instead, to the huge black-lead stove and put the kettle on to boil. Then she laughed drily.

'I don't know why I'm bothering to make tea,' she said. 'He only wants whisky as a rule.'

'He's been thirsty a long time, then,' Della offered, but Lilwen didn't smile.

'You'd be surprised what you can get if you know where to go,' she commented sharply. Della was about to make a similar remark regarding Lena's nylon stockings but she happened to look down and saw that Lilwen was wearing a similar pair. She thought quickly.

'So, are you going to try Christian Dior's New Look?' she asked. 'Spend all your coupons on the material for one skirt?' Lilwen sighed.

'No, I'm not. I'm enough of a mushroom as it is. But it would suit you.' And she went to look in a cupboard, giving Della the chance to glance through the window again.

The three men, by now, were standing outside the building furthest from the house. Aneurin pulled a packet from his breast pocket and offered cigarettes all round. Neither of the others refused, and then they went into the building, closing the door behind them. Damn, thought Della. That was a priceless opportunity lost, but what could she do?

She followed Lilwen into the little parlour where they'd eaten their dinner. There had been no sign of the three prisoners of war since she'd arrived but she knew, from the plates she'd washed, that they too had had roast lamb. She stood at the parlour window while Lilwen laid out the whisky bottle and three glasses on the table. She saw her lift the bottle and study it.

'There won't be much of this left by teatime,' she muttered giving an odd shudder. Della supposed she was thinking of the unpleasant task facing the men in the shed, but she said nothing.

Despite the strong smell of spirits that permeated the small car, the doctor gave no sign of being drunk as he drove Della home slowly over the narrow, slippery roads. She'd been shown into the passenger seat, although Aneurin didn't look very comfortable in the back. None of the three had said one word of what they had seen in the building throughout the hours in the parlour, although Della had sat very quietly indeed hoping that they would forget she was there. She watched the hedgerows go past, with the snow like melting icing dripping off the greenery, half listening to Aneurin complaining about his corns behind her.

'This dreadful weather's kept you busy, I expect, Doctor?' she said when there was a pause in the grumbling.

'Not half as busy as I'll be from July onwards,' he answered, flicking the stub of a cigarette out of the gap at the top of the window.

Aneurin gave his squeaky laugh.

'They'll be queuing out of the door for medicine when the National Health comes in.'

The doctor turned his grey profile towards him.

'And you and your ilk will be the first in the waiting room,' he said over his shoulder. 'I've got three years to go before I retire. I doubt I'll live to see the day.'

They'd nearly reached School House.

'And you'll be next,' he said peering at Della from the corner of his eye as he lit another cigarette. 'You'll lose them all to the County School at eleven. There'll be nobody to carry coal. Nobody to keep an eye on the little ones – and all of them convinced they're going to be the next prime minister, even the girls!'

'We could do with a little ambition,' answered Della. 'Every child deserves a chance.'

Aneurin could be seen nodding enthusiastically in the rear view mirror.

'Huh!' said the doctor, but he didn't argue.

Outside her back door, she paused. The evening stretched out ahead of her, in Lena's company, with the wireless perpetually tuned to the Light Programme instead of the Home Service, which Della preferred. A kind of invisible current of suspicion and incompatibility created an atmosphere between them, although they were both civil, from the teeth outwards. As it was a Sunday, the Hut would be closed. She went into the back kitchen and listened. Silence. She went through the house, taking off her best coat, expecting to see her every second, but she wasn't there. She knocked on her bedroom door and then pushed it open. Her eyes took in the unholy mess. Lena hadn't gone forever then, more was the pity. She heard the parlour clock strike half past five. Della sat on her own bed and slipped off her shoes, trying to work out where on earth Lena could be. She stopped herself. Lena was quite able to take care of herself and quite cute enough not to tell Della that she'd planned to go anywhere. Anyway, she had more than enough to worry about. She felt bloated after the big meal and all the tea she'd drunk, and would have liked to lie down for half an hour, but an idea was slowly forming in her head. Did she dare?

At a quarter to six she was loitering by the kitchen window with her torch in her pocket, her bag ready and Glenys's boots on her feet. She didn't know if she was brave enough to do this, but she could always turn back at any point. Five minutes later the mare's head came into view, trotting up the lane, and Della ducked back behind the lace curtain to watch it go by. Eirug Rees and Lilwen sat on the front bench on their way to chapel as she'd expected, but two dark heads could be seen huddling down in the back of the cart. They were hidden by the privet hedge before she could see exactly who they were. She swore and ran as fast as she could through to the parlour window where she might get a second glance. Thank goodness, she thought, Giuseppe and Salvatore. If Enzo had fancied a ride in the cart, that would have been the end of her plan. As it was she'd have to hurry.

'*Signorina!*'

Enzo smiled from the farmhouse door and watched her pick her way like a chicken over the yard where the snow had turned to mud and slush. 'Not forgotten anything, I hope?'

Breathless from having run as much of the way as she could, Della could not answer for a second.

'I've got half an hour at the most,' she said. 'I want to see the bodies and be home before anyone sees me.' The smile disappeared.

'Lamp,' he said, and turned on his heel back into the house.

Della stamped her feet to warm them on the threshold, but he was back in an instant with a paraffin lamp. He showed her a large key and Della smiled.

'Did you see the doctor and the policeman this afternoon?' she asked as she followed him out to the furthest building. Enzo nodded.

'Hetty been already last night. Napoleone send her. She wash and wash them.'

He was evidently not pleased at this.

'Deliberately, before the doctor saw them?' asked Della.

He shrugged and turned the key in the lock. Della took a deep breath. She had a pretty good idea of what to expect but you could never prepare yourself completely. Enzo shone the lamp around the high-ceilinged, empty space and the stone walls. Some kind of bier had been fashioned from wooden planks for the two corpses that lay side by side under old sheets. She had good reason to be glad of the bitter cold. Only the faintest unmistakeable smell of death reached her nostrils. She set down her bag and pulled out her torch.

'Right then,' she said, sounding far more confident than she felt. 'We'll start with Glenys.'

Hetty had left Glenys in her nightgown, and Della felt embarrassed as she lifted and started to play the merciless light over her bare skin. The beam caught the blue veins like ropes on her legs, her flat breasts and the sad grey hair between her legs. All the while Enzo watched her carefully. She moved over to Leonard and did the same.

'There isn't a mark on them,' she said at last. 'Not a bruise or a scratch. They didn't fight, they weren't strangled or beaten.'

Enzo stepped forward and grasped Leonard's hands, looking keenly at the nails. Della left him to it, and went through Glenys's hair minutely, but there was no sign of a blow to the skin nor any soft impression in her skull. As Leonard was bald, it had been easier to conduct the same inspection on him. She looked over and saw that Enzo had opened Leonard's mouth and taken out the cotton wool inside it. Hetty's thorough work was visible on both. The smell of disinfectant came out with the cotton.

'Die in bed,' said the Italian. 'No false teeth.' He held the chin down so that Della could peer inside. She pointed the torch to the back of the throat.

'But he's bitten his tongue,' she said. 'And look, there's blood on the cotton wool.' She picked up the piece and studied it. 'From the look of it, this came from the back and not his tongue.'

Enzo leaned over and smelt it, then shook his head.

'Soap,' he said miserably. 'Hetty wash too much.'

'What were you expecting to smell?'

'Something else. Something they swallow, burn throat maybe.'

Della thought about this. If someone had poisoned their food or drink, it was surely unlikely that they would have gone to bed and died peacefully in their sleep, seeing that Leonard at least had been in sufficient pain to bite his tongue. It was time to put her theory to the test, although she had hoped not to have to do so. She went to her bag and reached inside. When she came back, Enzo stared in alarm at what she held.

'This is an experiment,' she explained. 'It was something I noticed in their kitchen.'

She picked out the cotton wool carefully from Leonard's nostrils with her eyebrow tweezers and looked at both pieces in turn. Blood spots had dried on one. She did the same to Glenys and showed them to Enzo. More blood was visible on these.

'This is where the blood on the landing came from,' she said. 'It flowed when she was carried to Leonard's room, like you said.'

'Less blood from him because he don't get moved,' said Enzo and nodded with a degree of satisfaction.

Della picked up the second instrument that she'd taken from her bag.

'I don't think I'm strong enough to do this,' she said, 'You'll have to. But if I'm right, it should go in reasonably easily.'

Enzo took the fine knitting needle from her and turned it over in his hands. He didn't look at all keen, but then he seemed to come to a decision and went to Glenys. He put his hand on her forehead and thrust the needle an inch into her right nostril.

'Slowly!' hissed Della. 'It's got to follow the same path as it did the first time. Otherwise we've proved nothing.'

The Italian swallowed and gritted his teeth, trying again, but feeling more and pushing less. After initial resistance, he shifted the needle slightly to the right and it slid in, with ghastly ease, up to half its length. Enzo measured this with his fingers apart, nodding to himself, and then pulled the needle out. He moved to Leonard and repeated the process, his face expressionless. Finally he'd finished and stood holding the filthy instrument. Della saw that his hands were shaking and she quickly wrapped the needle in an old handkerchief.

Hurrying now, they put everything back into place without exchanging another word. While Enzo was relocking the door Della said, 'I'll have to tell Huw Richards.'

He pulled a face. 'Maybe he knows,' he whispered sourly. For some reason she felt she had to defend him.

'He couldn't possibly know about this!' she said, lifting the bag that held the needle. 'Remember, there was nothing to be seen on either of them. The doctor didn't spot anything.'

Enzo lifted his fist like someone holding a pint glass so that she should be in doubt of his opinion of the medical man. Then his face slid back into its usual impenetrable state. Della stared at him.

'Do you really think that Napoleone knows who did this?' she asked urgently. 'And Eirug Rees too? Does everyone know except us?'

He placed his hand on her arm reassuringly. 'No,' he murmured, 'Nobody knows. Nobody wants to know.'

Della ran the last hundred yards to the house. With every turn in the road she'd expected to see the mare and the travellers returning. She crept past the entrance to Jean's cottage and jumped when she heard childish voices but they faded almost instantly. She stood at the top of the slate steps once again and allowed her heart to slow down. If Lena had returned she would take it for granted that Della had been to chapel. However, when she opened the door, the house was as silent as it had been on her departure.

She dropped the disgusting needle in its handkerchief into the sink immediately and let the water pour over it with a fistful of soda. She watched the pitiful remains of blood and brain matter flow down the plug hole before taking off her coat and scrubbing her hands until they were red. Then she took the wet handkerchief to the fire where it hissed and turned black before finally burning. She dried the needle carefully on the flat hotplate until it was almost too hot to hold and then put it back with its twin in her knitting bag. Crouched by the flames to try to warm up, she realised that she wasn't just physically cold. Her mind whirled constantly around the events of the previous two hours. Had it been foolish to admit to Enzo that she had found the bodies? Yet, had she killed them, would she have taken such pains to show him how it was done? Wasn't that some kind of proof that she was innocent? He'd found the sight of the knitting needle shocking. She rubbed her shins and thought. Enzo didn't like Huw Richards. Was that because he had such status and influence, or because he believed he was a murderer? But he couldn't be. He could not have crept silently up the stairs nor carried Glenys from one room to the other. Not unless his gammy leg was a complete fraud. And if he had done it, why put himself to the extra trouble of putting the woman back in her own bed? If she hadn't found them – and not even a clairvoyant could have predicted that – that's how they would have been found, with all its implications. She had no doubt that their being found in the same bed was quite deliberate. Someone hated them enough to want everyone to think they were incestuous.

The mysterious cash payments into the bank had to lie at the root of it all. Enzo had told her that all the land was rented out but that several fields were not used. So, payments were being made in an outwardly public manner, but for other, more private, reasons. She couldn't think of any individual in the neighbourhood who could afford to pay thirty pounds a month – it was much more than her own salary. That suggested that there were a good number of people involved.

Was that the secret, that several of them had got together to rid the community of a couple who bled their victims dry? If so, it would explain Enzo's attitude. He appeared keen to know the truth, but frustratingly did not wish to do anything with the knowledge. Perhaps that was her role, in his eyes, as a newcomer. At least, perhaps it had been until she'd blurted out her own part in the tragedy.

The wind rose again, and howled in the chimney. She wondered whether the person who'd killed the pair knew that it was she who had found them, and not Eirug. Had they been keeping an eye on her throughout? Had she and Enzo been seen going back to the farm? And she'd have to go there again, worse luck, unless Aneurin forgot. She didn't want to go at all, but at least she would be safe in the policeman's company. Some of the sticks on the fire cracked suddenly and collapsed into the fire. It was time to fetch some more.

She got up and carried the bucket to the back of the long lean-to. The door to the garden shook on its hinges and the candle flickered. As quickly as she could, she gathered up a few sticks. When she heard an unexpected noise she stood still. The latch on the side door was slowly being lifted. Her heart beat loud in her ears. The wind couldn't have done that. She extinguished the candle and held the bottom of the bucket ready to throw the contents at whoever came in. The door was pushed open by inches and one high-heeled foot appeared over the threshold. Della stood to one side in the shadows watching it. Lena sneaked in, closing the door silently. Perhaps she hoped that Della would have gone to bed. She was going to be disappointed, if so.

'Oh heck!' said Della loudly, snatching up the dead candle from the bench. Then she pretended to see her for the first time. 'You're home!' she said, all smiles. 'I was just about to put the kettle on.'

She bustled through to the fire without waiting for a reply

and laid the sticks on it. Lena stayed in the scullery. Della knew she was trying to think of something to say, but she took her time arranging the fuel. She got up when she heard her footsteps behind her.

'You must be frozen stiff,' she said. 'And the wind's got up tonight again.'

'Yes, it has,' said Lena in a small voice. 'It's terribly cold.' To tell the truth, she looked grey under the heavy make-up. She stood awkwardly, tugging at her left glove, then giving up and leaving it on her hand.

'I don't think I want any tea, thanks all the same,' she said. 'I'm going to bed.'

Della let her go. She didn't know why, exactly, but she was pleased to have caught her coming in, when she so obviously hadn't wanted to be seen. It was childish, but after all the hide and seek she herself had played recently, it was comforting to know she wasn't the only one. But where on earth had Lena been all day?

CHAPTER ELEVEN

After lunch on the following Monday, Della stood in the front doorway of the school with her cup of tea, keeping an eye on the children. Behind her she could hear Norman stoking the fire. The snow had cleared sufficiently to allow the boys to kick a ball about on the higher ground behind the school. Gareth had already brought down someone tearful who had scraped his knees, and was proving a dab hand with iodine and plaster. Who could have imagined that one small first-aid box would have saved her from being locked in a perpetual battle of wills with him? Or perhaps he was just maturing. He'd stayed behind very willingly the previous Wednesday in order to start learning more about the complexities of bandaging, and according to his mother was building a rudimentary stretcher in the barn.

In front of her, away from the wildly kicked leather ball, the girls were playing a game involving running around a circle and chanting. The ones who were 'out' sat quite happily on the wall until that round was finished. Her eye was caught by a movement in the master's old bedroom window. So Lena had finally dragged herself out of bed. Most probably she'd been woken by the children's noise. About time, too.

'Miss! Miss!'

A forest of arms was pointing eagerly towards the gate and Della saw the figure of Huw Richards, in his sinister hat, with one hand on the latch. She hurried over, trying to smile.

'Good afternoon, Mr Richards,' she said in as welcoming a manner as she could muster, while her mind flitted over the state of the classroom.

'Good afternoon to you all,' he answered. 'I'm quite surprised to find you here. You didn't decide to go on a nature walk then.'

'Never on Mondays,' replied Della and turned to one of the older girls. 'What do we do on a Monday, Rhonwen?'

'Sums and tables and reading, Miss.'

Della smiled at her.

'Quite right. Will you come in Mr Richards? I'm sure there's tea left in the teapot.'

She led him towards the building. She saw his gaze flick up towards the bedroom window opposite. Lena could clearly be seen with her leg up on a chair, smoothing on her stocking and attaching it to her suspender belt. He pulled his hat down further over his forehead, but could easily have been watching her for the last fifty yards before reaching the gate.

'It looks like it's thawing at long last,' said Della once they were safely in the porch.

'Yes indeed, warming up amazingly,' he answered, hanging his coat on the hook.

She left him by the fire and went to look for an additional cup from Lilwen's room. She found her busy washing down the blackboard, standing on tiptoe to reach the top corners.

'The minister's here,' hissed Della warningly.

She received a fearful glance which rather shocked her but then she remembered the weeks that Lilwen had had to spend here in his company.

'Don't worry,' she said. 'I'll keep him busy.'

Back in her own classroom she found him sitting in her chair, leafing through the exercise books on her desk. He looked up.

'Odd isn't it,' he said, settling himself more comfortably, 'how the concept of number is apparently totally alien to many children, and yet they manage to do calculations on the farm regarding crops and milk and what have you.'

'They see the point of that,' Della replied. 'The problems set in the arithmetic books aren't relevant to their lives. If it takes an hour for one man to fill a bath, how long will it take two

115

men – what's the point if you don't have a bath?' She didn't mention that Gareth had asked in his most practised fake-innocent tone whether somebody had put the plug in.

The minister nodded.

'They're practical aren't they, rather than intellectual.'

'In my experience, that's the case wherever you go. It's the truly literary and academic child who's unusual almost everywhere. But people change and develop you know, sometimes much later in life, especially boys.' She smiled at him. 'The trick is to give them enough basic skills to build on, in a way that doesn't kill every urge to learn.'

He smiled back coldly.

'It's encouraging to hear you haven't been utterly defeated.'

Della handed him his tea. She very much doubted whether that last statement was true. He would be delighted to have an excuse to come down often and start ordering her around.

'I'm never defeated,' she said quietly. She glanced up at the clock. Another ten minutes to go before ringing the bell. The minister took this as a sign that she was wondering when he would leave.

'I don't intend to be here under your feet,' he said. 'Nor to interfere in the school either. It's quite obvious everything's under control. I actually came down to tell you that the Parish Council is meeting this week. And before you ask, you're on it, by virtue of your job.'

Della could not suppress a groan.

'What for?' she asked. 'What do I have to offer? I've only been here five minutes.'

He looked as if he was in complete agreement, but continued.

'There are big moves afoot to bring in electricity.'

That, for once, was good news.

'Wonderful! I'm sure people will be very pleased.'

'That's what I thought too when I made the initial enquiries, but there's a problem. You have to have a number of subscribers who sign to say they're willing to pay a certain sum every quarter. The farmers are extremely reluctant to do so. Whoever does the canvassing will need tremendous powers of persuasion.'

Della knew what was coming.

'Me and who else?' she asked.

'Eirug Rees or Jim Griffiths, or perhaps both. But you definitely, to talk to the wives.'

It was on the tip of her tongue to ask ironically why he himself was not one of the chosen few, but he'd finished his tea and was preparing to leave. This was when she noticed that he was wearing a black tie with his normal dark suit.

'On your way to conduct a funeral?' she asked, following him out to the porch.

He stood on the spot for a second, with one hand outstretched for his hat.

'A sad occasion,' he said over his shoulder.

'Really? I would imagine you'd be dancing on the grave.'

When he turned his face was like thunder, but Della didn't care.

'Tasteless?' she said before he had a chance to speak. 'But there we are, the whole thing's tasteless. A policeman with little experience in such matters, a conveniently unconcerned doctor, and the bodies carefully prepared before he had a look at them.'

'I suggested a post-mortem,' he said defensively.

Della snorted contemptuously.

'At arm's length I'll venture – and who would want to hold one in a barn in midwinter?'

'There was no mark on them. I looked myself.'

'You didn't look hard enough. They were murdered.'

'Oh, were they?' He was pushing his arms into the sleeves of his overcoat. 'And by whom?'

'That's what I intend to find out. And I notice you don't

ask how it was done, which makes me doubly suspicious that you want to bury them quickly in case they were poisoned or smothered.'

She knew she'd hit the nail on the head from the black scowl she received.

'But that's not how they were killed,' she continued. 'They were stabbed.'

'Where?' She could hear the incredulity in his voice.

Della did not answer directly.

'Did Hetty have any comments to make about the bodies? And I'm sure you asked her.'

She saw him consider denying this, but then he said reluctantly, 'She mentioned that both had had some kind of flow of blood from the throat or back of the nose. She'd seen it before with stroke victims. She thought it must have been brought on by the intense cold.'

'She didn't think it odd that both were affected in the same way?'

'Yes, she did – but the doctor signed the death certificate.'

'It's a shame not everyone is as thorough as Hetty, isn't it? It wasn't a stroke. They were stabbed through the nose straight into the brain.'

'But with what?'

'One of Glenys's knitting needles. Then she was carried through to Leonard's room and left there, so that people would think that incest was one of their vices, among everything else.'

Watching him digest this information she went on, relentlessly.

'Did you ever rent any land from them?'

'Heavens above, what for?'

He sounded sincere. She shrugged.

'That's what everyone will say, but a lot of folk around here have benefited from their deaths.'

Huw Richards was breathing heavily but he turned towards the heavy front door.

'I would be very careful, if I were you,' he murmured. 'I wouldn't recommend that you share your theories with anyone else.'

The implicit threat in this annoyed her.

'Actually I was thinking of sharing my theories with the coroner. Perhaps you won't be allowed to bury them out of sight so quickly after all.'

He shook his head.

'Too late,' he said, opening the door. 'They've been underground since eight o'clock this morning.' He couldn't hide the hint of triumph in his words but then he suddenly stepped back. Lena was standing on the doorstep. He raised his hat courteously and Della hurried to fill the awkward pause by introducing them.

'This is Miss Lena Jones, the master's sister. And this is Mr Richards, the minister.'

Lena held out a beringed hand which was formally, if briefly, shaken.

'Lovely to meet you,' she simpered, batting her eyelashes. Huw Richards's reaction was almost comical in his haste to get out of there.

'Very nice,' he muttered, and then was gone.

'Preacher is he?' said Lena after he'd gone through the gate, 'More like Laurence Olivier in *Wuthering Heights*. You know, Heathcliff. I like them dark like that.'

God help us, thought Della, but forced a smile.

'Anything wrong?' she asked.

Lena dragged her eyes away from the figure in the hat limping up the lane.

'Phone,' she said. 'For you. Somebody called Aneurin. Boyfriend?'

As his son was standing mere feet away, Della could only glare at her for a second before running to the house.

'There are odd marks here, Mr Jenkins. Come and see.'

Della stood on the landing of Glenys and Leonard's farmhouse once again. She'd gone through all the motions of pretending to see things for the first time, gone through the drawers again and left the lumber room until last. She let him find the photograph of Glenys and Robin, but was pleased to see him tuck it into his breast pocket. Despite this, he would have completely ignored the heavy leather case if she hadn't pointed it out to him. Now he was taking forever to go through its contents. He looked up from his task.

'Good stuff here,' he said as if he hadn't heard her. 'But no will.'

'Shame,' said Della and indicated the drops of blood on the skirting board. 'What are these spots here?'

Slowly, with one eye on the bank statements in his hand, Aneurin came out and glanced at them.

'Rust,' he said, with an air of finality. Della bit her tongue. Rust on a wooden length of skirting without a nail in sight.

'You don't think they could possibly be blood?' she asked humbly.

He shook his head, following one line of figures to the end with his fat finger.

'If it is, they carried it in on their feet,' he answered. Then he smiled patronisingly at her. 'The country's a dirty old place, see Miss Arthur. Not like the town.'

Della gave up trying after that. It was like walking through treacle. They went back down the stairs with Aneurin pushing some of the documents inside his jacket. To think that she had been worried he'd notice that the case wasn't locked!

'I know where to go now,' he said as they crossed the kitchen. 'Perhaps the bank can tell me more. And perhaps that's where the will is. But I can't fathom why they hid everything away and I'd love to know where they got all their money.'

Della wasn't listening. She'd suddenly realised that even more things had gone from the house. She hadn't had a chance to look at the tins of food but the dresser had nothing like the previous number of jugs and ornaments on it. If someone did eventually come to claim ownership of the farm, would there be anything left? She would never have believed this to be a thieving community, but perhaps the neighbourhood had merely taken their own possessions back, having been obliged to 'give' them to the pair when they had no cash. Aneurin was right about one thing. The country was a dirty old place.

The policeman pushed his bike along to see her back to School House, as it was now getting dark. There was no question but that he considered the visit a great success and he chatted cheerily all the way. Della could not share his optimism and so she just made polite noises. When the house came into sight in the distance she turned, intending to thank him and take her leave. However, the words were snatched from her lips by the startling sound of gun shots over in the fields to the left. Another sound came over the hedge, feet this time, and they watched as a dark figure, running as if for his life, came scrambling down and bounding into the ditch, ran across the road and then climbed the opposite hedge before disappearing. They could hear him galloping over the hard earth as if hunting dogs were on his trail.

'What on earth was that?' whispered Della, shocked. 'Do you think someone's been hurt?'

'In a manner of speaking,' answered the policeman sadly. 'That was Norman, poor dab.' He carried on walking.

Della hurried to catch up with him.

'Shouldn't we go and see?'

'No point. They're only shooting rabbits. He can't help it.

121

Pity for him. It was the bombing, see, when he was a little scrap. Did you know his mother and father were killed in the war?'

No, she hadn't known, and she felt ashamed that she hadn't wondered why Norman lived with his aunt. She'd taken it for granted that he had parents somewhere.

'Thank you for telling me. I had no idea.'

'They pulled him out alive, thank goodness. But they say he was trapped under the rubble for a good while.'

Della looked up at his red face and forgave him at once for his slowness. Even in the gathering dark she could see that the thought of this caused him pain.

'It's no wonder he runs then, is it?' she said quietly.

'No. It's a miracle he's as good as he is, tell the truth. But what sort of future does he have?'

'It might not be so bad,' said Della encouragingly. 'Who knows, perhaps he's the heir to Glenys and Leonard's farm. He was allowed to keep his chickens there after all. Nobody else was welcome there, I'm told.'

Aneurin laughed drily.

'Only because he's simple,' he answered and then sighed. 'At least he didn't find the bodies. That would have had a terrible effect on him.'

He said goodbye to her at the gate of the school and then threw a heavy leg over the bar of his bike and cycled off. Della went into the house. She'd seen the curtains being pulled back a smidgeon in Lena's room and let fall back into place. Evidently Aneurin was not worthy to receive the same show as Huw Richards.

CHAPTER TWELVE

The parlour clock struck eleven and Della rubbed her eyes. Lena would be home before long. She looked down at the pages in front of her. Another week had gone by and now it was Thursday evening again and the first opportunity she'd had to put pen to paper to write to Tydfil and Nest. She reread the last paragraph to make sure she'd said nothing that would make them worry. No, there was nothing there but a plain description of going out canvassing for the electricity in Eirug Rees's company earlier that evening. She hadn't mentioned Lena once. After all, there was a shortage of paper. That would have to wait until she could get Nest on her own with Tydfil out of the house for at least two hours. She didn't want him to know about the cherry brandy or the nylon stockings in case she got a lecture on her duty to save such a lost soul. She fancied that was beyond her powers. But it would be nice to see them both. Before the urge passed she grabbed the pen and added a sentence asking whether it would be convenient for her to visit for a weekend sometime.

She felt her weariness increase as she got up and went to stand at the kitchen window. She didn't fancy more tea. She'd had quite enough in the two farms that she and Eirug Rees had visited. It didn't matter how reluctant they were to sign the forms, they were extraordinarily generous regarding tea and Welsh cakes.

'You want feeding, Miss Arthur,' had been the chorus.

She'd be like a barrel before the first pylons appeared, if they managed to persuade anyone. By the time she'd climbed onto the bench in the cart to go home, she'd started to think there was no point continuing.

'Don't you worry,' Eirug had said. 'We only want one or two and the rest will follow.'

'Do you really think so?'

He'd smiled and clicked his tongue at the mare.

'They won't want anybody else to have an advantage, you'll see. They're terribly sharp like that.'

True enough, Della had thought, watching the trees shiver in the wind. According to the chat she'd had with Leisa, the farmer's wife down in Corsfelen, they were not that concerned about the legality of something either, if there was profit in it. Leisa had noticed the mare being led to shelter by the stable hand.

'I don't know why Eirug doesn't use his van,' she said. 'You must be dying of cold on the cart.'

As Della hadn't known he possessed such a thing, she was rather surprised but managed to answer.

'I suppose it's because petrol's so hard to get.'

The plump lady had laughed at such innocence and shaken her thick grey curls.

'There's always the pink diesel. I know it's for farm use, but good God, who's to know?'

'But what if Aneurin caught him?'

This invoked more head shaking.

'A fowl and a pound of salt bacon, and he'd hear no more. But there you are, you see, Eirug and Mr Richards are like bugs in a rug. And that one's a very serious law-abiding man.'

Della hadn't mentioned that conversation with Rees himself but it did make her wonder why exactly he was so friendly with the minister, when most other people regarded him with awe and more than a little fear. Perhaps, as Tydfil used to remark about the occasional deacon, Eirug Rees was a friend to all ministers of religion, with an exaggerated respect for the job, no matter who held it. And just how far did his loyalty stretch? Her chance to enquire further came as they went past the lane to the farm where the bodies had been found.

'That's Glenys and Leonard in their grave then,' she'd said, deliberately thoughtfully.

Rees had nodded slowly.

'At last,' he'd said. 'It was an awful job to dig it. We didn't finish until late on Sunday night, and they'd started on Saturday. I never saw the ground so hard.'

So that's what Giuseppe and Salvatore were doing in the back of the cart. The preparations had been put in hand long before the doctor had seen them, and the grave dug under cover of darkness. There was no need to ask whose bright idea that was.

'I would have come,' she said, 'but everything was over and done with when I heard about it on Monday afternoon.'

'Yes, well, it was awkward. Considering everything.'

She could easily believe that. Huw Richards's warning had rung loud in her ears at that point about being careful to whom she spoke, but she'd ploughed on.

'I don't think we know the whole truth about how they died,' she ventured. 'Don't you think it's strange that they both went at the same time?'

Rees's answer had come as a shock.

'I'm inclined to agree with you.'

Having received such unexpected backing, she'd smiled at him.

'Mr Richards doesn't,' she'd answered. 'I was told off good and proper. We had quite a row.'

From the small noise he made in his throat, it was evident he knew about that, too.

'It's a shame for you two to quarrel about this.'

Della couldn't see why and said so, but the farmer thought long and hard before replying.

'I had hoped that it had died with them. Perhaps you didn't know this, but Leonard, in particular, had a way of putting people at each other's throats, even though it was Glenys that

125

carried the gossip home to him. But there we are. Perhaps that's our inheritance from them. Ill-feeling.'

Della had let the silence grow between them. She was torn between shame in the face of such sincerity and naked curiosity. She could see the dark shape of the school emerging from the darkness.

'Aneurin has high hopes of finding a will,' she'd said as Rees pulled on the reins to slow the mare.

'Yes, he does. But I don't think there is one. No family member ever came here to see them. Although someone did say years ago that it was some tragedy that had made them move here, but then you can't believe everything.'

'What sort of tragedy? Something they'd done and had to leave because of it?'

'That's quite possible. And there again, if Aneurin does find a will, do we want more like Glenys and Leonard coming to live here?'

Della had dismounted carefully and thanked him. The farmer glanced up at the house but it was dark and silent.

'Your visitor's out then,' he remarked.

Della clucked disapprovingly.

'She's a regular at the Hut,' she said. 'And tonight she'd stolen some of my scent before going. The place is stinking of *Soir de Paris*.'

Rees had smiled wryly.

'Was it expensive?'

'That doesn't matter so much, but it was the last present I had from my fiancé Eifion before he was killed. I've been keeping it for as long as I can. I hope they appreciate it in the pub.'

'It's the little things that are important,' he said at last, and then added perceptively, 'It shows a lack of consideration. But when someone has their heart in the right place, you can forgive them a lot. That's why you should try not to quarrel with Mr Richards. We're all of us walking wounded to some extent.' And with that he flicked the reins and went on his way.

Della thought about his strange words as she stared into the darkness from the kitchen window. She recalled Hetty telling her that Eirug Rees was a widower. Perhaps he too had something he kept because his wife had given it to him. Lilwen – his most precious treasure. It was no surprise that he watched her every move. What was a bottle of *Soir de Paris* and a bundle of letters to compare with that?

She realised that she hadn't thought of Eifion at all since arriving at Nant-yr Eithin. What would he have thought of all this? Would he have encouraged her to continue with her enquiries, or warned her to leave things alone? No, he would have done nothing but shake his head and continue to play the piano with his long white hands. That was how she saw him in her memory, or rushing back down the hill from the station having been to Swansea to buy more musical scores. He would come into the Manse like a whirlwind and sit down to play without even taking off his coat. If he'd had to choose between her and the music, Della knew which one he would have found it easiest to give up. There was a time when that had been painful to admit, but by now it was a kind of relief, in an odd way.

She'd come to realise, even though they'd got on famously, that their relationship would never be more than a comfortable situation between two people who'd not managed to find anybody better. Away in the world of Brahms and Chopin, Eifion was a passionate man. With her, he'd been rather sleepy and quiet, very happy for her to take the lead, like Eirug Rees's mare. If he'd lived, they would have married and had to manage, more or less, on her salary – if she'd been allowed to keep her job. Eifion would have given piano lessons to children with fingers like sausages, with one eye always on the clock, and found his release in accompanying male voice choirs and playing the organ in chapel. It would have been her responsibility to keep their heads above water financially and to raise any children that might have appeared. Did Eifion know that? Had he let her express her interest in him quite deliberately, seeing her merely as someone who allow him to live just as he wanted? That was unfair. He wasn't devious, he didn't analyse or judge. He just accepted. But she could see herself in twenty years' time, sour and tired of having to shoulder every domestic burden to the endless accompaniment of Rachmaninov from the parlour. It was your fault, she told herself in the darkness. You decided that he was your last chance of a husband. Part of her was glad he didn't live to suffer the slow, inevitable disillusionment of watching her turn into a merciless harridan before his eyes. She hadn't read his letters for a long time. She would do so now in memory of him. She owed him that much.

Up in her bedroom the smell of perfume still lingered. She took the old tin box from the bottom of the drawer and sat on the bed. There were only three bundles of letters, and one of them contained the letters she'd written, which had been returned to her with his few effects, by some kind official. She could remember writing them late at night, exhausted from days organising evacuees or trying to teach enormous classes of children, before having to rush out to her fire-watching duties or to the shelter when the siren sounded. She untied the first packet and then stopped. The knot was loose and the ribbon crinkled as if it had been retied recently in a slightly different place. She looked at the others, but the knots there were tight. She recalled bundling them up small so that they would fit into the tin. She stared at them angrily. Someone had opened them and read her most private correspondence. Damn you Lena, she thought, with your grasping red nails and your greedy eyes. She could see her leaning on the bar in the Hut, drinking gin with a cigarette in her hand.

'She did have a boyfriend once,' she heard her say and saw

the astonishment on the faces of the men loitering nearby. 'You'd never think so, would you, to look at her. But it was all very lukewarm. You can bet he was glad to escape to the army.'

She felt sick. She scooped up all the bundles and ran down to the kitchen. The fire was still smouldering and she pushed one bundle straight in. Crouching, she pushed it deeper under the sticks and then added another. A tear landed on her hand and she wiped it away impatiently, but they continued to fall. She let herself drop on the floor and sat there. This was pure weakness, she thought, struggling to keep hold of herself. She looked down at the last bundle in her hand and saw Eifion's handwriting. She swallowed her tears. If she burned these Lena would have won. She pressed the bundle tightly to her and got up, determined to find somewhere much safer to hide them. It might not have been the white-hot love affair of her youthful dreams, but it was the only one she had, and it deserved a better fate than the flames.

When she heard Lena return some time later, she lay very still. She would have hit her had she seen her at that moment. Some man had seen her home, she could tell from the voices.

'Ta-ta now then!' she heard. 'And remember, we'll have a big booze-up before you go. You shan't go back to Italy sober!'

The door was closed and soon she heard her creeping up the stairs and into her own room. It sounded as if the Italians had received important news. With the huge task of bringing the soldiers back from Europe and the Far East, they would have been the last to get transport home. And if Giuseppe and Salvatore were going, that meant that Enzo would go as well, back to be a real policeman, with cases that he had the authority to investigate. That would be the end of following any trails here. Without him, what hope did she have? Don't be so pathetic, she chided herself fiercely, but despite that the pillow was damp next morning when she dragged herself out of bed to make breakfast, while Lena snored on regardless above her head.

Chapter Thirteen
May 1947

'Miss Arthur!'

Della turned on the threshold of the chapel and saw Aneurin standing with his bike at the cemetery gate, wiping the sweat from his brow. The weather had changed completely during the last few weeks and as she'd run all the way from School House having swallowed a quick tea, she could sympathise with him. She was already late, but two more minutes would make little difference.

'Busy again with the rehearsals for the Whitsun Meetings?' said the policeman.

Della nodded hurriedly.

'I won't keep you,' he added. 'I only wanted to let you know that there's a notice going into the paper – about the will.'

'No luck with the bank and the solicitors then,' she answered.

'No. And these solicitors are like clams. They won't tell you what day of the week it is. Perhaps somebody will see the notice – *To Whom It May Concern.*'

'And if you don't get a response, nobody can say you haven't tried until you're blue in the face.'

Aneurin laughed and looked down at his uniform.

'Blue in the face. Very good. Perhaps we'll find out a bit more about them. Somebody somewhere must know something.'

Della pushed open the chapel door and heard voices. Waiting for her would not have crossed Huw Richards's mind. She looked up and saw rows of children along the right hand side of the gallery, the smallest peering over the high parapet, while the bigger ones loafed at the back. She fancied she saw an expression of relief cross the faces of one or two as she appeared, but it might just be that they were hoping to hear her argue with the minister, in order to waste time. She'd really tried to keep matters on an even keel between them, but she hadn't always succeeded. And he had a distinct advantage in that she wasn't familiar with this type of Whitsun Meetings which were sessions of theological questions and answers for children and adults, on given themes. There was a distinctly competitive edge to them, as several chapels gathered together and the preparations were thorough. She'd thought the worst was over with the *Gymanfa Ganu* or Singing Festival at Easter, but that had only been a matter of practising a couple of 'items' with a small recitation party. This was on an entirely different scale. Whitsun would be upon them shortly, and the children's session still needed a lot of work.

She climbed the stairs and crossed over quietly to her usual seat next to Huw Richards on the left hand side. She was ignored.

'Say it again Eleri, but louder,' he said.

Eleri could barely be seen above the parapet but was sucking her lip nervously. The minister sighed theatrically under his breath and then asked in a voice like thunder, 'Who saw the burning bush?'

'Moses saw the burning bush,' Eleri chanted in a monotone after her older sister had given her an encouraging poke. Della smiled at her.

'That was very nice,' she said loudly. 'And remember to sit close to Eiddwen in case you forget.'

The mite nodded seriously and clambered back onto her pew with difficulty, displaying quite a lot of knicker.

'Heaven help us!' murmured the minister and Della made a mental note to tell Eiddwen to help her sister sit in a less exhibitionist manner.

At least he'd cut down on the endless paragraphs which were impossible to remember in his original script. One by one they went through their answers, some more successfully than others, but with each of them hiding scraps of paper in their fists. The clock ticked sleepily on the wall and the building was still and airless. The youngest ones of all had already started sucking their thumbs, and Eleri, after the strain of giving her one and only reply, was openly leaning against her neighbour, asleep. Gareth sat with Norman on the highest tier of pews, with their backs against the wall, throwing the occasional rebellious glance out of the window, where the sun shone and the leaves glistened in the breeze. Della sympathised. It was a close afternoon and they didn't want to be there any more than she herself did. Huw Richards followed the order on the page, making minute notes from time to time. Then he raised his eyes again.

'What does the psalmist tell us of God's purpose for man?' he barked in Norman's direction.

There was complete silence, and the boy's face turned red. He looked around him wildly. The next second, with no warning, Norman had grabbed Gareth by the shirt and punched him in the stomach. The girls fell back, shrieking like piglets while Gareth roared his head off. Instinctively, Della ran over towards them, but by the time she reached them Norman, breathing heavily, had dropped his victim and was standing over him. Gareth was doubled up.

'Norman! What on earth?' said Della, placing herself between them. From the corner of her eye she could see Huw Richards had put his head in his hands. Thanks for the support, she thought.

'He stole my paper!' shouted Norman hoarsely. 'He knows I can't remember it without my paper. He knows!'

This was true, for clutched in Gareth's hand that essential aide-memoire could be seen. Della scowled at him.

'Did you? On purpose?'

Gareth puffed and blew and rubbed his stomach before straightening.

'Yes I did,' he said, not sounding in the least apologetic. 'There you are, there's your old paper.'

Norman snatched it away and held it tightly. Then he stared fiercely at the minister.

'I'm ready now,' he said. 'What was the question again, please?'

'What in the world came over you to take his bit of paper?' asked Della crossly when she found Gareth sitting on one of the gravestones after the rehearsal was over. Norman had long galloped off.

'I'd had a bellyful,' he answered simply. 'And it's high time they all knew their words. I bet you anything there won't be any papers next time.'

'But was it worth getting thumped in the stomach for? You were hurt.'

Gareth smiled knowingly.

'I'll have a bruise like a saucer tomorrow morning. Hell's bells, he punches harder than Tommy Farr.' He got up. 'I might have a burst appendix,' he added joyfully. 'See you tomorrow, Miss.'

Della watched him open-mouthed as he limped towards the road. She realised that Huw Richards was waiting for her and turned towards the Manse.

'Boys!' she commented feelingly. 'What can you do with them? Jean told me to give him a clout when I first arrived. Perhaps I should have listened to her.'

The minister smiled less coldly than usual.

'No need,' he said, 'seeing as Norman's done it for you. If they could get on they'd be frightening. The brain and the brawn acting together, as it were. I'm ready for a cup of tea after all that excitement.'

Della didn't know whether it was all the carry-on in the gallery that was responsible but everyone was in a good mood over their tea in the Manse kitchen that evening. Hetty had witnessed it all from her position at the harmonium.

'Serve him right, I say,' she remarked robustly. 'But he doesn't give tuppence, at any rate. I once saw Stevie, drunk, trying to wallop him and missing every time. And then he caught hold of his father's arm and led him home like a pet lamb.'

Della sipped her tea appreciating the breeze that blew in through the open back door.

'That's the first time I've seen blows exchanged between him and Norman,' she ventured. 'I have to admit I didn't expect Norman to turn on him so suddenly.'

The other two smiled at each other.

'There are others who have had a taste of Norman's fists,' said the minister and Hetty nodded.

'He gave Tecwyn a lump on his forehead like a goose's egg, a couple of years back.'

'Wasn't it Carwyn that time?' asked Huw Richards.

'Who can tell? Anyhow, serve him right too, whichever it was. They're old enough to know better. I notice they don't provoke him as much since then.'

Della thought about this.

'The children in school don't make fun of him.'

Hetty snorted.

'Would you, if you knew he'd thumped a man in his twenties?'

Della turned to Huw Richards.

'Was that why you stayed where you were?' she asked lightly. 'In case you were thrown over the edge of the gallery?'

For the first time she heard him laugh, although quietly and into his teacup.

'Quite possibly,' he answered. 'Apart from the fact that it would be unseemly for a minister of religion to start fighting lads in the house of the Lord. The last time I saw anything like it, the two soldiers who belted seven bells out of each other were the best of friends in a quarter of an hour. Let's hope that's how it turns out here.'

The teapot was filled again, and yet again, and the next time Della glanced out through the back door, it was already night. She'd got up, meaning to go home around nine, but then she was pressed to have a sandwich by Hetty, and to come to see the historical volumes that Huw Richards had just bought. When he rushed off to the study, Della had turned to Hetty and said, 'But I can't sit here eating your food!'

'Nonsense!' came the reply, and then she added conspiratorially, 'He doesn't have many visitors, apart from people wanting something. Nobody round here understands what he's talking about half the time. I'll bring the sandwich into the study for you.'

She had not imagined that he would have such a collection of books. She was careful to treat them with respect, especially the very oldest ones. He turned one volume tenderly in his hands as he explained that he had bought it in Cardiff at the end of the war.

'Of course,' he said, 'I'm just benefiting from other people's bad luck. A lot more books came on the market as a result of the bombing. And I don't like to think how many priceless treasures were lost forever.' He looked rather guilty and sad.

Della hastily tried to think of something encouraging. 'I'm sure the original owners would be glad that they're appreciated, at least.'

'That's what I tell myself, but in their place I'd be spitting.'

When knocking was heard at the front door, he lifted his head and sighed. Hetty's footsteps came down the passage to open it, and within seconds she was at the door to the study.

'Problems,' she said. 'Come and see.'

Iori from the shop stood long-faced and worried on the

doorstep. Past him, down on the road, a figure danced whirling her handbag round and round. Iori nodded to Della.

'Awfully sorry and all that,' he muttered. 'But someone told me this is where you were.'

Even though she had tried to refuse the offer of help made by the minister, in the end she was relieved that there were two of them. She would not have been able to march Lena down to School House otherwise. Between the further attempts at dancing and the loud indecent songs, they had their hands full. She was never gladder to put her key in the front door. Lena hurried to the stairs immediately and blew a vague kiss in the direction of Huw Richards, who had mercifully stayed outside.

'Toodle-oo, Heathcliff!' she warbled and started climbing the stairs on her hands and knees. Della joined him on the front path, carefully closing the door.

'You'd think she'd be able to hold her drink by now,' she commented drily. Richards just raised his eyebrows.

'I didn't know there were other words to 'I Am a Little Soldier',' he answered with one eye on the open window of Lena's bedroom above their heads. Della wondered whether he was hoping for another peep show. Then he turned to her.

'Is this the first time?' he asked.

'For her to be stinking drunk on the road, yes it is, but the level in the cherry brandy bottle goes down alarmingly every day.'

'She topes in your house then?' he said disapprovingly.

'Yes she does. But then I sit on her chairs, don't I?'

'On Dafydd's chairs,' he corrected her. ' It seems to be family of drinkers. I just hope she doesn't end up in the same place.'

'Where is he exactly?' she asked.

He paused before answering.

'Didn't the education authorities tell you?' he asked and when she shook her head he tutted. 'That's very unfair.

Although, perhaps they believed they were respecting his right to privacy should he recover and want to teach again. He's in the mental asylum in Carmarthen. I pop over to see him now and again. They tell me it's a nervous breakdown, but I really don't know.'

For the second time that night, he looked downcast.

'It's very hard to see good friends suffer and be powerless to help,' said Della, feeling that she was getting to the end of her store of ready-made helpful remarks.

'It is. Dafydd is a nice old boy, sober or drunk.'

'Unlike his sister.' Della jerked her thumb towards the house. 'I think she's looking for something belonging to him. And I wouldn't be at all surprised if a removals van arrived one day and took all the furniture.'

'I'd say that was unlikely. From all accounts she plans to stay, now that she's got a job at the Hut.'

It was Della's turn to raise her eyebrows.

'Where did you hear that?'

'From Iori, but he doubts that it'll last. She may draw in the men, but she also drinks the profit.'

'I find it rather odd,' remarked Della, 'that Iori didn't volunteer to bring her all the way home.'

'He wouldn't dare. Ceinwen is notoriously jealous.'

She watched him for a moment making his way back up the road before turning. She knew very well why she'd been the last to hear of the job at the Hut. The atmosphere in the house had definitely worsened, not that it had ever been cosy. We're chalk and cheese, she thought, and neither of us can imagine living like the other. At least she hadn't started bringing men home. Not yet.

She hung her light jacket on the hallstand. The bathroom door was ajar and she could hear unmistakeable vomiting noises. She hurried to light the paraffin lamp. Goodness knew what mess Lena would be making in the dark.

'Lena?' she called quietly. 'Are you alright?'

The heartfelt groan that greeted her made her push the door open, and she could see and smell why. Lena knelt over the toilet bowl, her golden curls hanging, smeared, over her face.

'Bugger off!' she growled. 'I'm dying.'

Della ignored this and busied herself the sink, filling a glass with water and wetting a flannel.

'Come on now,' she said bending over her, pulling back her hair and placing the flannel on her forehead. Another wave of nausea gripped the other woman and Della waited for it to pass. From the evidence on the floor and in the bowl there wasn't much more to come. Lena dry-heaved for a few seconds and then fell back, seated, against the wall.

She stared up with red, tear-filled eyes and reluctantly took the glass that Della held out to her.

'He's not still here is he?' she asked suddenly.

'Who, Mr Richards? No, he's gone home.'

Lena sipped at the water and sniffed noisily.

'Better if he'd stayed there,' she said.

Della thought this was stunningly ungrateful.

'Would you rather have collapsed in the hedge and be found by the children on their way to school?' she asked sharply.

Lena didn't answer, but shut her eyes. In her present state she looked years older. It was surprising how effective lipstick and thick powder could be. Lena must have read her mind.

'And you can wipe that holy look off your face,' she hissed. 'I suppose you've never been the worse for wear.'

'No I haven't. Not that I can recall. Is it worth it?'

Lena put the glass down shakily.

'Yes it is,' she said defiantly. 'But never touch Turkish gin. It's lethal.'

'Is that what you drank tonight?' enquired Della wondering where one would find such a liquid in the village.

'No, I mixed them.' She winked up at her even though the

focus of her gaze was not exact. 'And have one yourself Lena! Very kind.'

'One of the drawbacks of the job,' murmured Della.

Lena laughed.

'There's more than one of those,' she said. She swallowed more water, letting some flow down her chin. 'When men get drunk they grow three extra pairs of hands.' She smiled secretly into the glass. 'And that's something else outside your experience, I'll bet.'

'You'd be surprised.'

'Yes, I would actually,' she said. 'And I don't mean holding hands and reciting poetry. God almighty, there's more to love than that!'

Della bit her lip.

'And there's more to life than throwing up down the toilet!' she answered.

'Like what, for example? What else has this arsehole of a place got to offer? The women look down their noses at you if you go to the only pub for miles and the men are all stupid!'

'Not all of them, surely?'

A sly look crossed Lena's features.

'No,' she admitted, 'perhaps not all. There are one or two. But they're the most dangerous of all.' She waved an uncoordinated hand. 'You take the Reverend Huw Richards now.'

Della refused to react in haste.

'But I thought you quite fancied him?'

Lena held out the glass to her and she refilled it.

'I do, but he's a deep one,' she said, taking it from Della's hand. 'Why is he here anyway? With his college certificates he could be anywhere. But no, he's buried himself here, far away from the big wide world.'

'Perhaps this is where he wants to be,' said Della, even though she'd asked herself the same question several times.

Lena just laughed and shook her head.

'He's here because nobody else wants him.'

The 'history' at last, thought Della, but she didn't need to prompt. Lena was more than ready to spill the beans.

'You know why,' she said without waiting for an answer. 'Because he killed his wife.'

Della sat down on the edge of the bath, unable to trust her legs. She was about to respond but Lena hadn't finished.

'As good as killed her anyway.'

Della swallowed hard. A buzzing noise in her head made her dizzy.

'How did he do that?' she asked, surprised that her voice sounded just as usual.

'He left her after she lost a baby. She was low, see, and she walked into the river. What did he have to join the army for in the first place? His place was at home with her. There's a Christian for you!'

Lena turned, without apparently noticing that the colour had drained from Della's face, and still on all fours, crept out of the room, leaving her among her thoughts and the pools of vomit.

Chapter Fourteen

Della looked at her watch and walked faster. She hadn't bought her ticket yet and the train would be leaving in less than five minutes. This was all Lena's fault. If it hadn't been for her drunken revelations the night before last, Della would not have rung Tydfil and Nest at eight the next morning to ask whether she could spend the weekend there. She had heard the instant worry in Nest's voice.

'Is everything alright?'

She'd almost postponed the visit there and then, but after taking a deep breath, managed not to. The only one who knew she was going to Cwm y Glo was Jean, and that was only because she'd remembered at the last minute to tell Gareth, who might or might not relay the message, depending on his mood. She would be missing another rehearsal tonight but she didn't care. She didn't think she could face another two hours in the chapel gallery listening to 'And who saw the burning bush?' in her present state of mind. She started to run as she saw the station roof through the trees.

Standing on the platform, with her ticket in her hand, still out of breath, she could feel the sweat trickling down her spine.

'Off somewhere nice?'

She turned in the direction of the voice and saw Aneurin pushing his bike towards her. Him again, she thought, but smiled.

'Only for a couple of days to see the people I used to lodge with.'

'Lovely. It's important to keep in touch.'

He too looked hot. He fumbled in his pocket and took out a cutting from a newspaper.

'It went in quickly,' he said. 'But I don't know whether it'll do any good.'

Della glanced over it.

'We can but hope,' she said.

Aneurin looked dubious.

'I'm not convinced. I heard from that solicitor this morning. There is a niece, he says. In Australia would you believe?' He took the paper back and folded it carefully. 'Do they read the *Western Mail* in Australia? No, of course they don't. If I knew where they came from originally, I'd go and ask about them. There's a story there, I'm sure.'   Then he winked significantly. 'High jinks the other night, so I'm told. Dancing on the square and all.'

Della pulled a long face.

'Don't talk! It was lucky I was in the Manse.'

'Wasn't it though? Ceinwen hasn't shut up about it since. That Lena's a case!'

'Perhaps she'll get tired of us before long and go home,' said Della hopefully.

'Doubt it. She was coming out of the bank in Cardigan when I was there making enquiries last week. I'd say she's opened an account. She'll be with us a good while yet. And they say Music Hall is dead! They should try living round here.'

The train puffed into sight that second and Della was saved from having to reply. Perhaps Aneurin was not as ineffectual as she had persuaded herself. He was tenacious for one thing and Glenys and Leonard's mysterious background had evidently piqued his curiosity. He lifted her case into the Ladies Only compartment for her. Through the window, she watched him wheeling his bike in the direction of the stationmaster's office and sat down with relief. She wouldn't have to think about any of it for two whole days.

'Tydfil will be away all day Sunday, you know,' said Nest breathlessly, having insisted on carrying Della's case up the wide staircase. 'He's got Yearly Meetings all day in Beraca, Cae'r Meirch.'

'But you normally go with him to Yearly Meetings! It's a day out for you,' protested Della as she followed her. She felt guilty for having unknowingly spoilt a treat. 'Why didn't you say on the phone? I could easily have come some other time.'

Nest pushed open the door of Della's old bedroom and grunted as she lifted the case onto the bed.

'Here we are,' she said and waited for Della to come in. Then she shut the door and gave her a hard look.

'It doesn't matter about the Meetings,' she said quietly. 'When I heard your voice I knew you needed to come home. There's something wrong, isn't there?'

Della threw her handbag onto the eiderdown and sat down.

'I don't know where to start,' she said.

Nest had either warned Tydfil to keep quiet, or he had depths of sensitivity hitherto unimagined for he didn't offer Della a lecture or any hackneyed advice. He sat silently listening to her tale over supper, and apart from a sharp hiss when she described her experiments with the knitting needle, he showed little emotion. It was Nest who exclaimed and who prompted encouragingly. Looking at them over her teacup Della could have sworn they had traded personalities for the occasion. She would have liked to hear the discussion that had given rise to this huge sea change in the normal order.

When, at last, he spoke, his words were surprising.

'This girl Lena,' he said sucking his pipe. 'I suppose there's no underhand way of making her shift? One couldn't write to the education authority and complain?'

'Not without creating a lot of trouble for myself,' answered Della. 'As Dafydd Jones's sister she's got a right to the furniture and she could take the lot.'

'But it's his furniture, not hers,' offered Nest.

'That's what Huw Richards said,' Della answered.

'But with the poor dab in the asylum, I think she can do what she likes.'

Tydfil considered a moment.

'Where did they come from, the two that died? From the Valleys somewhere?'

'I don't think so,' said Della shaking her head. 'Nobody seems very sure. From around Llanelly is the best suggestion I've heard.'

The other two exchanged glances.

'That settles it then,' said Nest. 'Come with us to Cae'r Meirch on Sunday. It's only a hop from there to Llanelly and if they did live there, someone will have heard of them. It'll be a chance for you to learn more about them, and if people won't talk to you, they shall answer to Tydfil!'

Before Della could respond, the telephone rang in the study and Tydfil got up automatically to answer it. She waited for the study door to close behind him.

'You don't have to do this you know,' she whispered. 'It could be really unpleasant. They were not nice people.'

Nest was already clearing the table.

'No indeed they weren't! But the truth is important, and you're the only one making any effort to discover it.'

She stared down at her, pleadingly.

'Please let us help you as much as we can. You'd be doing us a great favour. Since we lost Eifion, we've felt so useless.'

Della was alarmed to see her eyes fill, and rose to comfort her, but Nest brushed the tears away impatiently.

'I'm sorry,' she said. 'You had altogether too much of that while you were here. It's not knowing the truth, you see, about how exactly he died. It eats away at you. We accept that we'll probably never know, and that may be a good thing. But with your two blackmailers we've got the chance to do something.'

Who would have imagined such a thing, thought Della, remembering her words amidst the chatter and clatter of china in the vestry after the morning service the following day. Tydfil had preached powerfully and purposefully for forty-five minutes, and everyone was ready for their dinner. She smiled as she recalled his theme – justice for the unjust – and he'd certainly worked up a good head of steam and shaken the rafters on the topic. Napoleone should have been there to learn how to hold a congregation in your hand in one easy lesson. And now, here was Nest, the other side of the long room by the red hot boilers asking questions and listening, all polite attention, to the replies. She'd been watching her for some time and had seen one man shake his head sadly. No luck so far then.

Della turned to her nearest neighbour.

'Have you come far, or are you a member here?' she asked.

The man swallowed some of his bread and butter.

'We came on the train,' he said. 'Mary Anne's legs aren't what they were.'

The tiny woman with the thick spectacles sitting next to him nodded enthusiastically.

'We used to walk all the way, didn't we John? But not now.'

'You've lived in the area for some time then?'

'Since always,' said John, chewing. 'You're not from round here, are you?'

'No, but I come originally from the Swansea area. At the moment I live in Pembrokeshire, in Nant-yr Eithin. It's quite far from everywhere.'

'So you had it bad in the snow then, I expect,' said Mary Anne.

Della brightened up considerably. This was the entry she needed.

'I'll say we did!' she said raising her voice slightly. 'It was terrible. Three people died. A farmer who went looking for his sheep, and two others, a brother and sister, in their own house. Think of it!'

Mary Anne sucked her false teeth but showed no flash

of recognition. John just ploughed into another fish paste sandwich.

'That's nasty,' said Mary Anne.

Della tried again.

'You're right. And now they have the added difficulty, with the two who died in their house, of having to find the relatives. There's no will you see.' She pretended to think. 'I believe they've put a notice in the *Western Mail*, asking people to come forward.'

Happening to look up, she noticed that a woman standing at the other end of the table was looking curiously at her, which spurred her on.

'D'you know, something tells me that they were from round here originally. Glenys and Leonard Hughes.'

Mary Anne poked her husband in the arm.

'Were they on your round?' she asked. 'He was a postman until last year, see.'

'Not that I remember,' he answered and held his cup and saucer over his shoulder for one of the serving women to take and refill. The woman took the cup and Della noticed that it was the same curious lady, but she showed nothing in her face.

Disappointingly, the conversation moved on to other things and Della finished her lunch. She hoped that Nest had had more luck. Tydfil was over on the high table with the other preachers, and had taken out his pipe. They appeared to be in the middle of some deep theological discussion, apart from the young pastor who was due to preach that afternoon. He looked worried, as if he had suddenly realised that he was only the filler between Tydfil's two big-hitting sermons, morning and night. Perhaps he was hoping to be offered a call to be pastor of a chapel in the area. She pitied him if so. Nobody would remember him.

Ten minutes later, as she stood at the vestry door, she saw

Nest out in the cemetery talking to one of the other pastor's wives and went over to them.

'I was only saying to Olwen here,' said Nest, 'how nice it is to have you home for the weekend. Della goes to Huw Richards' chapel now. Small world isn't it? It seems like only yesterday he used to come to you as a student.'

Olwen sniffed. She was a majestic, barrel-shaped lady.

'Does he acknowledge the existence of the New Testament these days?' she asked in a rich contralto.

'From time to time,' answered Della, laughing. 'But the tribes of Gath are his main interest.'

A serious faraway smile crossed the large lady's face fleetingly.

'Plenty in his head, mind you,' she said. 'But inclined to be obstinate in the face of all reason.' She lowered her voice and addressed Nest. 'Remember that girl he married? Did you ever see anyone more unsuitable to be a minister's wife in your life? What was she, eighteen?'

Nest considered.

'I'm not sure – but she was certainly very childlike.'

'Personally I wondered if she was all there, but perhaps that was the innocence of youth. She had no idea anyway, and she was a bundle of nerves.'

Olwen did not look as if nerves played any part in her own life.

'It was a great pity,' said Nest, glancing around. 'It's time we took our seats. It's ten to two already.'

'Any news?'

Della was consumed with curiosity, but all she got was a warning look from Nest. The pews either side were quickly filling up. This suggested that something was up.

'The secretary of the chapel has offered you a lift to the station before tea,' was her only remark, and Della had to be satisfied with that for now.

147

The young minister was by no means boring. Despite this, her mind wandered. Would Napoleone's childish wife have grown to be a pillar of the community if she'd lived? Or would she have retreated ever further into her 'nerves'? She sounded like the last person to be able to cope with being Huw Richards' wife. Like living with a steamroller, she thought. But you never knew how someone else's relationship worked, not really. Perhaps she loved him desperately and felt she had completely failed when she lost the child. Yet, she herself couldn't imagine walking into the river. Even in the black days after the telegram arrived and she knew she would never see Eifion again, suicide had never crossed her mind. Perhaps, having lost her parents so young, she had been hardened to life's calamities to some extent. What must it be like not to see the point of living?

Outside, standing once more among the throng, she turned to Nest.

'The chapel secretary, did you say?'

'Yes, there he is over there.' She pointed to the gate where a tall man waited. He saw them and raised his hand. 'Have you got your case handy? It won't be fair if he misses his tea.'

Della ran straight to the vestry where she had left it safely at the back of the raised stage. The tables had been cleared and relaid during the service. Standing by the boiler was the woman she had noticed staring at her during lunch.

'Excuse me – could I just fetch my case from the back? The secretary has offered me a lift to the station and I don't want to keep him waiting.'

The woman nodded and handed it down to her. Then she took off her apron and folded it.

'I'll come with you,' she said unexpectedly. 'I'm his wife.'

Della didn't know whether this was encouraging or not, but she took her leave of Tydfil and Nest and climbed into the Austin Seven. The woman got into the back and Della could not have failed to notice the look that passed between husband and wife. Had she come in order to shut him up? Della hoped not.

They had left the chapel and the crowds far behind before anybody spoke.

'They say we're going to have a very hot summer,' remarked the woman.

'To make up for the dreadful winter, perhaps,' answered Della gratefully.

The secretary nodded and cleared his throat.

'You had it bad down in Pembrokeshire, so I heard.'

'We did. I haven't been there long, but it seems that heavy snow is fairly common, and from the way they organised themselves it was obvious they'd had plenty of practice.'

There was a silence while Della considered how she could introduce the all-important topic, but she didn't have to. The woman leaned over the seat towards her.

'So Glenys and Leonard died with you then?' she said. 'They used to live on the same street as Irfon's mother.'

Della caught her breath and saw Irfon glowering at his wife in the rear view mirror. She would have to tread carefully, or she'd get nothing.

'Yes, they did,' she said evenly, 'and now the local bobby is struggling to find relatives so that the farm doesn't lie empty.'

'There aren't any,' said Irfon staring ahead. 'Not round here anyway. Their niece Susan has been in Australia for years. When did she go, Janet?'

The woman answered immediately.

'Six months before the war started. Her mother Edna, who was Glenys and Leonard's sister, died in thirty-four. And she was a widow. I never heard of any other family.'

The secretary nodded and there was another pause. Della knew that there was much more to be learned, but how could she tap into it? In her mind's eye she saw the little snapshot of the boy with Glenys.

'What about Robin?' she ventured. 'Glenys was very fond of him.'

'She was daft about him,' answered Janet, 'and his grandmother was too. He was the be-all and end-all, considering he was illegitimate. Susan was nearly thirty when he was born. Everyone was shocked. Lucky Edna went before the accident. She'd never have got over it.'

'There was an accident?'

The man nodded again.

'Yes, a terrible thing. He was on his new bike on the road just after Christmas. Hit by a car, but nobody saw the driver. He didn't have a chance. He was only ten.'

Della thought sadly about the photograph. It was quite possibly taken just days before the child was killed. No wonder Glenys had kept it so carefully. She was drawn back to the present by Janet's voice.

'In less than a year they'd all gone,' she said. 'First of all Susan just disappeared and then one day there was a big van outside the house and nobody saw or heard anything about them after that. The notice in the paper was the first time I'd seen their names in years.'

'So how did you know that Susan was in Australia?'

'You heard, didn't you Irfon?'

He nodded reluctantly.

'Yes. I've got a brother in the police. He saw her leaving early one morning as he was walking home from his night shift and happened to ask where she was going. The enquiries were still going on at that time you see.' He glanced over at Della for the first time. 'Everybody felt for Susan.'

'But not so much for her aunt and uncle?' ventured Della.

There was another pause, but then Irfon answered, as if he'd given up on trying to keep mum.

'I worked for some years with Leonard,' he said slowly. 'He was not popular.'

A dry laugh was heard from the back seat.

'Tell the truth, Irfon, my love. He was a right devil. I've lost count of the people he cheated and the money he got out of them.' She tapped Della on the shoulder to emphasize her point. 'He had his claws in everyone. That's why I said nothing in the vestry. Half a dozen of them could have been his victims. Was he still the same? Had the leopard changed his spots, or were they beating saucepans on the road when they heard he'd gone, like they did here?'

Irfon scowled again but did not contradict.

'He was just the same, from what I've heard,' said Della. 'So he was the chief villain, was he? What about Glenys?'

'She was sly,' answered Janet.

'And under her brother's thumb completely,' added her husband. 'According to some, there was something not right about their relationship, if you know what I mean.' He pondered, as if unwilling to follow that train of thought. Then he added, 'It's odd that they ended up down in Pembrokeshire. Do you remember the number plate, Jan? Edwin my brother had great hopes for that number plate. Somebody saw an unfamiliar car with a DE number – that's Pembrokeshire – but it didn't belong to any vehicle they could find registered which is strange, because there aren't that many, are there? Everything came to a full stop after that.'

'Great shame,' murmured Della although her mind was still working. 'Who was Robin's father? Was he a local man?'

Irfon played the drum on the steering wheel.

'That's the strangest thing of all,' he said. 'Susan never let on. Everyone suspected that he was a married man. Anyway, she lost her job and all, even though Glenys and Edna were more than willing to look after the little one. She worked in a shop afterwards I know. Perhaps she was able to go back to her proper job in Australia. Let's hope so. She was a good teacher from all accounts and they're rare enough.'

Chapter Fifteen

Janet saw her onto the platform while Irfon stayed in the car. She pressed a paper bag into her hand.

'Couple of Welsh cakes for the journey,' she said.

'I'm very grateful to you,' replied Della. 'You've both been so kind. What would I have done without you?'

Mischief sparkled in Janet's eyes.

'If I hadn't been there, you would only have had a lift from Irfon. His mother knew everybody's business, but Irfon doesn't believe in gossip – not since he became chapel secretary.'

'Well at least I've got something to tell Aneurin our local policeman now. Perhaps he can get onto Susan's trail with this information. After all, there's a big farm waiting for her.'

Janet smiled.

'And the best of luck to her. She deserves it.'

The train's plume of steam came into sight and Della prepared to leave. After she had climbed in, she leaned out of the window to say goodbye. She realised that Janet was thinking. She moved out of the way to let a latecomer go past her and then she asked, 'Is there something else?'

'Only one thing,' said Janet wrinkling her nose. 'I was trying to think who Robin's father could have been. Irfon's mother had plenty of suggestions, but Susan was quite a lady, you know. Whoever he was, he wouldn't have been a road digger. He would have had an education. And round here there's only two places where she could meet someone like that – the chapel or the school.'

Good grief, thought Della, staring at the country going past, what a Gordian knot of complexities. She'd have to call Nest after getting home and let her know. Then she remembered it was Sunday night and that Lena would be there. Hell! As usual the train was packed full but somehow she'd managed to get a window seat. Janet's words stayed with her and she pondered with some amazement the fact that half a dozen of those respectable, religious people drinking their tea in the vestry could have been paying Leonard to keep something quiet. He had had a lifelong talent for discovering people's sore spots, and the overwhelming desire to pick at them. But if Irfon represented the area's inhabitants generally, hardly anybody knew they had moved to Nant-yr Eithin. So, it was fairly unlikely, even though not impossible, that someone had made the journey down with the purpose of killing them.

Yet, considering how the bodies had been found, his remark about the nature of the relationship had been interesting, and she could not rid herself of the feeling that there was some connection here, something that she was not seeing, especially in the light of the number plate. The two had chosen the village quite deliberately. It wasn't a place you happened to chance upon. Had they discovered who had killed Robin? How, if the police hadn't been able to trace the driver? She didn't believe they did much without it being of direct advantage to them. Susan sounded different. It was obvious that she had chosen to get as far away as she could and start a new life, where nobody knew her. Did Glenys and Leonard know she was intending to go? The fact that Irfon's brother had seen her leave early in the morning on her own suggested that they didn't. She wished that she'd had more time to question Janet.

She tried to put the events in order. Susan had left in spring of thirty-nine, as Robin had been killed the Christmas before, and they were all gone before the end of the year. She had an idea that their decision to move had somehow been spurred by Susan's departure, but of course they would have had to sell the house in Cae'r Meirch and find a suitable new home. It was just such a pity that Susan had not disclosed the name of Robin's father.

She leant back in her seat and closed her eyes for a second, the better to imagine the scene. Had there been an almighty row? Had Susan shouted out the father's name and her intention to leave? No, that was far too melodramatic, considering that she had determinedly kept the secret for over ten years. She opened her eyes suddenly as she realised why Susan had remained so silent. She hadn't been afraid of the world knowing. It was her own family she feared. Glenys and Leonard would have used the information, as they used all information, for profit.

Della tried to put herself in her place. Susan had planned it, packed what she could carry, and slipped out of the house without a word of explanation or farewell, long before anyone got up. She imagined their astonishment and rage when they found she'd gone. Perhaps they hadn't been told for days that she'd sailed for Australia. She knew too what she would have done in the aunt and uncle's place, which was to go through anything she'd left behind minutely, and question everyone who knew Susan. As she'd gone in such a hurry, it was possible she'd left a letter or a document behind, or perhaps they'd succeeded in getting more out of people once she'd gone and was safe out of their reach. Whatever happened, they learned something that sent them to Nant-yr Eithin, something they hadn't known before.

The train lost speed and Della saw that they were slowly approaching Carmarthen station. If Janet was right and Robin's father was an educated man, only one person in the village matched the description, and that was Napoleone himself. But at the time of Robin's birth at the end of the twenties, he would have been in theological college, barely out of his teens. Didn't Olwen say that she remembered him as a student? They did come to preach at chapels far from home, she knew that. Susan could have met him. The brakes screeched but Della barely noticed. She supposed it was possible that a love affair could have blossomed over a weekend, but Susan was at least ten years older than him. She tried to remember what Robin looked like, but apart from the scowl, he didn't resemble Huw Richards at all.

Some of the people got up and left the compartment. Who else was there, she pondered watching them go with half an eye. Iori, Eurig Rees, Jim Griffiths, Drunken Stevie, Norman's Nuncle, although not one jumped out as a credible candidate. Perhaps Janet was wrong. The man might have been from some other place close by, or he might not live in the village any more.

The instant the words formed in her mind, she leapt to her feet and pulled her case from the overhead luggage net. The guard had his whistle to his lips, and he was startled to see her throwing the door open and kicking her case from the train to the platform.

'For crying out loud, woman!' he shouted. 'Where were you? We've been standing here a good five minutes!'

Della apologised hastily and muttered something about falling asleep. Out of his sight, she forced herself to stop and take stock. She needed to leave her case at the station and check the time of the last train down to the west to ensure that she could get home that night. While she was at the Left Luggage counter, she asked in addition for directions to the mental hospital, which she got with a sympathetic look. Oh dear, she thought. She walked out into the sunshine and tried to think of the right questions to ask.

When the door was locked behind her, Della shivered. She had, of course, heard of such places, the 'locked wards' that people whispered about, but she'd never expected to visit one. And yet, nobody she'd seen so far had looked dangerous. Rather, they were lost souls, wandering purposelessly and pathetically.

'Hands, John!' said the sharp little nurse who was showing

her the way, and Della shied like a frightened pony. The nurse just smiled knowingly.

'Don't worry,' she said. 'He'll only touch himself, not you.'

She unlocked another door and went through it first.

'How is Mr Jones?' asked Della as she waited for her to lock it again.

'Up and down,' answered the nurse. 'Perhaps you'll be lucky. Perhaps not.'

She glanced around the wide, light room.

'That's him there in the corner,' she said pointing. 'Knock when you're ready to leave. I won't be far away.'

Della crossed the floor carefully past one or two who rocked rhythmically back and forth on their chairs. Others stared through the barred windows, but none of them said anything. Actually, she doubted whether they even saw her. The man in the corner had a book open on his knee, but wasn't looking at it.

'Mr Jones?' asked Della. 'Dafydd Jones?'

The man didn't react at all. Della looked round for the nurse but she'd disappeared. From far away could be heard faint wailing. She was on her own. She pulled up a spare chair and sat down.

'Mr Jones?' she tried again. 'Master?'

A vague light came into the man's eyes. He raised a shaky hand and rubbed it over his face. Someone had shaved him in the last few days, and his hair was reasonably short, but it couldn't conceal that he was little more than a ruin. Skeletally thin, the bones of his knees made sharp angles in the fabric of his trousers. Della fumbled for the paper bag of griddle cakes and felt his gaze upon her. She placed them on the table by his side.

'Do I know you?' he asked in a deep, husky voice.

'No you don't,' said Della shaking her head and smiling. 'But I've heard a lot about you. I'm the new teacher at Nant-yr Eithin. Della Arthur.'

She extended her hand, and instinctively, without taking his eyes from her face, he shook it. She saw that he was trying to think of something to say. After a long pause, he succeeded.

'How are the children?' he asked.

As she chatted and described, to herself mostly, she realised that he was slowly beginning to pay attention. She tried to include names that would be familiar to him, like Jean and Mrs Jefferies, and she thought she saw a tiny smile when she mentioned the latter of these.

'At the moment, we're busy preparing for the Whitsun Meetings, and Mr Richards the minister has written a good question and answer session for the children.'

He laughed suddenly, showing yellow false teeth.

'Don't tell fibs,' he said. 'Good session, my eye! Huw couldn't write for children to save his life.' Then, just as suddenly, his eyes filled with tears. 'I shouldn't have said that. That was unforgivable. He's been a faithful friend to me. You won't tell him, will you?'

Della hastened to allay his fears, but his mood had changed completely. He started to rock back and forth and mutter to himself. She thought she could make out the words 'useless, useless' repeated endlessly. This was dreadful. In an attempt to pull him back from whatever dark place he had gone to in his mind, Della grasped his hand. The rocking slowed but he no longer met her gaze.

'Listen,' she said. 'Everybody wishes to be remembered to you. They all thought very highly of you in Nant-yr Eithin.'

He didn't believe her, she could tell, but she ploughed on.

'You were very kind to Norman, weren't you? And it was he who showed me the way the day I arrived and told me about you.'

He leaned forward.

'Poor Norman,' he whispered. 'Innocent. Orphaned.'

Della nodded and tried to catch his eye.

'We all have a responsibility to look after Norman, don't we?' she said.

'Yes we do. But I failed in that as in everything else.' He looked at her anxiously.

'Did you? When was that?'

She saw him think.

'When he was killed,' he said. 'On his bike.'

Della bit her lip. All her careful thinking of questions had been in vain. She'd been answered without even asking.

'That wasn't Norman, Mr Jones,' she said quietly. 'That was Robin. Susan's son. Glenys and Leonard's nephew.'

He shot her look of sheer terror.

'Are they here?' he asked looking around.

'No. They've been dead for months.'

He leaned ever closer and she could smell his sour breath. For some reason, she got the impression that he already knew this.

'But have they been buried deep enough?' he hissed.

'In the depths of the earth,' said Della. 'They won't plague anybody ever again. They made your life a misery, didn't they?'

He gave the slightest of nods but the fear hadn't left his face.

'They came looking for me,' he said. 'Like the Hounds of Hell. After the Angel left. She kept them at bay until then, you see.'

'Was Susan the Angel?' asked Della but he didn't answer. He was far away once more.

'My fault you see. Poor little Robin. On his new red bike. We didn't see where he went.'

She didn't know what to take literally from all this.

'Were you there when Robin was killed?' she asked urgently. 'Was it you who saw the number plate of the car?'

Someone scraped a chair behind them and his eyes wandered in the direction of the noise. She'd lost him again. She cast an impatient look over her shoulder and was nailed to the spot. Standing, leaning insolently against the far wall, was Lena. She let go of his hand and grabbed her bag.

'I'd better go,' she said. 'You've got another visitor.' But he was already halfway out of his seat.

She too got up and walked towards the door. She was about to greet the newcomer, but as she drew nearer she saw Lena's eyes open wide. Dafydd Jones had followed Della, and in front of her, he took hold of Lena and kissed her long and full on the mouth. It didn't matter how much she struggled and pushed him away she could not escape him. A strong smell began to emanate from somewhere and Della looked down. Between his feet a large yellow pool dripped and widened. She knocked frantically on the door and called for the nurse. With huge relief she saw her running towards them through the glass pulling a long chain of keys from her pocket.

Della did not wait to see what happened after that. With pounding heart she made off, not stopping until she could see the station in front of her. Her stomach churned every time she thought of the scene she had witnessed. The buffet was closed, so there was nothing to do but reclaim her case and sit down to wait on the platform. She was profoundly grateful that he hadn't taken it into his head to kiss her. His mental state was so unstable he could easily have done so. He'd behaved very properly towards her, luckily. Perhaps she just wasn't the sort of woman that men grabbed without warning. She couldn't remember anyone ever doing so. The hot sun was less dazzling now, but she could still feel the damp under her collar and around her hatband. She leaned back against the warm wood of the bench, relieved that it was all over.

'You!' said a voice above her head. 'How did you get in to see him? You're not family. What right have you got?'

Lena stood over her, her red lipstick staining her mouth and chin.

'The same right as anyone else, I'd say,' replied Della evenly.

'But you didn't know him! Bothering him like that, with him so weak. What did you have to go and upset him for?'

'It was seeing you that upset him,' answered Della. 'He was fine before that. Talking nicely about the school and the children.' Although this was not strictly true, she wasn't going to yield an inch to her. 'And another thing, he didn't look all that weak when he took hold of you.'

Lena looked furious and Della considered her thoughtfully. Her suspicions grew that things were not so simple as Lena insisted. She recalled her creeping cautiously into the house on that other Sunday evening months before. Had she travelled up here then too? Why did she feel the need to keep it secret?

'I'm not the only one from Nant-yr Eithin who visits him you know,' she said. 'The minister calls. They were good friends.'

For a second Lena looked almost afraid. She plucked a cigarette from her bag and lit it. That seemed to give her renewed strength.

'You're all just poking your noses in!' she spat.

'You think so?' Her attitude was puzzling. 'Don't you think that knowing that he hasn't been forgotten is a comfort to him? He must be lonely. He's a clever man – he was reading when I got there. Perhaps I'll bring him a book, next time I come.'

That was sheer mischief on her part, but she couldn't help it. She didn't in any way relish the thought of going into that ward again, but if it annoyed Lena, she would do it. She was pleased to see her adversary turn an unpleasant pink colour.

'Why don't you just tell the truth?' said Lena maliciously. 'You went there to see whether there was any hope of his coming back and taking your job!'

Della rose. Standing, she was the taller by several inches. Lena stepped back slightly.

'Don't judge everyone by your own low standards,' said Della. 'I notice that neither he nor anyone else in the neighbourhood saw hide or hair of you while he was well. You're more interested in the furniture than you are in him.'

'He's pleased to see me!' came the challenging reply.

'Heavens above, I'll say he is!' retorted Della sarcastically. 'He's so glad, he wets himself with excitement.' Then she stopped, as for the second time that day, light dawned.

'He isn't your brother at all, is he?' she murmured. 'Where did you meet him? In a pub before or during the war? And how did you find out where he was?'

Lena set her lips in a straight line. She fumbled around in her bag and took a cheap ruby ring out of a small box.

'Engaged, see!' she hissed. 'For years and years. So I've got rights. We're very close, me and Dai.'

'If you're so close, why did you never get married? Did he see the light, I wonder, or did he meet someone else?'

There was no need to ask whom he'd met that made him change his mind about Lena – Susan the Angel.

'What did you do when he tried to break off the engagement? Threaten him with breach of promise?'

Lena didn't want to answer. She turned her head away and glared at the opposite platform. Della went on, sure now that she was on the right track.

'And now that he's ill here you are again. What for? Are you still trying to persuade him to marry you? For the sake of a mahogany sideboard? Good grief!'

Lena blew a plume of smoke from her lips and then dropped the stub and ground it under her heel.

'Fine for you to talk – I've got nothing! There are no good jobs now nor places to rent. But then, you wouldn't have noticed in your nice little house being paid every month, would you?'

Della now knew what all the cleaning and going to the bank had been about.

'You've been looking for his money,' she said.

'I've got to live like everyone else. But he hasn't got a red cent anywhere. Where did it all go to, you tell me? Nobody could have drunk the lot. He's been there for fifteen years, and there's nothing in that bloody village to spend your money on, is there?'

Della could have told her where Dafydd Jones's money had disappeared to but she did not dare. Who knew what she would do with the information?

'But you can't seriously want to marry him,' she said. 'Not just for that. Nobody's as desperate and unprincipled as that. Not even you.'

She didn't see the blow coming. One moment she was standing and the next she was sitting on the floor. She heard a man shout and the sound of running feet. When she looked up a porter had grabbed Lena's arm and pulled her away. Another porter bent over her.

'Are you hurt?' he asked anxiously. 'Do you want us to call the police?'

No, Della did not want that.

'Give me a minute,' she heard herself say as birds sang in her left ear. By the time she had been helped to stand and then put back on the bench, Lena had been led to the far end of the platform. It sounded as if she was being roundly berated.

'Thank you very much,' Della murmured. 'You're very kind.'

She saw that the porter was still regarding her carefully.

'That was assault and battery,' he said, adding, 'Since the war, we see her type oftener. A ruddy whore if ever there was one, 'scuse my language.'

Della smiled at him.

'How do you know I'm not one too?' she asked.

He picked up her handbag and handed it to her. It had opened as it fell from her arm, revealing some of its contents.

'Because as a rule they don't carry hymn books,' he answered.

'I've just been to a Yearly Preaching Meeting,' she explained.

The man laughed drily.

'Well, that one over there hasn't been saved, more's the pity. But Mr Harris will give her a dose of fire and brimstone and a long list of her sins. Don't worry, we'll keep her here until you've gone. You won't have to travel with her.'

Chapter Sixteen

A couple of hours later Della stood outside her home station and listened to the train whistling its departure. In the toilets, she had been relieved to see that her ear was not swollen, even though she had a sore red mark near her forehead. She had rearranged her hair to cover it and decided not to wear her hat for the rest of the journey.

'*Signorina!*'

She turned to see Enzo loitering, hands in pockets. She smiled, pleased to see him.

'Are you going on a trip somewhere?' she asked.

He shook his head and reached out his hand to take her case.

'I just walk,' he said. 'You go to School House? I accompany you.'

He said this with a hint of pride at having remembered the word. In a few moments they had left the station behind and the high green hedges closed around them.

'You'll be leaving soon, they tell me,' said Della conversationally. 'It'll be wonderful to go home to Italy and see your family. How long have you been here?'

'Four years,' he replied. 'I think everything change now. Mussolini dead. New Italy.'

'Didn't you like Il Duce?'

He chuckled sourly.

'No,' he said and spat.

'So why did you join the army?'

Enzo pulled a stalk from the hedge with his free hand.

'Everywhere dangerous. Home. Army. In my town, people disappear.'

He drew his finger across his throat.

'So you took your chance as a soldier.'

'I want to live. More hope in army.'

There was silence between them for a while.

'You been to see your family?' he asked suddenly.

'The only family I have,' answered Della. 'The parents of the man I was going to marry. He was killed in the war.'

The Italian sighed sympathetically.

'Why he go to army?'

'He had to. He was called up. As a music teacher he had no choice. He died as a Japanese prisoner of war in Singapore.'

She didn't have to explain to him what that meant. He shook his head and waved his arm to encompass the whole neighbourhood.

'Farmer don't have to go,' he said. 'Special job.'

'Reserved occupation. I know. The coal miners where I come from didn't have to go either,' agreed Della. 'But a lot of boys went all the same. The minister fought in India, did you know?'

'Of course. Napoleone always fight.' He smiled showing his perfect teeth. He put one hand inside his jacket in a mocking gesture.

There was another pause.

'I saw Dafydd Jones, the old master this afternoon,' said Della into the silence. 'In the hospital in Carmarthen. And Lena too. Did you know that she wasn't his sister?'

His face lit up as if she'd given him a present. He gave a low whistle.

'You ask him this?' he said admiringly.

'Not exactly. But I heard a long story which includes Glenys and Leonard, if you have the time to hear it.'

They had reached a breach in the hedge with a stile which led to a wooded slope. Without hesitation, Enzo climbed over and extended his hand for Della to follow.

'We talk where nobody see us,' he said.

He led her through the brambles to a stand of beech trees.

He took off his jacket and spread it on the ground. They sat and Della told him everything about her exciting weekend. From time to time he would ask a question, but mostly he let her talk. When she came to the information she'd been given by Janet and Irfon, he rubbed his hands in satisfaction.

'I thought that would fill some of the gaps for you,' said Della, smiling, before resuming her tale. With such an appreciative audience it was even easy to describe the events at the hospital and the station without emotion, almost laughingly.

'She hit you?' he asked, astonished.

'Yes she did. A really good thump. Look.' And she pulled back her hair to show him.

With gentle fingers he touched the bruised spot.

'Ach, bad woman,' he whispered, and then leant forward and kissed it.

Della felt her stomach give a little jump. She wasn't a hopelessly dry old spinster after all. There was a good, sober, clever man who found her attractive. She put her arm around his neck and returned his kiss enthusiastically. She could not feel any stubble against her cheek and he smelled clean and of soap. She closed her eyes when he kissed her throat and felt his fingers lightly trace the line of her jaw. Enzo was humming a tune under his breath.

'*Con brio*?' whispered Della and saw him open his clear grey eyes.

He shook his head mock seriously.

'*Con passione!*' he answered and kissed her more deeply sliding his hand down over her breast. Oddly, she felt no fear when she sensed his fingers dancing over her knee and under the top of her stocking. She stared unseeing through the intense green of the leaves overhead and sighed softly. When he suddenly pulled away she stiffened, thinking she had done something wrong in this unfamiliar game, but his eyes were alarmed, scanning the crest of the slope behind them.

'What?' she whispered, but he shook his head urgently and put his finger on her lips.

She listened, hearing voices in the distance, but coming nearer. A blush rose from her neck up over her face. Damn it, she thought. Enzo's face held a watchful, guilty, worried look. Fair play to him for thinking of her and not displaying his conquest like a green adolescent. He didn't move either, but his gaze followed whoever he could see every step of the way. Della held her breath until the voices faded and the Italian nodded. Then he got up carefully, and placing a finger on his own lips as a warning, helped her up.

Down through the scrub they crept, with Della praying she wouldn't trip in her Sunday heels. Neither of them spoke until they were back over the stile and on the road again.

'Who was it?' she mouthed, although there was nobody around to overhear.

'Lilwen and Tecwyn-Carwyn.' Enzo still looked perturbed.

'Tecwyn is her boyfriend I think,' said Della.

Apart from making an ambiguous noise in his throat, he didn't explain further. Anyway, the spell was broken, and they walked on, only breaking the silence with the occasional remark. School House rose before them as the road curved and Della reached for her case.

'I'll be fine from here on,' she said and Enzo nodded, handing it over.

'I see you again before we go,' he said. 'They make party for us.'

'Really?' This was news, and she could see he found it surprising too.

'We'll all miss you,' she said.

He made a small apologetic gesture and smiled.

'Don't want to go now,' he said. 'Difficult time.'

She took it that he was referring to the deaths in the farmhouse.

'You were a great help,' she said.

Once again he touched her cheek and she thought she saw real regret in his eyes.

'Not forget,' he answered, and then turned on his heel back towards Clawdd Coch. She watched him go for a while but when he didn't turn back, she went on her way.

She climbed the steps to the back door. The sun was finally setting on this dreadful, triumphant day in a suitably flamboyant manner. She felt quite light-headed. Would she ever experience another day like it? She'd learned so much – about herself as well – and the world looked different because of it. She'd been struck and kissed all within two hours.

She climbed the back steps. If the porter kept his word Lena wouldn't be home for a while which was another reason to be cheerful. She put down her case and hat and took off the jacket of her costume before going into the kitchen and fetching the kettle. She was filling it at the tap in the scullery, humming a tune when she heard a noise. She stopped and stared into the darkness of the long lean-to shed, but she could see nothing. Then the noise came again and she felt her heart thump in her throat.

'Hello?' she called. 'Who's there?'

There was nothing but a brooding silence. Suddenly, she was very afraid. Had somebody slipped into the house to wait for her? She dashed back into the kitchen and grabbed the coal shovel. Standing in the doorway to the lean-to, she glared into the shadows.

'Come out of there now this minute!' she commanded in her schoolyard voice.

Nothing moved for a long time and then she heard a snuffling, weeping sound. Still suspicious she entered, hearing her heels clicking on the slate slabs. She had nearly reached the coal pile at the far end when she saw a figure, bundled up against the door that led out to the garden. Relief swept over her like a tidal wave.

'Norman!' she said. 'What on earth are you doing out here? You could have sat in the kitchen.'

He lifted his heavy head from the haven of his folded arms.

'Didn't like to,' he muttered. 'You weren't here.'

She leaned over him and rubbed his head.

'I'm here now,' she said. 'Let's go and have a cup of tea, and you can tell me what's wrong.'

He looked up at her in bleak despair.

'All my chickens are dead,' he said.

It took two cups of hot, strong tea, and a clean handkerchief before she managed to stop the tears and get the whole story. When he'd gone to open up that morning, he had found them all killed.

'A fox, I expect,' said Della in an attempt to comfort him. 'I've heard that all the fluttering and squawking drives them into a frenzy and they kill them all.'

Norman inclined his head to his tea cup which he held in the frayed cuff of his jumper.

'Something red anyway,' he said indistinctly, but at least he was no longer sobbing. 'I've buried them. And sung a hymn.'

Della nodded wisely.

'That was the right thing to do. Now then, how about if I take you home. I can understand why you didn't want to go there at once. You didn't want to upset them, did you? Not with your uncle so poorly.'

The poor lad took a deep breath.

'No,' he said, wrinkling his brow, as if this hadn't actually struck him.

'You don't need to worry. I'll explain everything. You won't get into trouble.'

Della had not crossed the threshold of Norman's home before, not even as she went from farm to farm with Eurig

Rees. She'd thought it odd at the time, and had mentioned it, but Rees had only shaken his head.

'There's no point even asking,' he'd said. 'It would be kinder not to.'

She understood why the moment she walked into the farmhouse. Even though none of the farms she had visited had been luxurious, this place screamed of neglect and poverty. Despite the fire that burned in the black-lead grate and the residual heat of that warm day, the walls sweated damp with a pungent odour. Nanty hurried towards her, a tired wren of a woman, wiping her red hands on her sacking apron.

'I've brought Norman home,' said Della apologetically. 'He's had a bit of a shock.' She was aware of him standing behind her like a huge shadow as she spoke. Nanty's brown eyes swept over them.

'Oh dear, poor old Norman,' she said. 'Come on, I'll warm you up a cup of milk. You shall drink it in bed, like when you were little.'

Della watched as they climbed the uncarpeted stairs, with the aunt holding the lad's hand as if he was five years old.

'Come in then! Don't stand there in the draught.'

The croak came from the wooden settle by the fire. Because of its high sides and back Della had not realised that there was anybody sitting there. She approached a pile of blankets and shawls. The man who sat swaddled in them, despite the heat, turned and grinned at her like a skull.

'Sit down, sit down. I don't often get visitors.'

Della pulled up a hard chair and sat facing him. He was as yellow as a sovereign and the bones of his face were visible under the skin. He pointed a bony finger at her.

'You're a teacher, aren't you? You look like a schoolmistress. I hope you're strict with them.'

Della smiled.

'I shout like a sergeant major,' she said.

He giggled and wheezed until a bout of coughing nearly choked him and wiped his damp mouth on the corner of a shawl.

'Do you give them the cane?'

'No, never.'

'You should. If sense won't go in one end of the little buggers, it'll go in the other.'

'Yes, but if you can't keep order without the cane, what hope have you got of teaching them anything?'

He chewed the cud on this for a moment.

'I used to get the cane often,' he said. 'Six whacks on my arse.'

'Did it do you any good?'

'No.' And he laughed quietly to himself.

Della hoped that Nanty would appear soon. It was difficult to know whether it was his illness that made him so repulsive, or whether he'd always been like this. With relief, she heard footsteps coming down the stairs. Nanty was shaking her head.

'God help him,' she said, evidently having received a precis of the story. 'He thought the world of those chickens. I'm sorry you've had to go to such trouble.'

Della got up, eager to leave.

'Not at all,' she said. 'I owe Norman a debt for all the coal he's carried for me. And he never forgets either.'

His aunt was pleased by this. She smiled shyly for the first time.

'He lays the fire for me here every morning while I milk.' she said. 'Summer and winter, no matter what.'

She leaned on the table briefly. Quite probably, she had a host of tasks to complete before turning in that night. Where did the twins come into the scheme of things, pondered Della. With three great lads about the place, there should surely have been no need for her to milk. Her eye was caught by something fluttering above her head. A row of silk rosettes in red and blue hung from a high shelf.

'Who won these?' she asked.

Nanty tutted dismissively but her husband answered. 'The boys and me,' he said. 'When I could, I used to show horses, see. Welsh cobs. And we used to go to races all over.'

'That's their delight,' said his wife. 'We don't keep horses any more, but that's where they are when they get the chance.'

'How interesting,' said Della. 'A good horse is a very pretty animal.'

'A good wife would be prettier,' said Nanty, ignoring her husband clicking his tongue. 'Yes, indeed it would. They're getting on for thirty, both of them. It's high time they settled down with a tidy girl apiece.'

Before Della could mention that one of them, at least, did have a 'tidy girl', another impatient croak came from the settle.

'Let them have their youth while they can, woman!'

Out of the old man's line of sight, they smiled at each other.

'I won't keep you,' said Della and turned for the door.

Out on the yard Nanty thanked her again, speaking more freely than she had in the house.

'Norman's had such losses,' she said sadly. 'Did you know that my sister and her husband were killed in the bombing?'

Della nodded sympathetically.

'He was only seven, poor little mite,' his aunt continued. 'It's no wonder he gets so upset at everything. He was there all night in the house with the two bodies. Enough to send anyone off their heads.'

'He's amazingly good, in that case,' said Della sincerely.

The other woman wiped her hands again on her apron. Della supposed that she did it automatically a hundred times a day.

'What's to become of him? We have so little to give him.'

Della tried to reassure her.

'You care for him, and you understand his problems,' she said. 'That goes a very long way, believe me.'

She extended her hand and Nanty shook it with her rough paw.

'Come again,' she said. 'Don't be a stranger.'

On reaching the gate at the far end of the farmyard, Della turned and waved. Such tenacity was humbling. She didn't think she could get up in the morning in Nanty's situation. Walking down the lane, deep in thought, she didn't notice the figure coming towards her at once. It was one of the twins.

'All right then, Miss?' he said and smiled, reminding Della of his father.

'Fine thanks,' she replied, and then, emboldened, asked, 'Which one are you, exactly?'

He had already passed her but turned and put his finger to his nose.

'Wouldn't you like to know?' he answered and carried on walking.

Yes, I would actually, she thought, being of the opinion, like their mother, that it was time they grew up.

She knew Lena was home the second she opened the door. From somewhere above her head came the sound of dance music. There was a gap on the shelf where the wireless and its big battery usually stood. She was too tired to go and claim it back tonight. Picking up her case and hat from where she'd left them she slowly climbed the stairs to the top landing. The door to Dafydd Jones's old room was slightly open, but as she crossed to her own bedroom it was slammed shut. No truce then. To hell with her, the common little cow.

CHAPTER SEVENTEEN

Della came within a hair's breadth of being late next morning again. She had to rush across the yard without breakfast.

'Thank goodness!' she said seeing Lilwen there already filling the teapot. 'I'm in dire need of that.'

Lilwen looked up with her large blue eyes, immaculately turned out as usual.

'How do you always manage to look so well groomed?' asked Della. 'I'm like a scarecrow. And I have nobody but myself to organise.'

The girl smiled sweetly and stirred her tea slowly.

'When you have to get up at six, you've got a lot of time to spare,' she answered. 'And once the Italians go it'll be even earlier to milk, unless my father finds someone else. That reminds me, did you know that a party's been arranged in the hall, for Saturday night?'

'I did hear something,' said Della, not wishing to disclose from whom. 'It's a very kind thought.'

'We were going to hold it at home, but we can't fit everybody in. The whole neighbourhood wants to come. Everybody will be cooking full out. Aneurin's wife has promised a banana cake.'

'Where on earth has she found bananas?' Della asked in astonishment.

Lilwen pulled a rueful face.

'She hasn't,' she said. 'Not real bananas. She uses parsnips and banana flavouring.'

So that was something to look out for and avoid, but she too would have to think of something to offer. A jam sponge perhaps, if she could beg butter and eggs from somewhere. She might just be able to use her margarine, but now that Norman no longer had his chickens, eggs might be a problem. She glanced at the fire. It looked far smaller than usual and the scuttle was empty, too.

'Norman saves fuel does he, this time of year?' she enquired.

'No,' said Lilwen. 'I set the fire this morning. I don't think he's here.'

She spoke the truth. There was no sign of him that day, nor any message to explain his absence.

Two days went by, and perhaps because there was no need for a blaze Della didn't miss him as much as she would have done in the winter. However, on the Wednesday morning, when she called his name on the register, with no response, she raised her eyes and looked around the room.

'Has anyone heard if Norman's ill?' she asked.

The younger children seated at the front shook their heads, but she saw Rhonwen at the back look significantly at Gareth, who kept his head resolutely down. Now was not the time to make detailed enquiries. Her opportunity would come at the end of the school day when Gareth stayed behind to go through another chapter of the first aid book. She caught herself watching him out of the corner of her eye. He had seemed preoccupied all week, she realised. There could be a number of reasons for this. He was, after all, coming to the end of his last term at school. She did not imagine he relished the thought of taking up the reins on the smallholding, and having to work side by side with his father. Perhaps he'd have to go to some other farm to work – possibly to Eurig Rees. Even though she had mentally earmarked Norman for that job, there could potentially be room for them both, if they could get on. Rees would not be happy if they started fighting as they had in the chapel gallery. Oh heavens above, she thought suddenly. What if it was Gareth who had killed the chickens?

'The general consensus of opinion regarding the treatment of shock,' read Della, 'is that alcohol should not be given. Do you know why?'

Gareth shook his head and then paused to consider.

'So that they don't get drunk on top of everything else?' he ventured.

Della smiled. He was thawing slowly. The first fifteen minutes of their usual lesson had been hard going.

'That's a good point, but I think that the reason is to avoid drawing the blood to the stomach from the brain and the heart. It's important to keep them working.'

Gareth studied the black and white illustrations of people wrapped in blankets.

'If that's true,' he said in his normal, challenging tone of voice, 'you shouldn't give them hot, sweet tea either then, should you?'

This hadn't struck Della.

'Perhaps you're right,' she answered, 'although the people who were bombed out of their houses in Swansea drank gallons of it. Shock can kill, you know, if the person's in poor health to start with.'

She got up and fetched a pencil to make a note in the margin, aware that Gareth was watching her.

'Do you think Norman's in shock?' he asked suddenly. 'After losing his chickens.'

'A sort of shock, possibly,' she said carefully. 'Did you know that he held a funeral for them?'

Gareth shook his head and pulled a loose thread from the cuff of his shirt. His face looked tight and closed. Then he stared straight at her.

'I did not kill the chickens,' he said slowly.

Della pretended to be totally shocked at this.

'I thought a fox had done it,' she said.

The boy laughed harshly.

'That's because you come from the town,' he said. 'Norman knows that it wasn't a fox, and he knows it wasn't me either. But everyone else thinks it was.'

'You've seen him since it happened, have you?'

He nodded anxiously.

'He hangs about near that old coop as if he hopes they'll come alive again, you know, like that whatsisname in the Bible, Lazarus. Is that just shock? Or is he really off his head this time?'

Della had to admit she didn't know.

'That might be his way of grieving,' she suggested. 'Norman's had such a lot of terrible experiences in his life. He won't always react like other people.'

Gareth wriggled impatiently in his seat.

'There are three things that set him off,' he said. 'Loud noise, fire and blood. If he hears loud noises he runs. Fire, he hides in the corner and cries, and blood he faints flat out.'

Despite this observed analysis, Della had to protest.

'But he fetches coal and feeds the fire here every day!'

Gareth leaned forward, in the same manner as Della's old Latin teacher used to do.

'Haven't you noticed that he forces himself to do it? You watch him next time. He's really, really careful. Red hot cinders never fall on the floor when he does it. He doesn't trust anybody else to do it properly. It took me a long time to twig that. Last year, I was dying to have a go, while Master was ill, but when I started, Norman used to stand over me, breathing hard and muttering, "Not like that, not like that." It wasn't worth the trouble in the end.'

It had to be admitted that this made sense.

'And now people think you killed his chickens,' said Della.

Gareth drew a long, miserable breath.

'Yes, they do. And they shake their heads at me.' He placed his hands on the table. 'I couldn't kill twenty hens. For God's sake, I can't wring the neck of one without feeling sick.' He shuddered in revulsion. 'It's the only thing my father can do that I can't.'

'So at least your parents believe you.'

He pulled a long face.

'I heard them arguing about it last night. For once, Dad was on my side, and Mam was saying, "He could still have hit them with a stick." Think of it! My own mother!'

He folded his arms and aimed a kick at the nearest chair leg.

'I believe you,' she said, hoping she would not live to regret it.

'Do you? Why should you?'

What could she say that would not complicate matters further?

'Look,' she said, 'whoever did this is cruel. And you may be a little devil at times, but I don't think you'd do anything to hurt Norman like that. The question is, what has Norman done that someone would deliberately take away the one pleasure he has?'

Gareth sniffed contemptuously.

'He wouldn't have to do anything at all. Once they're tanked up round here, they'll do all sorts. Killing chickens is nothing. Norman was just unlucky that he kept them away from home.'

Perhaps so, thought Della, downcast at the casual callousness of this, but a small voice in her subconscious told her that it hadn't been a matter of chance. She came to a decision.

'Will you do me a favour?' she asked. 'Will you keep an eye on him for me? And if you see something that bothers you, come and tell me straight away. It doesn't matter when.'

Gareth gave this some thought.

'Do you think he's going to do something daft?'

'I really don't know, but I don't want anything else to happen to him, and I don't think you do either.'

Then, in an attempt to lighten the atmosphere, she added, 'I saw the master over the weekend. He wished to be remembered to you.'

The lad gave her a sharp, incredulous look.

'Last time I saw him he was worse than Norman,' he said. 'Has he got a lot better, then?'

In the face of such unsentimental hard-headedness it was pointless to lie.

'Only at times,' she admitted. 'But he did say that we all have a duty to look after Norman.'

He smiled knowingly.

'That's the most sensible thing he's said in months,' he said and got up to leave.

Della watched him cross the yard. He was such a perplexing mixture of man and boy, she sincerely hoped that her faith in him was not misplaced. If he had killed the chickens, then he was an excellent actor. But then, as Jean, his mother, had said, they were cunning at that age.

It had been a long Saturday evening, and it wasn't over yet. Eurig Rees climbed awkwardly onto the table. The whole neighbourhood ebbed and flowed around him and the children ran mad races in and out of the door of the hall. Della glanced down at the tables, pleased to see that her sponge had all gone apart from one lonely slice. There was enough food left, even in these restricted times for them to have another meal. In the corner by the stage sat the three Italians, each holding a glass of home-brewed beer and looking rather stunned. It was hard to tell whether it was the drink, the valedictory verses, the singing, or just the accumulated effect of the party that was responsible. She'd been very careful to stay away and not catch Enzo's eye too often.

'Right then,' said Rees. 'How about a bit of hush!'

The chatter grew a little quieter, but not much. From her standpoint next to the boiler, Della could see the mothers pulling their offspring to them, and the lads who had been having a sly fag outside appearing at the open door. Rees coughed and wiped the perspiration from his face.

'I won't keep you long,' he began, smiling at the general groan. 'We have gathered together tonight to say farewell to our friends Giuseppe, Salvatore and Enzo before they catch the train to London.'

A shout from the back interrupted him.

'Hurry up then Eurig, or they'll be here for another week!'

Rees rolled his eyes.

'Personally, I would be very happy if they didn't go at all, but I don't arrange these things. They've been good workers and good neighbours, ready to lend a hand and easy to handle.'

This drew enthusiastic clapping from the floor and Eurig Rees nodded in recognition. He took three envelopes from his waistcoat pocket and turned to the three.

'As a gesture of our friendship and appreciation, we've been collecting. It isn't much, but perhaps it'll be of some help.'

They came up in turn to receive their gift. Giuseppe and Salvatore only managed to mumble a few words of thanks but Enzo was a different matter. He cleared his throat.

'Thank you very much all of you, and you Mr Rees,' he said clearly and the whole place suddenly became silent. 'We were, none of us, expecting this. We came here as prisoners of war, but we leave as friends. We will never forget your kindness. *Mille grazie*. A thousand thanks.'

In the middle of the deafening applause and whistling, Della felt a presence at her shoulder. Huw Richards stood there, regarding Enzo through narrowed eyes.

'There was a lot more in that one's head than anyone imagined,' he muttered between his teeth. 'Of course, you wrote his speech for him.'

'No I didn't,' answered Della. 'I thought it must have been you.'

He shook his head.

'He wouldn't have asked me. I have an idea he's not too keen on ministers of religion. Perhaps he's a communist.'

'We'll never know,' said Della with a smile. 'Everybody came to say goodbye, fair play to them.'

'Almost everyone. There are some significant absences. Norman and his family and your lodger, for example.'

Della hadn't noticed.

'Lena's no loss, but it's a shame Norman and his aunt aren't here. The twins have put in an appearance though.' She gestured towards the door where she could see the two of them standing like reflections in a mirror. They seemed to be enjoying a joke with the other young men, taking quick nips at roll up cigarettes, almost hidden in their fingers. Napoleone followed her gaze and they saw one of them smile, turn away and disappear into the darkness. His brother waved at someone, took a last look round and went after him.

'Not enough home-brewed?' suggested Della.

'Possibly.'

The men accompanied the Italians all the way to the station, while the vast majority of the women stayed behind to wash up and put away. Della stood at the back of the crowd by the school gates, knowing that she could not go to the station without drawing attention to herself. There was no way of saying farewell to Enzo privately, so it was better not to try. She smiled and waved her teacloth with the rest, and for an instant she fancied the grey eyes met hers, but it was dark and then they were gone.

The women turned and straggled back up the slope to the hall. A couple of the younger ones were tearful.

'More work clearing again,' commented Jean who walked next to her.

She fanned herself with her cloth and puffed her red cheeks.

'And the children are wound up like springs. But there we are, at least I didn't have to make them supper. You'll find it quiet now.'

Della froze within. To what was she referring? Had she been seen in Enzo's company. Her silence must have struck Jean.

'Without that one,' she said, jerking her thumb in the direction of the house. She saw that Della did not understand. 'She left this morning. Around eleven. And got Stevie to carry her case. Didn't you see her go?'

'Lena's gone?' Della could only shake her head in surprise. 'I've been up at the hall preparing since before ten. I've only been home for ten minutes to change, around six – and she's often gone to the Hut before then.'

'Didn't you notice her things were gone?'

'No, but I was in a hurry. Mind you, she might come back.'

'I don't think so. The case weighed a ton, according to Stevie.' She pulled a long, comical face. 'Perhaps she's made off with the cutlery.'

Among the women in the kitchen, Della digested the news. She took another wet cup from Hetty, who was up to her elbows in soapy water, and dried it thoughtfully. That lady glanced sideways at her and blew a stray lock of hair from her eyes.

'She's slung her hook then,' she said.

'It looks that way,' said Della. 'She never said a word.'

'She's found another way of living for nothing,' she said. 'Nobody round here will miss her.'

'But she'll linger long in the memory, despite that,' said Della, looking around. 'Did Lilwen go home on the cart?'

'Yes. She looked done in.'

'I'm not surprised. I lost count of the sandwiches she cut.'

Hetty smiled.

'About time you went home too,' she said.

'Do I look that bad then?'

'No you don't. But you'll need to have a good look round to see what's gone from the house. Lena's kind never leave empty-handed.'

In the silence of her own kitchen some time later, Della

considered her words. As far as she could see there was nothing missing. Lena had disappeared completely, as if she had never been there. Lamp in hand, she went through the rooms. Everything was exactly as she remembered in the china cabinet and all the pictures remained on the walls. She climbed the stairs and pushed open the door to Dafydd Jones's old bedroom. Lena had stripped the bed and folded the clothes neatly, which was unexpected to say the least. The jam pot she used to stub out her cigarettes had been washed. The room looked as bare as it had before she arrived.

She went back to her own room and searched for Eifion's scent bottle which she had hidden carefully. It was as she'd left it, as was the bundle of his letters, with the special knot she'd made, undisturbed. Tired, she sat on the bed and kicked off her shoes. Perhaps this was Lena's parting shot – nothing at all to say. She hung up her blouse and skirt. In her petticoat, she pulled back the coverlet to fetch her nightdress. There was a blank envelope on the pillow. Without touching it, she finished undressing and went to the bathroom. Then she rolled her hair in rags and cold-creamed her face just as normal.

She settled herself comfortably in bed and then she opened the envelope. She'd been rather expecting an avalanche of paper, but Lena had succeeded in reining herself in. In neat, rather childish handwriting on one sheet which had pencil lines painstakingly drawn across it, Della read her lodger's words of farewell:

Dear Miss D. Arthur

I am going far away. There is nothing here to keep me. There is more hope elsewhere. I will call and see Dai when I can. We could have been friends. You are no better than me.

Kind regards

Lena Protheroe (Miss)

Della turned the paper over but there was nothing else. She was filled with a kind of nebulous sadness and pity that she had never felt in Lena's company. She had, after all, gone to some trouble to write a missive that would not arouse Della's mockery. The amazing thing was that she cared enough to do so. Perhaps I deserved to be walloped, thought Della, placing the letter on the bedside table. I should not have called her unprincipled. She came from a different world, with different morals. She extinguished the lamp and lay in the darkness. Well, she'd never have to think about her again and her home was her own once more. She just hoped that Lena too had a roof over her head that night.

Chapter Eighteen

Wednesday already, thought Della, yawning as she poured tea early in the morning. The week had just slipped by unnoticed. The Italians would be home by now, unless they were delayed in transit. The party seemed to have taken place a long time ago. She'd been late getting to bed the night before once again owing to another parish council meeting. At least there was no longer any need to go from farm to farm about the electricity supply. By some miracle the required number of subscribers had been obtained, and they'd spent the meeting drafting a triumphant letter to the relevant authorities. When a formal vote of thanks to her and Eurig Rees had been proposed she had stated that her own contribution had been minimal and that a plaque bearing his name should be put on the first pylon.

'All I did was drink tea,' she had said. 'Mr Rees is the hero of the hour.'

The blush that spread from his neck to the top of his head had been worth seeing and even the minister had smiled.

She took a little margarine mixed with butter from the saucer and spread it on a slice of bread. She still had half of the pot of jam Nest had given her, the other half having gone to fill her sponge for the party. It would have to last a long time. It would be wonderful not to have to count every spoonful of sugar, but there was no sign so far of the rationing easing. However, with the departure of the Italian prisoners of war and the promise of an electricity supply, she could see that things were slowly improving.

She'd have to hurry. There had been no sign of Norman for the second week in succession. Lilwen had given up setting the fire and it was Della's turn today to bring in a flask of tea. She put the kettle on to boil for it.

She was in the living room a few minutes later, gathering up the exercise books she was in the process of marking, when she heard frantic knocking on the front door. Surely, she couldn't be late already? She rushed to answer it and heard someone call her name.

'Miss Arthur? Is anyone at home? Is she here?'

On the path stood Eurig Rees and Huw Richards, the former purple in the face, and the latter even more surprisingly, without a tie. Rees would have bounced into the house past her had not his companion put a hand on his arm to stop him. But he could not stop his anguished cry.

'Lilwen's gone! Is she here? I don't know where to turn. You aren't hiding her, are you?'

Della would have given much, at that moment, to confess that she was, but she could not.

'I haven't seen her since yesterday afternoon,' she said, adding, 'Come in. The kettle's just boiling.'

Rees would not have stayed, but the minister led him firmly into the house. He stood bewildered, like an evacuee on a station platform, in the middle of the living room, peering around him as if he expected to see her lurking behind the furniture.

'But where could she be?' he muttered, to himself as much as to anyone else.

Standing behind him Huw Richards raised one dark eyebrow at Della. She hurried out to fill the teapot with the boiling water intended for the flask.

'Have you phoned Aneurin?' she called from the kitchen. 'Use the telephone here. He can contact more people than we can.'

She heard them discuss this briefly and Rees's footsteps going out to the hall. She turned and saw that the minister was standing in the doorway.

'Clothes gone, and a case?' she asked quietly and saw him nod.

'Sometime last night, while we were at the meeting. He came home late and thought she'd long gone to bed.'

He coughed embarrassedly.

'She didn't say anything to you, did she, that might give us a clue? He's out of his mind with worry.'

'Not a word,' said Della, 'and believe me I would tell you if I had any idea.'

He appeared to accept this.

'That's what I've been telling him – but he got a bee in his bonnet that she might have come here … to another woman, you know …'

She stared at him, but the farmer reappeared at the moment.

'Aneurin's going to ask,' he said, 'and call other stations.'

Della set cups of tea before them.

'Sit down a second,' she said. 'Tell me, have you got family somewhere else?'

He pulled out a chair and sat, twisting his cap in his hands as he thought.

'The wife's cousin lives outside Aberystwyth and I've got an old uncle down the south of the county. Do you think she could have gone to one of them?'

'I'd say it was worth asking. And what about old friends from college or school?'

He considered this and nodded but she could see he was as yet unable to accept that she had chosen to leave her home at all. The minister looked at his watch.

'It's time you went to ring the bell,' he said briskly to Della. 'I'll come back later. Perhaps we will have learnt something by then.'

The younger children showed surprisingly little curiosity as to why their teacher was not there that morning. Della put the oldest of her own class, Gareth and Delyth, in charge of the infants' room as caretakers and tried to behave normally, but it was difficult. Part of her felt guilty that she had not been able to make friends sufficiently with Lilwen for the girl to divulge her feelings and fears, but then you couldn't force people to talk to you. Lilwen was the second to disappear within a week, thought Della, and she had failed with both of them.

She set them mathematical problems to be getting on with, giving her the opportunity to finish the marking she had started the night before, but perturbing thoughts insisted on intruding, and she was glad when she heard a knock on the front door. Aneurin stood there, out of breath.

'She went on the train,' he stated without the least preamble. 'Last night. Ticket to London. Mr Richards will come down later on to give you a hand.' He turned and started pushing his bike towards the gate. Della ran after him.

'Mr Jenkins! Hang on a minute,' she called. 'Has she emptied her bank account?'

'No idea,' he said. 'Is it important?'

'I'm not sure,' she said, not wishing to waste his time on a wild goose chase, 'but perhaps it would give us an idea of what she was planning to do.'

'We know that already,' he said reasonably. 'She's on her way to London. But I will ask.'

She watched him cycle away. She realised that she would feel happier if Lilwen had drawn all her money out. At least it would mean that she had left deliberately, and that she had a plan worked out beforehand. If she hadn't taken money it suggested all manner of other, more alarming, possibilities.

It was lunchtime before Huw Richards returned. The furrows between his brows had deepened. With the little ones running races around them on the yard they couldn't say very much, but the look on his face spoke volumes. She left him with the older class and took up the reins with the infants. The warm afternoon slid by painfully slowly, and like the smallest children of all Della would have been very glad just to lay her head on her arms on the desk and snooze as the flies buzzed lazily against the windows. She had never been happier to see half past three, and she led them out for the evening prayer, but the minister was already on his way through the back door.

'We'll discuss this again,' he murmured. 'I can't leave Eurig on his own.'

'Where is he now, then?' asked Della.

'He was up at the Manse with Hetty, telephoning everybody. But he's got cows to milk and nobody to do it.'

He hurried off, raising his hat to Jean and her bucket. Back in her classroom ten minutes later, after the last child had gone, Della began her usual tidying. Glancing up she saw that Jean was standing by the door, with a worried expression. She jerked her thumb towards the other classroom.

'London, then,' she said. 'What's she going to do there?'

'She'll probably get work,' Della answered. 'Perhaps not teaching, but some kind of job, I expect.'

Jean pulled a dubious face.

'Not with a baby,' she said, and then seeing Della's eyes open in astonishment, she added, 'I don't know for sure, mind, but having had seven you do tend to notice the signs.'

Della sat down, the better to process this latest revelation.

'How long have you suspected?' she asked.

'A little while now. She was in Cardigan the other day buying summer clothes – Eirian my eldest girl told me – and she didn't want anything too tight. I thought then there was something wrong.' She sniffed, 'I can see now that she was preparing to leave. Poor old Rees.'

Della saw too and perhaps even more than Jean. She needed to think about this. In order to change the subject she said, 'Talking of people disappearing, has anyone seen Norman?'

Jean made a sound in the back of her throat.

'He's about the place, but always too far away for you to do anything about it. This business with the chickens has sent him right off the deep end.' She leaned on her mop. 'Gareth swears blind it wasn't him, but I really don't know.'

'I don't think Gareth's responsible,' said Della as firmly as she could. The boy had not been exaggerating when he claimed that his own mother didn't believe him.

Jean considered this, but Della could see that her defence of him was having some effect.

'If it wasn't him, who was it?' she asked. 'Although, his father's as sure as you are. According to Stevie, Gareth can't kill chickens. Did you ever hear such a thing?'

'And that's not all,' said Della. 'Gareth is mischievous, but he isn't cruel. Whoever did this either didn't care about what it would do to Norman, or they wanted him to suffer on purpose.'

'What, kill the chickens to drive him mad?'

Della nodded and was pleased to see Jean shiver a little. So she wasn't completely unfeeling.

'Ugh!' she said. 'That's nasty.' Then she shook herself. 'It was probably just lads who'd been on the home-brewed. Drunken stupidity.'

And as she was an expert in that regard also, Della didn't argue.

She couldn't settle to anything that night. She sat at the table by the living room window to make best use of the light, and tried to write to Tydfil and Nest, but she had no enthusiasm for it, despite the shocking news. Her thoughts insisted on returning to Lilwen's predicament. If Jean was right, and who could possibly be a more reliable predictor of pregnancy, then it was easy to see why Lilwen had chosen to leave. As her father's pride and joy how could she stay and bear a fatherless child? She could, of course, have married the father. That was usually the answer to the problem, so why hadn't she done so? Something told Della that Lilwen had doubts. So she'd gone, in a similar manner to Susan, Robin's mother, even though that one had waited ten years before making her escape.

Perhaps neither of them had actually wished to tie themselves to their child's father. In the case of Susan and Dafydd Jones, perhaps Lena had stood as a barrier between them, but if he could be believed, he saw and spent time with Susan and Robin throughout the years. However, she could not see Rees permitting that kind of arrangement between his daughter and Tecwyn. If Lilwen had admitted to him that she was expecting, he would have gone straight to Nanty and Nuncle and would have insisted on a wedding as soon as possible. It looked more and more likely that Lilwen did not want to marry Tecwyn. He was fine as a boyfriend, to have some fun with, but unsuitable as a husband and father, and Della could not blame her for that. Some relevant memory was knocking on the door of her consciousness, but she couldn't quite get to it.

Frustrated, she went looking for food and took a spoonful of rhubarb tart, given to her by one of the children. With Lena gone, she could stand there and eat it out of the dish. No, she could not reproach Lilwen for not wanting to marry Tec, but life would certainly not be easy in London. To tell the truth, it would be virtually impossible, but perhaps Lilwen hadn't really given that part much consideration in her hurry to go. And if she hadn't told her father, had she actually told Tecwyn? Perhaps she had, and he had reacted badly, which was another reason for her to escape to London.

She thought of the last time she had seen Tecwyn and Lilwen together, which had been in the copse. There had been no way of hearing their conversation, but she couldn't remember hearing a quarrel either. She recalled how embarrassed she and Enzo had been, coming so close to being discovered. Enzo had been worse than she, although perhaps he had been concerned for her reputation. By then he knew he was leaving, but she would have to stay and face the gossip. But the more she considered this, the odder it was. Did not the two couples (as far as she knew regarding Enzo's marital state) have a perfect right to be together? Yet Enzo had been very anxious for the other two not to see them. Did Lilwen know that he had a wife in Italy? Was that it? The memory she could not grasp came close again. What exactly had he said? Something about Tecwyn and Carwyn. That was it, he had suggested that there was no difference between them. Or did he mean that Lilwen couldn't tell them apart?

She took another spoonful of tart and chewed thoughtfully. Was it actually possible that, unknown to Lilwen, they had been taking turns and either of them could be the father of her child? If so, she pitied her. She could imagine Enzo watching them and starting to suspect they were playing tricks on her. Had he told her, or had she come to the same conclusion independently? Or, perhaps, when Lilwen told Tecwyn she was pregnant, it was he who admitted that Carwyn could also be responsible. He wouldn't have admitted it, he would have announced it, throwing the information in her face as a reason why he didn't have to marry her. Lilwen could never prove which one was the father, and she couldn't marry them both. Poor Lilwen, she thought, why on earth didn't you tell someone? She must have endured agonies of worry, hiding it all from everyone.

But however much she cast around in her mind, she could not recall a single instance when Lilwen had shown the least anxiety. How on earth had she managed to accomplish that? She was either a superb actress, or she wasn't worried at all. There was something wrong with the whole idea of her desperate flight to the great anonymous city, to live and raise a child totally alone, or arrange for it to be adopted. Lilwen had been tenderly cared for all her life, her path made smooth in every respect. She aroused protective instincts in people. Enzo, thought Della with a jolt. Enzo had offered to take care of her and the child. That was why he'd been in a lather with her in the woods. That's why he had said he didn't like leaving people in a difficult situation. He was not referring to Della and the dead bodies. He was talking about Lilwen.

Della pushed open the Manse gate but stood still for an instant to think. Was this all madness? Would she be far wiser to go home and keep quiet? Should she have gone to Jean and discussed her ideas with her first? No, Jean might be sharp but she did not believe that there were people who couldn't kill chickens. Only Napoleone would understand all the implications at once without her having to spell it out endlessly.

'Where's Hetty tonight then?'

The man himself had answered the door in his shirtsleeves. He smelt of fried bacon. 'Down with Eurig. After seeing the state he was in, she didn't think he should be on his own tonight.'

'Did you manage the milking?' she asked.

'I didn't have to. Half the neighbourhood turned up. I was lucky to be allowed to feed the cat. People round here don't need a telephone. They can smell news on the wind.'

She followed him into the study and sat by the empty fireplace.

'I'm afraid I have no fresh information,' he said. 'The last we heard was Aneurin saying she'd taken the London train last night.'

Della nodded.

'I don't think we'll hear anything for about six months,' she said.

'Why six months?'

Now that she had said this, she had to go on, but with his dark eyes fixed on her suspiciously, she felt even less confident than before.

'I can't be completely sure. Perhaps we'll hear before then, but from my calculations, that's how long it will take her to marry and have the baby.'

He chewed his lower lip and scowled.

'Why didn't you say that this morning?'

'I didn't know this morning. And I'm only guessing, mind you. I spoke to Jean this afternoon. She strongly suspects that Lilwen's pregnant.'

He considered this.

'She's definitely pregnant if Jean says so.'

'Quite.'

There was a pause as Huw Richards worked through the implications in his mind.

'She can't tell her father because of the shame,' he muttered under his breath, 'so, she escapes.' He looked at her curiously. 'Do we expect Tecwyn to disappear up to London too in the next few weeks?'

'No, we don't. She's not going to marry Tecwyn. And she won't be in London for long. She's on her way to Italy.'

'Italy?' Huw Richards took a deep breath. 'To one of the prisoners of war? But they were illiterate peasants ...' He interrupted himself and clicked his fingers. 'Apart from one ... the one who learned his speech of thanks perfectly.'

'Enzo Mazzati,' said Della. 'Who was far from being illiterate. He was actually a policeman.'

The minister sat up straight in his chair.

'He told you that? When?'

'I guessed, to tell the truth. When we were experimenting to find out how Glenys and Leonard were killed.'

He snorted through his nose.

'So you actually put your theories to the test with someone equally nosy? Those weren't the only experiments he was conducting if Lilwen's expecting.'

This annoyed Della. 'He's not the father. He's taken pity on her and offered to save her from an impossible situation.'

'I wouldn't say it was impossible. Eurig would have been bitterly disappointed, of course, but it would only have been half an hour's work to arrange a quiet, early morning wedding.'

'Not if you're not sure who the groom should be.'

The silence lasted far longer this time. For the first time in her experience he was stunned into speechlessness. She decided to help him.

'Lots of people have told me how difficult it is to tell the twins apart. I heard a suggestion that Lilwen didn't know who she was with half the time. If that's true, how can she prove which of them is the father? She can't. And after discovering the games they've played with her, would she want to tie herself to one or the other? I doubt it very much. I wouldn't, in her place.'

He was nodding slowly as he followed the thread of her argument.

'So she tells the Italian,' he said. 'Or if he's sharp, it's he who warns her. But it's too late. Grief, what a mess!'

'This is all guesswork.' Della felt she had to impress this upon him. 'I could be totally wrong. But if I'm right, at least she's safe.'

'Yes. If the Italian can be trusted.' He looked at her as if he had just realised something. 'You obviously got to know him pretty well.'

Della pulled a wry face that was not entirely insincere.

'As well as you can know anyone when you don't really have a common language. But in comparison with Aneurin, Enzo Mazzati is a clever man.'

She outlined his theories regarding the blood on the landing.

'Aneurin thinks they're rust,' she said.

Huw Richards looked at his hands. He appeared to be less sure of himself than previously.

'It looks as if you've gone into it in some detail,' he murmured.

'Oh, I have,' replied Della, 'and not only here in the village. This isn't where it all started. Did you know, for example, that

Dafydd Jones was the father of a child by a woman called Susan, who is Glenys and Leonard's niece. She's the one who inherits the farm now, but she's in Australia. The child, Robin, was killed in an accident before the war.'

If he had been astonished by the news regarding Lilwen's disappearance, it was nothing compared to his reaction to this news. He rubbed his leg and for once she could read his thoughts clearly.

'I did know about the child,' he admitted at last. 'But not about the connection. He never said a word about that, even when he was maudlin drunk, which he often was.'

'You can easily understand why,' said Della. 'I think they moved down here with the sole purpose of bleeding him dry. It's no wonder Lena failed to find any cash.'

'So that's why she left,' he mused. 'Having cracked the nut and found it empty.' He cleared his throat and she thought she saw the old competitive light come back to his eyes. 'She wasn't his sister, of course,' he said.

'Heavens above, no!' replied Della. 'A one-time girlfriend. Claiming that they were engaged, and had been for years. She showed me a ruby ring and, although I wouldn't believe Lena on her death bed, I do think that he, at least, believes that he proposed to her at some point. He was probably too drunk to remember. And she held it over his head. Lena's the reason he and Susan never married.'

'When did you get to see the ring?'

'On the station in Carmarthen, seconds before she hit me for calling her unprincipled. She'd been trying to persuade him to marry her again but the man is seriously mentally ill. I was just telling her the truth.'

She saw him run his hand over his face and realised he was trying to hide a smile.

'It wasn't funny at all at the time!' she said crossly.

'I'm sorry,' he said making an effort to compose his expression. 'May I ask how you've managed to find out all this?'

Around ten, they went out into the kitchen and made tea, but although he listened and suggested throughout her explanation, Della did not feel she was any nearer to knowing whether he planned to act on her information regarding the deaths. Neither did he say anything about what ought to be done next regarding Lilwen. He absorbs everything like a sponge, she thought, but you have to squeeze hard with both hands to get anything out of him. Yet, some of his questions were interesting.

'How long do you think Lena was standing at the back of the room listening to you talk to Dafydd before you noticed her?'

'I couldn't say,' she answered. 'But the second he saw her, he was on his feet.'

'Can you recall where the conversation had got to when you saw she was there?'

She had to think about that.

'Talking about Robin's death I believe. I'm not sure whether he was mistaken but he seemed to say that he and Susan were talking when the child was killed. The guilt is playing on his mind, but perhaps his illness has caused him to put two different occasions together.'

'That's quite possible. He did go and see her – he told me that much. Do you think Lena will actually continue to visit him?'

'Perhaps. But if there's no hope of getting any money …' She shrugged without finishing her sentence.

He sighed quietly.

'There seems to be no end to humanity's ability to shock or inspire. On the one hand you have Lena unashamedly milking a sick man, and on the other you have an enemy alien taking on another man's child and giving it and the mother a home. What was he, a saint?'

Della had to smile.

'I don't think it'll be much hardship to be married to Lilwen. Quite apart from her beauty, she's a farm girl used to hard work, and a teacher with an education. Enzo's getting a bargain I'd say.'

It surprised her to find that she believed this fairly sincerely. She wasn't really jealous of her colleague. It had been very nice to be made to feel attractive, she had to admit, after such a long, lonely time, but it wasn't love. Perhaps Enzo had been lonely too, and had thought that Lilwen was still out of reach. He might well have been smitten with her for years. The more she thought about it, the more likely it seemed. She could only hope that the girl learned to love and appreciate him. It was Lilwen who was getting a bargain in reality, not Enzo. She suddenly noticed that the minister was squirming on his chair.

'You never know,' he said. 'I just hope he won't regret acting impulsively in that chivalrous way. Sometimes it doesn't work out.'

There was something uncomfortable about his entire demeanour that made Della sit very still. He looked over at her as if coming to a decision.

'I did something similar once, you know, even though Enfys wasn't in the same pickle as Lilwen. I thought I could rescue her, make everything all right. But I couldn't.'

He fell silent and Della felt she had to say something.

'Your compulsions were entirely honourable I'm sure.'

He gave a short bark of humourless laughter.

'It was the arrogant pride of a young man,' he said sourly. 'At almost thirty! She was only eighteen, such a pretty girl, from a difficult home with a nasty bully of a father. I thought that her background was responsible for her childish nature and that away from it she would develop and mature, but if I'd slowed down and considered, I would have seen that wasn't true. She would always have been like that.'

'How long were you married?'

'Three years. She was sick and tired of me after eighteen months. And Nant-yr Eithin didn't suit her one bit, and that was my fault too. I should never have brought her here pregnant. I should have left her with her aunt in town, never mind the bombing. She was happy there, spending her afternoons in the pictures with her friends.'

'But you were trying to keep her safe,' said Della.

'Was I? That's what I told myself at the time, but now I know differently. What I was actually trying to do was force her to grow up.'

He stared silently into the empty fireplace.

'She didn't want the child at all. She tried all sorts of things to get rid of it.'

'Why?'

'For a number of reasons I suppose. Basically she was too young emotionally to be a mother, and she certainly didn't want to be tied to me. But where could she go, saddled with a baby? She was dying to get into the WAAFs. She fancied the uniform I expect – that was about her level. The minute she got here she started making enquiries from various people, Hetty among others, about how to procure an abortion.'

Della opened her eyes as she thought of what the reaction to this must have been.

'And you got to hear of it?'

'Oh yes.' He rested his elbows on his knees. 'There was a knock on the door one dark night and there was Leonard. Wanting a little word. What would the Baptist Union think if they knew, and so on?'

Della felt as if someone had thrown cold water over her.

'So you paid?' she asked quietly.

She was surprised by the ferocity of his response.

'No, I did not! I told him to go to hell!'

When he spoke again, his tones were more measured.

'That was another mistake. Perhaps I shouldn't have threatened him. Perhaps Enfys would still be alive if I hadn't shown him the door.'

'Did he tell the Baptist Union?'

He shook his head.

'No. But having failed to get anything out of me, he and Glenys started on Enfys. They threatened to tell the police, and all sorts. By the time the baby was born she was nearly mad with fear, and then the poor little mite died. He had a heart defect. She'd had her wish. She was free. She could leave when she liked.'

'Is that why you joined the army?'

He nodded thoughtfully.

'Yes, to give her an escape route,' he said, rubbing his leg. 'I thought that if I was around, then it would have been obvious, but with me away, she could have left in stages, pretending that she had war work to do, and people would have gradually grown used to the situation. I spent months waiting for a letter from her, saying that that she'd left me, but in the end it was Eurig who wrote, telling me that she was dead. Two days later I was cleaning a Bren gun, not paying attention, and I got this. A catalogue of stupidity and wilful blindness.'

Della walked slowly back down the lane towards School House. Now that she knew the whole story, she was not in the least bit surprised that Napoleone didn't give a fig about Glenys and Leonard's deaths. He must have buried them with a song in his heart. On the whole, knowing him, she was inclined to believe he was telling the truth. In all probability he had never given them a penny in silence money. But Dafydd Jones had paid for years, and who else? Nobody would admit it now. With Enzo back in Italy, she was the only one with any interest in getting to the truth. So many people had a reason to keep quiet. And if she was honest, the more she heard, the less she could blame them. They must have been driven to the point where they only had two choices, self-destruction or killing the blackmailers. Glenys and Leonard had been fortunate to survive as long as they had.

She went on, pleased to see the shape of the white house appear as she turned the corner. It was no wonder she found it difficult to get up in the morning, when she tramped along the roads night after night like this.

Chapter Nineteen

'I'm coming, I'm coming!'

Della tightened the belt of her dressing gown and came racing down the stairs in the dark. When she'd heard the thundering knocking first of all she been fast asleep, and it had reached her like the faint echo from a long tunnel. But it persisted, and she came to with a start and looked instinctively at her alarm clock. Who on earth could it be at half past one in the morning? She paused a moment at the foot of the stairs and lit the candle she kept by the telephone.

'Miss!' The flap of the letter box suddenly shot up, and she jumped. 'It's me, Gareth.'

She opened the door and saw him on the path, his hair in spikes and his eyes red with lack of sleep. Della grasped the neck of her gown.

'It's Norman, Miss,' said the boy. 'You said I was to tell you if I saw something.'

She led him into the house. She could see his pyjamas peeping out from the bottoms of his trouser legs.

'Where was he?' she asked.

'Down by our chicken shed. I heard a noise, see, because I sleep downstairs. I thought something had got in with the animals – a weasel or a fox – but it was him.' He shook his head. 'He isn't right, honest he isn't.'

Della was already halfway up the stairs.

'You stay there,' she said. 'I'll be two minutes.'

She was very glad of her torch, even though Gareth had no need of it. She followed him down the lane and past the sleeping cottage. They kept the chickens close by. Gareth pointed to a spot behind the coop.

'He was on his knees there,' he said, 'and when I asked him

what he was doing, he said "Hiding". But he'd eaten eggs from our hens because you can see the shells.'

Della shone the torch around but there was no sign of him and no sound of anyone pushing through the undergrowth in the copse nearby.

'Why does he need to hide?' she asked, keeping her voice low. 'Was somebody after him?'

Gareth pulled a face, visible in the weak light.

'Could be, 's'pose,' he answered dubiously. 'But perhaps only in his head. And another thing, Miss, he was dirty. As if he'd been out for days. He smelled.'

'Why doesn't he go home? His aunt would feed him and keep him clean.'

Gareth didn't know. He watched her point the torch here and there.

'D'you think he killed his own chickens?' he asked. 'That's what Roberts Maes Cryman did when he went off his head. Killed his stock.'

'Did he?' asked Della distantly. She was concentrating on why Norman would feel the need to hide.

'Yes. When the doctor called to see him, there was a whole pig's head on the mantelpiece.'

Della shook herself out of her contemplation.

'You've been listening to your parents talk again,' she said. 'Tell me, where else have you seen Norman?'

The boy puffed out his cheeks thoughtfully.

'Round about the place, you know,' he said. 'He's been loitering by Glenys and Leonard's. And he was in the wood.'

There was nothing for it but to go and look.

'You go back to bed,' she said. 'If he comes back tell him to come to School House. Tell him he can hide there.'

Gareth nodded unwillingly.

'I could come with you,' he offered.

'At two o'clock in the morning. No, indeed you couldn't!'

She walked back up the incline in the direction of her home. Would it really matter, she thought, if she postponed the search until daybreak? She was weary to her bones now. She reached the slate steps and paused, in two minds. No, she thought, a great deal could happen in a few hours and Gareth would not have come to fetch her if Norman's behaviour hadn't worried him. She'd forgotten to ask him whether he'd seen him down by the river. She nearly turned back to the cottage to ask him, but finally went the other way. She'd search the wood first and then the abandoned farm. If she had turned back she would have seen Gareth crouched in the dark shadow of the hedge watching her. Of the two of them, he looked by far the more wide awake.

Della climbed back over the stile that led from the wood to the road. Apart from a rough lair among the bushes, which she had discovered entirely by accident, stumbling about over the roots of the trees, there was nothing. She'd nearly fallen headlong several times on the slope and was glad to feel the hard road under her feet once again. Despite this, she was more determined now to keep on looking. Norman had been sleeping in the wood for days, she was sure. The fact that he was not there tonight was an indication that his mental state had changed, for better or worse. She knew that she wouldn't sleep now, having left matters half done, but if she didn't find him on the farm, she would have done her best and would go home.

Nobody had mended the gate to the farm and by now the hedge had grown through and over it. Della shone the light ahead and walked over to the old chicken coop. She felt soft earth under her feet as she got nearer. It was, most likely, the tomb of the unfortunate birds. Tentatively she opened the door, but it was quite empty. Someone had cleared away all the straw from the nesting boxes but it still smelled overwhelmingly strongly of its former tenants. The stink of chickens is not easily eradicated. She stood and looked around. Where might Norman go?

She picked her way across the yard, suddenly aware of the complete silence and the blackness. He could be anywhere, watching her from the shadows. She came to the row of buildings opposite. Most of them were locked and she had to shine her light, as best she could, through the windows which by now were thick with cobwebs. They were all empty, and anyway it was unlikely that Norman had a set of keys, unless he had gone into the house and found them. She moved, nevertheless, along the row until she reached the garage which was windowless. She shook the door, not expecting it to open, and it didn't, but under her fingers she felt cord. By the light of the torch she saw that the padlock had been broken. It lay on the floor now, and in its place binding twine had been woven in and out of the two metal rings on the door and the jamb. Why? It was no kind of defence. A pocket knife would have made short work of it, if she'd had one. Was this Norman's handiwork she wondered? What was he keeping in the garage that he didn't want anyone to find?

Tucking the torch under her arm she went to work untying the twine. Loosening it proved to be awkward. She nearly gave it up as a bad job, sucking her fingers as her nails caught on the fibres, but then it suddenly gave way and she was able to open the door. The car sat on wooden blocks under a huge tarpaulin, like some sleeping mammoth. The light breeze caught the door and slapped it shut behind her, making her jump. A scrabbling sound came from a far corner and she stood still. Rats? They'd be all over the farm in droves by now without anyone to keep them down. Keeping one hand on the tarpaulin she stepped around the car and directed the light to the place where the sound had come from. She thought she saw a long tail disappear through a gap at the base of the wall.

The car shuddered under her hand. She drew her fingers

away quickly and took a step back. Rats ate leather, didn't they? What if she lifted the cover and saw dozens of them running riot inside, chewing on the seats? She shivered and turned to leave the building. Coward, said the voice in her head. Perhaps the reason for the twine on the door lies inside the car. You've got to look. Fearfully, she raised a corner of the tarpaulin, and the shaking motion increased, including, this time, a couple of hard knocks against the door on the driver's side. Della swallowed, and flung it back over the roof of the car shining the torch in through the window. Great frightened eyes were the first thing that she saw, and under them a kind of white mask. She pulled on the door handle but it was locked.

'Kick, Norman!' she called. 'Kick hard!'

For what seemed like an age the boy didn't move at all but stared blindly at the light. Della realised that he couldn't see her and she shone it on her own face.

'It's me,' she said. 'Now kick as hard as you can!'

Although the door bulged outwards the lock refused to give and Della looked around for something to break the window. She remembered seeing large stones by the door and dashed to get one.

'I'm going to break the glass,' she yelled and mercifully he understood and turned his head away into the seat. It took two or three attempts before it even cracked, but finally she succeeded in getting her hand through and opened the door from the inside. She dragged him out by his feet and hurried to untie the cloth over his face. It was no surprise that he had been unable to shout for help – half of it had been stuffed in his mouth. Norman started to cough and splutter and Della left him to it while she turned her attention to his feet. From the tight knots that had been used to bind him, the same hand had improvised the locking of the door. The rough twine had bitten into his ankles and she rubbed them before helping him up. His hands had been tied behind his back and his wrists were even worse than his ankles. She noticed, with distress, that he had originally been tied with a cord leading from his hands to his feet, and that he had somehow broken that cord, which had enabled him to kick. He'd paid dearly for the effort, for the twine that had bound his wrists was bloodied.

'Who did this to you, Norman?' she hissed urgently, but he didn't answer. Rather, he stood there, painfully, licking and sucking his wrists like an injured dog.

'Come on,' she said. 'You need to get those wounds dressed. I'll take you home.'

She bent to pick up the torch from where she'd left it on an upturned bucket. The door clanged shut and she got up. Norman had gone. She rushed out of the garage but the farmyard was empty, and although she strained to hear, there was no sound of feet running nor anything that gave her any clue as to where he could be. She swore under her breath. He knew the farm so much better than she did. Where would she go in his position?

She stood in the middle of the yard trying to decide. I would hide rather than run, she thought. But every other building was locked. Behind her the farmhouse rose like a cliff. Unless things had changed tremendously since her last visit, he did have the means to get into the storeroom at the side. It was worth taking a look, although she did not hold out much hope of finding him there.

She was disappointed to find that the makeshift wooden barrier in front of the storeroom door was still in place. So he hadn't come this way. The kitchen curtains were closed preventing her from shining her light through into the room. She found a tiny chink between the curtains to the parlour, but there was nothing to see. With her nose on the glass trying to see through to the passage beyond, she thought she heard something. She pressed her ear to the window. She couldn't be sure. It could be nothing more than the natural creaking of an old house. Her torch was definitely giving out less light than before. She shook it impatiently, but instead of growing stronger, the beam faded away and died. What now? The only thing she could do was to go into the house and steal a candle.

Keeping one hand on the wall to steady herself, she moved carefully back towards the storeroom. She knew she would certainly find a candle in the kitchen. As her fingers touched the wood of the front door that led directly into the kitchen, she sensed a slight breeze from within. She stopped and pushed at it very slightly with one finger. It gave a couple of inches. It was open. With one foot on the doorstep she listened. Something told her she was not alone, but that was probably the aftermath of the shock of finding Norman. Despite this, she tiptoed over to the dresser as quietly as she could, and with fumbling fingers lit the candle stump that she knew was there. Perhaps indeed Norman was somewhere in the house. The trick would be to persuade him to come with her and have his injuries treated, should she actually find him. She didn't even want to start thinking about who had tied him up and left him until she had him safely in her kitchen.

The door to the passage was wide open and she crept through the gap. When she heard the unmistakable noise of feet crossing the landing above her head, she paused and shaded the flame with her hand, pressing herself against the wall, in case he should glance down over the banisters. The footsteps moved away and she heard bedclothes being lifted. Poor old Norman, she thought, trying to make himself a comfortable nest out of blankets that must be covered in mildew by now. She considered calling his name, but thought better of it. She didn't want to do anything that would make him wilder and more disturbed than he was already.

She peered up the stairs. He was in the room where the bodies had been found, although he probably didn't know that, and had half closed the door behind him. She climbed, one step at a time, as silently as she could. He was evidently arranging everything to suit, for furniture moving sounds could be heard now, which stifled any noise her feet might make. She crept closer and closer to the door. What should she do? Knock courteously perhaps, and ask if she could enter? That would be less threatening than walking in without warning.

She tapped twice on the upper panel and waited. Everything went very quiet. It was as if she could hear him standing there, listening. She cleared her throat.

'Hello?' she called and gave the door a gentle push.

At the far end of the room a figure was bent over the open bottom drawer of the dressing table. He stood up slowly with his back towards her, but Della knew without seeing his face that it wasn't Norman. He turned and smiled. Della's stomach tied itself into a tight knot.

'I'm looking for Norman,' she heard herself say. 'Have you seen him?'

Whichever one of the twins it was licked his lips, out of nervousness perhaps, but it wasn't a reassuring gesture.

'Looking for Norman,' he echoed. 'Is he missing then?'

'Yes he is. From school at any rate.'

He tutted, but she could see he was thinking. Then in a few short strides he was across the room with her. 'We'll go and see,' he said. 'We wouldn't want him to get the cane now, would we?' Before she could step back he had grasped her arm. 'I think I know where he might be,' he whispered conspiratorially. 'But we'll need to be very quiet. There's no need to frighten the poor dab, is there?'

Even though these were the very thoughts that had gone through her mind only seconds earlier, Della felt cold. His grip on her elbow was like a pincer.

When the shout came from the stairs, her first instinctive reaction was to duck closer to him, but she forced herself to stand firm and look. Norman stood there, carrying a heavy spade. He was furious.

'You leave Miss be!' he roared. 'You red devil! Leave her alone!'

When the twin didn't move, he lifted the implement by the handle and swung it wildly, but the man moved aside too quickly and it was Della who caught all the power of the metal edge on her shoulder. The pain shot through her like a hot poker and with a cry she dropped the candle and fell on her knees. Norman's shouts became anguished and he rushed towards her.

The twin leapt out of the way like a fugitive deer and headed for the stairs, but Norman swung again and caught him on his side. Even though he grabbed at the banister rail he could not gain his balance and before their horrified eyes he fell, painfully slowly all the way down the wooden staircase. Della heard a horrible crack and then silence.

For a long moment neither of them moved, then Della took a deep breath.

'Norman!' she called. 'Help me to get up.'

He looked down at her, his face shining with tears from the faint light coming from the high landing window.

'I didn't mean to …' he muttered hoarsely and reached out his hand.

She took it and pulled herself up.

'I know,' she said comfortingly. 'I know, Norman. It was all an accident. But we have to go to him.'

To her surprise he shook his head.

'We have to get out,' he said urgently. 'Come on. I'll light the candle so you can see.'

Her legs felt like rubber under her but somehow, leaning heavily on him, she got down the stairs.

'One of us has to go to get help for him,' she said when she saw that the twin's left foot was trembling. 'You go, you'll be quicker than me.'

Norman stared expressionlessly at his cousin.

'No point,' he said. 'He's broken his neck.'

'But he's still alive!'

'Not for long,' replied the boy, and indeed as he said this, the ghastly shuddering stopped. 'Chickens and pigs twitch after they've been killed. I've seen them.'

He hunkered down and pulled up the body's right eyelid. A blue eye gazed up at them, unseeing in the candlelight. Then he got up and wiped his hand on his trouser leg.

'What was he doing here?' whispered Della. 'Has he been stealing from the house? Did you catch him at it? Was it he who tied you up?'

Norman shrugged his shoulders like a bullock bothered by a fly.

'Him and the other one,' he said flatly. 'Fetching things back. And looking.'

Before she had time to consider the implications of this, they heard a noise from the storeroom. Norman stared about him desperately and then pulled her unceremoniously towards the parlour door, but it was too late. They were caught in the light of a powerful torch and the two of them stood like rabbits, completely dazzled.

Chapter Twenty

'You've gone and done it now, good boy.'

The other twin played the beam of the torch over his brother's body. It was as if the spirit of the dead man had arisen and spoken.

'We've got to get him a doctor,' said Della. 'Perhaps there's still hope.'

The twin pulled a thoughtful face and poked experimentally at the body with the toe of his heavy boot.

'No,' he said. 'He's gone.'

Della couldn't believe how unconcerned he sounded, but before she could say anything, he added, 'Serve him right, anyway.'

'Why?' So great was her surprise, Della could not stop herself. He stared coldly at her.

'Because he stole Lilwen. He always wanted whatever I had. Always wanted us to be the same. I saw her first.'

'That's not true!' said Norman, turning to her. 'Don't believe him. I saw you swapping clothes and laughing. You were as bad as each other. Whatever you did, it was together.'

His cousin showed his teeth.

'You don't know anything,' he growled. 'You're daft, you are.'

If he expected that to silence Norman, he was wrong.

'Daft or not, you haven't found it, have you?' answered Norman with a little smile. 'And it doesn't matter what you do to me, I'll never tell you where it is.'

Della saw the twin weighing the torch in the palm of his hand.

'You shouldn't have taken it,' he said slowly.

'Taken what?' asked Della.

'The number plate for the pick-up,' said Norman without

moving his gaze from his cousin's face, even though he hissed at him, threateningly. 'The one they've been using to go and steal things for years.'

'Shut your big old gob! What did you want it for, anyway?'

'What did you want to kill my chickens for? What did I ever do to you?'

Hearing the anguish in his voice, Della reached out for his hand, but the twin only rolled his eyes.

'You're a nuisance, forever hanging around here. No chickens, no reason for you to be here. We've got work to do here, and we need peace to do it.' He sounded as if his brother was still alive, but you could not discard the habit of a lifetime in five minutes. He turned to Della. 'And you're back and forth here as if you were on a piece of elastic. What's this now, the fourth time?'

He counted the occasions on his fingers so that she would know she had been seen each time.

'The night after they died, moving them out, with the Italian nosing around, if that's what you were doing all that time upstairs, and then back again with Aneurin. It's been a job to find the place empty.'

Della's mind whirled. He could not know that she had arrived the night after they died, unless he was there when they did die. Two of them, she thought. Of course, there had been two of them to go into the two bedrooms at the same time and use two knitting needles on their victims. One had already been loose in the bag but the other had had to be pulled out of the knitting, and put back hurriedly. And Norman hadn't lost his key at all, it was taken from his pocket and then returned so that Norman would find it and lock the door again before Eirug Rees turned up. She dragged herself back to the present. He'd talked about some work they had to do. From the evidence of her own eyes she suspected they were searching for something other than the number plate. It could only be one thing.

'Leonard's "rent" money is all in the bank,' she said simply. 'There's nothing for you here.'

He laughed drily.

'I don't believe you,' he said. 'He always used to say he didn't hold with banks. All tricksters, he said.'

Della groaned in frustration.

'But he was the biggest trickster of all,' she said. 'He put cash in the bank every month. I saw the statements.'

The twin scowled at her.

'Where? Where did you see them? There are no papers. We looked everywhere.'

Della could imagine them ferreting about in every out of the way corner without thinking of the junk room.

'I'll show you,' she said and turned towards the stairs.

The other two followed her. She hoped desperately that she was, by doing this, buying some time for herself and Norman. Yet she had no way of knowing exactly what his cousin had in mind for them. Did she dare hope that he would not be so brave without his brother?

She went straight to the pile of cases and pointed to the middle one.

'In there,' she said. Her arm hurt too much to lift it herself. The twin stood on the landing, holding the torch like a club. He still looked suspiciously at her.

'You go and get it,' he said to Norman. Della thought for a moment that he would refuse, but slowly he went in and picked it out.

'There's something in this one,' he said, surprised. 'It's heavy.'

'Bring it out here, then.'

The boy placed it on the landing floor. The twin clicked the buttons open easily. He looked up at Della.

'These were all locked,' he said. 'I remember.'

Della nodded.

'Aneurin got it open,' she lied, 'looking for a will.'

Even though it was not Aneurin who had opened it, he had taken away a number of documents. She crossed her fingers that there would still be enough left to be convincing.

He rifled through the untidy pile impatiently, pulling one out here and there and then throwing it aside.

'Nothing here,' he said angrily.

Della's heart sank but then she saw a familiar heading on one sheet, partly hidden.

'Look there!' she said. 'That's a bank document.'

She extended her good hand but it was slapped away.

'Keep your mitts to yourself.'

She stepped back obediently but as she did so saw that Norman, during their conversation, had picked up the spade from where it lay in the shadows. His face was quite blank. Her insides jolted painfully. The first twin's death had been an accident, and she was a witness to it, but twice? With a dry mouth she watched him move the spade from hand to hand slowly to get the best grip. What could she do? On the point of trying to attract Norman's attention to warn him not to be reckless, she jumped as the twin leapt up suddenly as Norman surged forward. But instead of using it as a weapon, he held it in front of him as a barrier and kicked the case into the junk room where Della had instinctively retreated from the battle. The twin tried to grab the spade, but Norman was much stronger and wrenched it free. Before his cousin could stop him, Norman had backed into the room with her and slammed the door on him. With one foot against it, he started to drag the furniture across.

'Put your weight on the door!' he panted, and Della obeyed as best she could.

The twin was hurling himself against the panels with all his strength, shrieking uncontrollably, convincing her that he would break through at any moment, but Norman had already crossed to the other side of the room. He paused, spat on his hands, and then grunting and sweating pushed the wardrobe from where it had stood for years, inch by inch, the heavy oak squeaking and protesting and leaving fresh grooves on the floor, until there was no longer any space for her to lean against, and she had to jump quickly out of the way. The huge cupboard slid into place, hiding the doorway completely. Then the boy sat in a heap with his back to it, breathing heavily.

'That's settled his hash!' he muttered.

Della listened to the man outside cursing and kicking in sheer frustration, but he might as well kick the wall as the wardrobe. The monolith gave no indication that he was making the slightest impression upon it.

'What if he goes to get an axe, Norman?' whispered Della. They might well be safe for a while, but how could they get out now?

He stared up at her.

'He'll be a long time getting through this,' he said, 'and I'll be waiting for him.' Della would have liked to share his faith in his physical prowess but she didn't want to think about what a fight between Norman's spade and his cousin's axe would entail.

The shouting, if not the hammering, continued.

'You were lying!' she heard. 'You've taken the lot, Miss bloody Arthur. Nobody comes back and forth here for no reason. And you Norman, you'll hang for what you did! Hang! They'll put a rope round your neck!'

But despite the hysteria, the words seemed to be coming from further away. Della put her ear to the gap between the wardrobe and the door. Was he looking for a way in from one of the adjacent rooms? Not from the footsteps.

'He's going down the stairs,' she said, realising that Norman was also listening. 'Do you think he might be leaving?'

She moved over to the window, disappointed to see how

small it was. Perhaps if they moved fast they could drag the wardrobe out of the way and escape.

'He's thought of something,' said Norman, and the tone of his voice made her look around. His face had changed completely. The confidence had disappeared to be replaced by despair. She could not let him give up.

'We'll get out of here somehow, don't you worry,' she said. 'We'll think of something too. If he has gone to get an axe, there are two of us after all.'

Norman shook his head as if it lay heavy on his shoulders.

'He's not fetching an axe,' he said distantly. 'He's fetching fire.'

Della struggled not to show her fear.

'Why would he do that?'

'That was their original plan, see. That's why he wasn't with the other one. He went to get petrol. They were going to burn down the garage.'

'With you tied up in the car? Why? What was the point of destroying the vehicle?'

He ran his fingers thoughtfully over the pattern on the lino.

'If they could get enough of a blaze going, the car would be destroyed and nobody would notice that the real number plates were gone. They could use those again, then.' He swallowed hard. 'And everybody would be too busy with my body to worry much about it anyway.'

He nodded slowly to himself and smiled sadly.

'This is all my fault,' he said. 'I shouldn't have run away when you got me out of the garage.'

Della crouched down beside him.

'I was the stupid one, telling you I was going to take you home,' she murmured. 'That was the last place you wanted to be, wasn't it?'

The sound of approaching feet could be heard again, and another noise, of something hard knocking against the banisters. A strong sour smell reached them, and the sound of a liquid being poured in spurts here and there on the landing. A small pool of it crept in under the wardrobe and started to spread. Della began to take off her coat, but then remembered the curtains.

'Pull those down,' she said, 'and break the window. Quick, Norman, we've haven't got much time.'

Norman got to his feet lethargically, but did as she asked. Della pushed the fabric between the door and the wardrobe but without expecting it to provide much defence in the face of the impending fire. Norman was walloping the glass with the spade and she heard it break. That gave her renewed hope, but the twin had heard it as well.

'You shan't get away!' he screamed, frighteningly close by. His mouth must be against the keyhole. Della ran to the window and called loudly for help, but the only reply was a dog barking far away. She saw that Norman had broken the frame as well as the pane to make the gap bigger.

'I could let you down,' came his voice in her ear. Della doubted that her shoulder would bear the strain, and there was no earthly way that he, twice her size, could push his way through.

'It's too far to fall,' she said, 'and anyway you couldn't follow me.'

He stared down in to the blackness below.

'Doesn't matter,' he said. 'Even if I get out of here, they'll only hang me.'

She turned on him fiercely.

'No they will not!' she hissed. 'I saw what happened. Those two were going to burn you alive!'

He rubbed his hand over his head.

'But will they believe you, Miss?' he asked.

'I'll make them believe me! And they will when I tell them that the twins killed Glenys and Leonard.'

Norman's brow furrowed.

'How do you know they did?'

Even though they had so little time, she had to convince him that it was worth the effort of trying to escape.

'I made enquiries,' she said, 'and I've seen the bodies. You remember Enzo, the Italian who worked down in Clawdd Coch?' She waited for him to nod. 'Well, he was a policeman in Italy, and he agreed with me.'

The lad looked at her with respect.

'So why did they kill them?' he asked. 'Was it because they were paying them all that money?'

Della had long given up being surprised at his flashes of perception.

'Yes. You knew didn't you? It had been going on for years.'

'Forever. They were desperate. That's why they stole, see. When the money ran out. The stock's nearly all gone. They used to tell Nanty that the cows weren't fetching much, but I know what you can get for a bullock or a heifer.' He paused and thought. 'But I never knew why they paid for the land. We don't need it.'

It was too much of a coincidence that the father of Susan's child and the twins were being blackmailed. There had to be a connection between them. She tried to concentrate.

'They used to go to horse races a lot, didn't they?'

The lad nodded.

'Just to enjoy the horses, they said, but I reckon they were laying out a lot in bets even then. They've always looked for quick money.'

'Did they go on their own, or did they take someone with them?'

She remembered suddenly that Norman was only a little boy during the war. He wouldn't have known. But he was thinking.

'Nanty said something once about how the master used to

go with them sometimes, before the war. But not after that. I don't know why he stopped.'

Of course, thought Della. It would have been convenient for him to get a lift from his former pupils, and he would have provided a respectable front for their journeys. After Robin died and his mother emigrated, there was no point. Perhaps Dafydd Jones's memory of having been speaking to Susan when Robin died was true, after all. By now, smoke was beginning to drift from under the wardrobe – not much, but a sign of things to come. Now that she'd received the answer she'd been looking for, Della hastened to explain, as a kind of insurance, so that at least one other person should know the truth.

'I think they killed a little boy on the road near Llanelly, years ago. He was Glenys and Leonard's nephew. That's why the number plate was so important to them.'

As Norman digested this she looked about her. She could see no means of escape. She suspected that the walls of such an old building were thick, but she knocked hopefully on all of them, to be sure. There was, as far as she could tell, no tell-tale hollow ring anywhere.

'I didn't know that,' said Norman seriously. 'It wasn't just horse racing, see. There were dog fights too. You're not supposed to do that. They used the plates when they went.'

'Where did the plates come from?'

'Down the south of the county. Somebody left an old tractor to rot, and they stole the plates from that. And then they started using the pink diesel, you know, during the war, and they needed the number plates for that, too, in case they were caught.'

Of course, thought Della. It was as simple as that.

'And they were dealing in things to pay Glenys and Leonard – on the black market I suppose.'

Norman nodded.

'Masses of stuff. They were nicking it mostly, and then

bringing it back to sell down here. They thought I didn't know about their store. That's where they'd hidden the number plates.'

She was encouraged to see him cheer up slightly. He did not appear to have noticed that the smoke was curling around their feet now. She looked up at the ceiling. Someone, Glenys most likely, had papered it neatly, but like all old houses, it was uneven. She raised the candle to get a better look. One place, in particular, seemed odd. It looked square, and her heart leapt.

'What's that, I wonder?' she murmured. 'Give it a poke with your spade, Norman.'

When they heard the metal strike wood, they exchanged glances.

'A trapdoor to the attic!' said Della, but Norman had already dragged a chest of drawers across the floor and was climbing onto it. With the edge of the spade he cut through the thick paper along the lines that marked out the square and then thrust upwards, hard. The piece of wood didn't want to yield easily but when he put his weight behind the handle and bent his knees, they heard a sudden crack and the trap door disappeared into the space above their heads.

Norman clambered down.

'You first, Miss,' he said.

Della thought she would never be able to pull herself one-handed through the narrow gap even with Norman holding her legs and pushing. The worst pain she had ever felt in her life shot through her shoulder every time she gained purchase with her left hand, but at last she found herself on her stomach lying across the huge beams that ran in parallel lines along the attic floor. The plaster ceiling between them looked fragile. She peered down through the hole. Norman had disappeared and for an awful moment she thought that he didn't intend to follow her, but then she saw the glow of the candle, and he passed it up to her, carefully.

'Watch you don't burn,' he said, without a hint of irony. Della put the candle safely to one side and then took the heavy spade, even though she wobbled on her narrow perch as she did so. Norman pulled himself effortlessly through the hole and then fitted the trapdoor back over it.

'Why would somebody paper over that?' asked Della.

'Draughts and dust from the roof,' he answered. 'And Glenys papered over everything anyway.'

Up to that point, the smoke hadn't penetrated their new haven, but Della knew it was only a matter of time. Above her head, great swathes of cobwebs hung, and dust lay thick all around. The beams stretched into the darkness each side. Della lifted the candle. To her left, the roof sloped down, but the right hand side stayed high to the far wall. Norman was on his feet, walking confidently over the rafters.

'There could be another trapdoor somewhere,' he called, but Della's mind was still on the shape of the roof, picturing the house's outer form in her mind's eye.

'The storeroom is that side, isn't it?' she said, pointing to the right.

'Yes.'

On all fours Della crawled along the beam. She dared not slip and break through the lath and plaster as she didn't know how far the fire had spread already.

'What do you think the storeroom would have been originally? In the old days, when the house was built.'

Norman's voice came out of the gloom.

'A place to winter the animals,' he said. 'Mr Jones said they lived with their stock. It kept them warm, but there must have been a terrible stink.'

'And they'd keep the fodder to feed them up above – and let it down?'

By now he was standing on the rafter next to hers. How on earth could he move so fast, when she feared every step?

'So you think there's another trapdoor here?'

Della answered him carefully, clenching her teeth against the pain.

'Perhaps, one that goes straight down to the ground floor. We'd only have to cross the storeroom then, and we'd be out.'

'He could be waiting for us,' said the boy.

Della spat a cobweb from her mouth and coughed. 'Not if he's in his right mind. If it was me, I'd be long gone.'

'But he isn't in his right mind, that's the problem,' answered Norman, poking about with the sharp edge of the spade.

The fire could be heard and smelt now. Further off to the left, the bedrooms were alight, and through tiny holes in the plaster came wisps of smoke as if hundreds of cigarettes were being smoked underneath them.

Della continued her shuffling journey. She knew her knees were scratched and bleeding but she could not risk standing. She turned her head to see if it was worse behind her. It came as little comfort to know that it was, but at least they were moving in the right direction.

'There's no trapdoor here,' said Norman. 'There used to be, but it's been taken out, and new pieces put in the beams.'

He was right. Even in the faint light the new wood looked different from the old. They stared mutely at them. This was extremely bad news.

'Pass the candle, Miss,' said Norman. 'So that I can see how they were put in place.'

She took the opportunity to sit up and think. Once the fire had burnt through the ceilings there was nowhere they could go. Would they have been wiser to try to climb out of the window? Could they do so, even now? Was there an exit through the roof tiles? Were they just wasting precious time trying to undermine the heavy beams? She didn't know. The decision was a cold weight on her stomach.

'Now then, let's see,' said Norman lifting his head and

coughing. 'We'll only need to break through one beam. There's enough room either side.'

He handed her the candle. There was barely an inch of it left. Then he rubbed his hands on the legs of his corduroy trousers and placed the blade of the shovel under the new part of the middle beam as a lever. Della could see, although dimly, that the old beam had been cut in two places on a slant, so that the new part could be slotted from the top. The new wood was wider at the upper end than the lower and had been nailed in place. Norman rocked back and forth on his heels, and then chopped down through the plaster on either side, to give the spade more room to slide under. The wood groaned and gave very slightly.

'Wait a second!' said Della.

As she was sitting down, she was nearer to the beam than he was. She stared down through the holes but there was no sign of the fire. Her straining ears picked up a slight sound and she froze. Someone was moving beneath them.

She raised her head and put her finger to her lips, aware of Norman watching her, fearfully. If the twin was still around, they dare not betray their presence. Would he look up and notice the glow from the candle? She listened. From afar, she could make out the sound of a motor. A rare car passing on the road perhaps? The twin making his getaway in the pick-up? No, it was more like an engine idling. Had he returned to see the outcome of his night's work? Then came a voice, although not clearly, and she recognised one word.

'Miss!'

Even then, she wasn't sure. Was it he, trying to entice them down from their hiding place by pretending to be one of her pupils? But Norman had no such doubts. He fell on his knees and put his mouth to the hole.

'Gareth!' he screamed. 'We're up here!'

A shadow appeared below and Della shone the candle down on it. Her young neighbour's face stared back up at her.

'Pass me the saw, Gareth – there's one on the wall,' shouted Norman taking up the blessed spade once more and cutting long swathes into the lath and plaster. Della hardly dared to breathe. They heard other voices. He was not on his own.

'Miss Arthur? Are you there?' It was Huw Richards's voice.

'Yes I am. But the upstairs is alight. Don't even think of going into the kitchen!'

There was no time to say more. The long blade of a saw appeared through one of the openings and Norman grabbed it and started sawing like a madman. Della shied away as the sawdust spat and scattered but one side was almost sawn through and Norman jumped with both feet on the beam to break the last fibres before beginning again near to the other join. Della couldn't tell whether the snapping and cracking sounds were coming from the beam or the fire. She looked back to see a sinister red haze engulfing the trapdoor behind them and yellow darts of flame licking at the gaps in the wood. She concentrated on the sound of the saw and forced herself to take shallow breaths.

With one almighty crack the nails released their grasp.

'Watch your heads!' yelled Norman and the yard of timber fell like thunder onto the slate floor beneath.

He picked her up unceremoniously under her arms as if she weighed nothing at all and lifted her so that her feet were directly above the hole.

'Down you go,' he said and held her until other hands grasped her legs and she was lowered safely onto her feet on the floor of the storeroom. She thought she smelt starch and Brylcreem but she opened her eyes and saw Gareth.

'Come on,' he said, grabbing her arm. She winced, but held her ground.

'Not until I see that Norman's safe,' she said.

They sat in a row on a low wall off to the side, away from the farmhouse, to get their breath back. Della clasped her injured arm and tried to fight the bile that rose in her throat. Men rushed back and forth with buckets and hosepipes, but it was obvious that the fire had long got a grip and was not intending to go out without a struggle. Della felt foolishly sad to think of all Glenys's skilful work, her one virtue, going up in flames.

She turned to Gareth who had been watching her with some concern.

'How did you know where I was?' she asked simply.

He smiled at her mischievously through the floating black smuts.

'I followed you,' he said. 'From afar.'

Della pretended to be angry.

'After I told you to go home?'

'Aren't you glad I'm a little devil?' he said, without the least shame.

He looked over to where Norman sat coughing like a horse. He had insisted on helping the other men, but had been ordered to sit and rest, when it became apparent that he was seriously overdoing it.

'He'll be fine now,' he murmured thoughtfully. 'He won't go off his head again.'

The fire fighters stood by the garage in a small tight knot. They appeared to have given up. Amongst them Napoleone could be seen, taller than most of the farmers around him. She wondered whether she could summon the energy and the courage to tell them that there was a body at the bottom of the stairs. The red ends of their cigarettes made arcs in the darkness as they talked. A loud thump heralded the fall of the roof, attracting their attention and she saw one or two shake their heads. They had known it was hopeless. Where was the other twin now? At home, pretending to be sound asleep in his bed or, more likely, driving for his life away from all this.

Aneurin was among the watchers. She had to warn him. She got up shakily.

'Sit down for goodness sake,' said Gareth. 'We don't want another body. We've got two already.'

She looked down at him.

'Two bodies?' she asked.

He nodded and bit his lip.

'Tecwyn and Carwyn,' he said quietly, and then, seeing that her legs would not support her, he reached out to stop her from falling. Della could not suppress a wail of pain and clutched at her shoulder.

The lad glared at her.

'Why didn't you say?' he asked fiercely. 'You want a sling for that arm.'

CHAPTER TWENTY-ONE

'Look at him,' said Hetty from the corner of her mouth, taking a swig of red hot tea and wincing.

Della followed her gaze and saw Norman, resplendent in a new dark suit, holding his aunt on his arm as if she were a china doll and seating her carefully at a table the other side of the vestry.

'I told Sara years ago that he'd be a blessing to them one day, and I was right. What would they do without him now? You should see that boy cut hay.'

Della nodded silently in agreement. With any luck, they'd never know how that had come to pass. In the few weeks since the tragedy, Norman had suddenly become a man. He stood tall now, instead of staring at his feet, blushing. He glanced over at her and smiled. She had not seen him in school since the fire, but had marked him present every day. He had a farm to run now, which was in her opinion, more important. He looked, quite literally, as if a huge weight had been lifted from his shoulders.

Her own shoulder was slowly improving, but she, like Norman, had no time to dwell on what was past. Her appearance, complete with sling, had been greeted with open mouths at school the day after the fire, but although she had spent some days in considerable pain, it had been worth the effort. Her commitment to her job had been seared into the minds of the children and their parents.

A gust of laughter came from the table next to the tea urns. A number of men stood there, amongst them Eirug Rees. He hadn't had to wait six months for a letter from Lilwen, and for once Della didn't mind getting the details wrong. She strongly suspected that Lilwen had been in contact with someone in the community all the time. It could not be a coincidence that Rees had received the letter so soon after the twins had died, telling him that she and Enzo were shortly to be married. And she didn't mind that either. He had been a means to self-discovery, and a friend in need, but she wouldn't have wanted to marry him.

She heard a chair being pulled back next to her and Huw Richards sat down.

'Pretty good show on the whole,' he said. 'And no bits of paper to be seen anywhere.'

He was referring to the children's question and answer session that morning.

'With Gareth giving a poke to anybody who needed it,' answered Della smiling. 'That one will go far.'

He thought about this.

'I don't think I want him to go too far,' he said.

Della stared at him crossly.

'I'm surprised at you. Surely you wouldn't want him to be a farm labourer all his days? They've only got three cows, and barely six acres of land.'

He laughed and looked down at his hands.

'You're starting to sound as if you were born in the country,' he said. 'I can't see Gareth as a doctor or a solicitor, but perhaps he could start his own business. Here in the village, not miles away. Places like Nant-yr Eithin are going to need every Gareth they can get soon enough. The ones with anything about them will leave in droves once they get a chance of secondary education.'

'Don't tell me you agree with Dr Davies, who doesn't think the proletariat should be educated!'

'No, indeed I don't. But there are long term implications to everything, you know.' He glanced around him, pensively. 'The world is moving on apace.'

There was an unaccustomed wistfulness in his tone that made her bite back her next sharp retort. Instead she asked,

'Speaking of Gareth, I've been wondering about one thing. How did he persuade you to come out the night of the fire?'

He smiled.

'He threatened me,' he replied. 'He said he would break every window in the chapel if I didn't get up that second and go with him.'

'There's a lot to be said for disobedience then.'

'And he's had plenty of practice.' He chewed on a sandwich. 'Isn't it strange how they can go either way, these lads? To the good or to the bad. There's really no predicting it.'

They sat in silence for a while. He was right, thought Della. When he next spoke she wasn't paying attention, and she couldn't quite believe that she'd heard him correctly.

'What?' she asked.

He looked embarrassed.

'I said that I'd been offered the pastorship of a chapel up north. Near Caernarvon.'

When she didn't react at once, he stared at his empty plate.

'Don't rush to congratulate me, will you?' he muttered.

Della came to with a jolt.

'I'm sorry,' she said stumbling over the words. 'It's just unexpected that's all. Very well done.'

She was rescued from having to think of any more platitudes by a movement at the vestry door. Aneurin the Policeman had arrived, in his uniform, and was looking around as if searching for someone.

Huw Richards stood, grateful for the diversion, she suspected, and went over to him. Della watched him go, astonished at her feelings regarding the news. She was furious. How could he even contemplate leaving Nant-yr Eithin? Was that the hidden agenda behind all the talk of Gareth? Did he intend leaving a fifteen-year-old boy as the leader of the community? Despite his numerous failings, he was the backbone of the village. To whom else could Gareth have gone that awful night, with the knowledge that he would act decisively? Who else had the authority and the intellect to organise and to think ahead? Some other pastor would take his place, she knew, but would he be willing to roll up his sleeves and stand in the breach in every situation, as Napoleone, blast him, had done at the school? It filled her with misery to think that after he had gone there would be nobody she could turn to, nobody she could speak to about important matters without having to weigh every word. And why now, of all times? There he stood, completely unconcerned, discussing something with Aneurin, knowing that he was leaving his congregation to fend for themselves. If he had been ten feet closer, she would have hit him.

'You're looking terribly serious, Miss Arthur.'

Della jumped but scraped a smile together from somewhere. Eirug Rees stood opposite her. She hadn't had the opportunity for a chat since she'd heard that Lilwen had written.

'Mr Rees,' she said, and gestured for him to sit down. One of the women hurried up to them with a cup of tea. The first wave of diners had finished their meal and gone. He leant his elbows on the table.

'I expect you've heard the good news,' he said, all smiles. As he would not be any happier to see Huw go than she, Della had to assume he was referring to his daughter.

'Yes I did, and I was so glad. It must be such a relief to you that she's safe and happy.'

'You're telling me! I didn't sleep for weeks.'

Della made sympathetic noises and Eirug looked around him carefully. Norman and his aunt were in the middle of their dinner among a sizeable crowd, but he lowered his voice nevertheless.

'I feel responsible, you know,' he said. 'For what happened to those boys.'

She couldn't for the life of her see why, so she raised an eyebrow to encourage him to continue.

'One of them was courting her, you see, on the sly.'

'Was he?' answered Della, innocent and ignorant.

Eirug nodded, guiltily.

'Yes. It caused a lot of ill-feeling in our house. I used to say to her, you can do better. And then when she disappeared …' He scratched his bald head. 'I thought all sorts of things. There was a time when it struck me that he'd hurt her and that's why she went.' He glanced over his shoulder. 'I was in school with Benj, their father. He was a nasty boy, even then. Sara had to marry him. And she's had a dog's life, between everything.'

Della had to agree. 'I can understand your fears. You wouldn't have wanted Lilwen to suffer like that.'

'No, and I suspected that he had one eye on our farm. There wasn't enough work for three of them on theirs.'

He evidently didn't know the truth. She sincerely hoped that the baby, when it arrived, did not have red hair. But Eirug had not finished.

'D'you think that's what sent them over the edge?' he asked worriedly. 'Tecwyn, at least, going there to steal and then setting the place alight? Because Lilwen had gone, I mean. And then the other one trying to rescue him and getting caught in the fire? If I hadn't gone on about her being too good for Tecwyn, she would have felt she could have told me about Enzo. Because if I didn't approve of Tec, then she must have thought I'd hit the roof about an Italian prisoner of war.'

Della wondered how much she could safely tell him. She knew that the official story, although perhaps not the one given to the twins' parents, was that the farmhouse had accidentally been set alight as the twins searched for Leonard's money, while Norman, in his fragile state had been using it as a shelter. She had happened to be there because she was searching for him. Norman, surprisingly, had been wise enough to deny remembering much about anything since his chickens died. He recalled sleeping in the farmhouse and waking to see her there with the place on fire. The sermon Huw Richards gave at the twins' funeral had been a masterpiece of things left unsaid, concentrating on their liveliness and zest for life. He'd succeeded in giving everyone happy memories of the two murderers. She turned her mind back to Eirug.

'I don't know exactly what happened,' she said, 'but to tell the truth, I don't think they could live apart.'

'No, perhaps not.' He didn't look particularly convinced. 'They were very close.'

'They were more than close,' answered Della. 'In many respects they were actually one person, and they would always be like that, I'm afraid. I can't see Lilwen having any kind of life in that situation. You were absolutely right to warn her, and she was wise to go.'

He sighed, but seemed easier in his mind. 'Well, at least I can do something to help Norman. Although, I don't know how much help he needs, tell the truth. If what it takes is hard work and a knack with animals, he'll do fine. But I'll be there if he needs me.'

Della knew that this was no empty promise. She was about to say so when she saw Aneurin and Huw Richards approaching. The policeman coughed.

'Could I have a brief word outside, Miss Arthur?' he asked.

She stared at him. Her first thought was that some suspicion had arisen about the deaths of the twins, but she pushed it aside. They had, like Glenys and Leonard, been respectably buried with all their secrets. Unless Norman had let something slip. She stood up, trying to hide her fear and followed him out through the vestry door.

The minister stood with his hands in his pockets. Della sat on a flat gravestone close by, trying to make sense of what she had heard. When she looked up Eirug had joined them.

Huw Richards took him to one side, but apart from a muted exclamation from Eirug, she did not hear what was said.

'And where was Lena exactly?' she asked. Aneurin the Policeman stood looking down at her, staring intently at her face.

'On a bomb site down by Swansea docks. Derelict, it seems. She would have been there a lot longer except that children go there to look for shrapnel. Did she say anything about going to Swansea?'

'Not a word,' said Della, truthfully. 'She left a brief note, that's all. How did they find out it was Lena?'

Aneurin paused. This news had changed him somehow, and had turned his usual genial quietness into something harder. She saw Huw Richards watching him closely. He'd seen it too, then.

'After they found her, they searched the area, and found her handbag buried under a pile of stones. There wasn't so much as a threepenny bit in it, but all her papers were there. And that was another odd thing – she hadn't registered to get her rations from Ceinwen and Iori, but in Cardigan – and d'you know why?' He didn't wait for an answer. 'Because she wasn't Lena Jones, but Lena Protheroe. She wasn't any relation of Dafydd Jones at all!'

He nodded to himself significantly as if that was a good enough reason in itself for her to be found dead.

The minister stepped forward. 'Tell me, who exactly did you talk to?'

'The sergeant in Cardigan – he's a distant cousin of the missus. They asked them to enquire in the shop where she was registered, see, in case anyone had seen her lately and she was alive and well. The bag could have belonged to someone apart from the corpse.'

He looked down kindly at Della.

'I don't think you'll have to go up and identify her or

anything. If they don't find any family, I'll go up. I saw Lena often enough, after all, and it would be a chance to have a chat with them about it.' A look of distaste came over his face. 'Although I don't know what she'll look like now. They said she had sustained multiple blows to the head and face.'

'Thank you,' murmured Della. She could have done without knowing that. She preferred to remember Lena with her blonde curls and red lipstick. Then she added, 'Can they tell when she was killed?'

'Quite a while. I wouldn't be surprised if she didn't last long after she got there.' He smoothed down the bulging front of his tunic. 'I've got to make enquiries this end. I've already been down to the station, but they can't remember seeing her on that particular day.'

'I'm not surprised,' said the minister. 'The day she left here was a busy Saturday. And of course, she used the train a lot. I don't think it's crucial anyway. She more than likely got drunk at one of the public houses near the docks and happened to cross the path of some desperate character. A sailor off one of the foreign ships, perhaps. Spent all his pay and thought he could get more.'

'I'll mention that to them,' said Aneurin hopefully, looking at his pocket watch. 'It's time I got going. I've got phone calls to make.' He paused again and looked at them both. 'Too many bodies by half,' he murmured ambiguously, 'and nobody knows anything.'

They watched him cycle ponderously down the road. Eirug excused himself and went to organise the moving of the piano for the afternoon service, but Huw Richards continued to stand at her side. Della waited for the farmer to disappear through the front door of the chapel.

'She didn't deserve to be murdered,' she said.

Huw sat down with his back to hers on the gravestone so that she could not see his face.

'No, she didn't,' he replied after a short pause. 'But when you go too close to the edge too often, you are liable to fall over it at some point.'

'Is that meant to be a warning to me?' asked Della, her anger rekindling.

She heard him laugh quietly.

'Not unless you're planning to get dead drunk on a regular basis from now on. I strongly suspect she went to the docks in the course of business, as it were.'

'Whoring,' said Della bluntly.

'The oldest profession of all.'

She shot him a glance over her shoulder. 'No you don't,' she said tartly. 'You don't suspect anything of the kind. You don't think she left here alive. She hadn't even had time to register her ration book in Swansea.'

'Stevie carried her case to the station for her,' he answered as if that was the final word in the argument, but Della just tossed her head.

'I never heard that he put her on the train.' She thought for a moment. 'We both have a pretty good idea of who could have offered her a lift to Swansea, on one of their illegal little jaunts.'

'But they were both there at the party for the Italians,' he objected. 'From early evening onwards. I saw them. And so did you.'

'I didn't say they actually took her to Swansea that day, did I? But I think she was dead by then, tucked away safely ready for transportation when it was convenient. She was probably standing listening to me talking to her so-called brother in the hospital for a lot longer than I thought. She had plenty of time to hear about the number plates. Lena would have noticed something like that. She had a nose for money and mischief. She would have bought black market goods from the twins – that's where the cherry brandy came from you can bet. Perhaps she saw them changing the plates at some point. Who knows?

If she thought she had a handle on them, she'd have pumped it for all she was worth.'

'This is just surmise,' he murmured, but Della was still turning it over in her mind.

'What's worrying you is that Aneurin will ask enough questions to persuade some sharp detective to come down from Swansea to make further enquiries. That's why you want everyone to believe that she died there. Although I don't know why you could care less. You won't be here.'

She felt his back stiffen against hers but before he could reply Jean came hurrying over the grass towards them. The news had spread with lightning speed as ever.

'Is it true about Lena?' she asked, her eyes wide. 'What a terrible thing!'

Della smiled at her sadly. 'Yes, isn't it,' she said.

Jean shook her head in bewilderment. 'And to think that Stevie shook her hand at the door to the station and wished her a good journey. She'd have been wiser to stay here. He said she looked nervous. There you are, see, since the war, you can't trust anybody.'

'Jean!' Someone called her name from the vestry door, and off she went.

'He just didn't want to wait for the train,' muttered Della under her breath. 'A waste of good drinking time.'

'Perhaps she was eager to get rid of him,' said the minister. 'And if I may say so, you've become very cynical.'

'I had a good teacher,' replied Della, and shoved him with her elbow.

When she heard him laugh again she got up.

'How can you?' she hissed to the back of his head.

He half turned, presenting her with his profile. He was no longer laughing.

'Don't be hypocritical,' he said. 'You couldn't stand her.'

'No I couldn't. She was dangerous and an absolute pain.

I admit that. But to think that she was beaten to death and dumped is appalling!'

He shrugged but not provocatively, and she thought she saw something like anguish in the lines of his face. 'Yes it is,' he said after a long pause. 'It's horrible. But it's a matter of choosing between bad and worse, isn't it? Do we really want the twins brought into this – far too late to be able to punish them? And even more importantly, do we want someone from the outside to come in and start asking questions about the circumstances of their deaths?'

Della felt again the cold fingers of fear on her spine. Had he guessed something regarding the events leading up to the fire? She had played dumb – and had not revealed the cause of the first twin's death to anyone at all. She should have known he would wonder. She realised that he had turned completely to face her.

'Would you rather the whole story, starting with Glenys and Leonard came out? Do you think you, and more critically, Norman, could cope?'

She stepped back from him, but he reached out and laid a finger on her arm.

'Listen,' he said. 'We can't bring anybody back. But we can protect the living. I knew that from the moment you walked into my study and told me what you'd found the night of the storm. Everything I've done has been with that in mind. But the choice is yours.'

Della knew that the colour had risen to her face as she listened to him. He had to understand what he was asking her to do. She took a deep breath.

'We can't influence what the police in Swansea decide to do,' she said slowly. 'If they come down here and start asking questions, we'll have to answer them.'

'I don't see why …'

'What? Because we're very likely to be arrested for not

telling the truth! Aneurin is already suspicious that it's not all quite as simple as the official version.'

Looking at his sardonic face, Della could see this was having absolutely no effect on him, and this enraged her. 'Do you not see what you're asking me to do?' she asked. 'I can't keep something like this going on my own.'

'Listen, Della.' He started to protest but she waved his words away.

'And don't tell me I can telephone you in Caernarvon! I need you here.'

She pulled herself up short when she realised what she'd said. She had betrayed herself to no purpose. It was humiliating. She stared wildly around her. Nobody seemed to have heard. She hardly noticed him getting to his feet until she smelt the starch and the Brylcreem again.

'Della?' he asked. 'Do you actually need me?' He spoke so quietly she almost didn't catch the words.

'Does it matter if I do?' she managed bitterly at last. 'Does it make any difference at all? Or do you just want the pleasure of hearing the words before you disappear over the horizon?'

She heard him give a deep sigh. 'I only said that I'd been offered another chapel. I didn't say I'd accepted it, did I?'

She got sufficient grip on herself to challenge him.

'But if you weren't intending to accept, why did you mention it at all?'

She had him there. She could tell by the way he frowned.

'To see,' he said reluctantly, as if the words were being wrung from him. 'To see whether you'd react.'

'Well, I've reacted. Happy now?'

He thrust his hands into his trouser pockets and looked at her from the corner of his eye.

'Yes, I suppose I am,' he said thoughtfully. 'But it's an unfamiliar sensation.'

The men had started to foregather for their last smoke

before the afternoon service, and through the open door of the vestry the women could be seen putting their hats back on and scrubbing their children's faces with handkerchiefs and spit. One or two of these were already running races through the graveyard after receiving their mothers' attentions and on the warm breeze their joyful cries and the deep voices of the smokers could be heard, teasing and leg-pulling. Della stood listening and watching. If the world knew the truth, would this precious community ever be the same?

They only had one hope, and he was standing there in front of her, sullen, hard to handle but ready to fight to the death for them. Was he her only hope too? Did she really need him?

'Perhaps, Huw, with a bit of help, we might both get used to happiness,' she said.